CASE
SENSITIVE

T0017904

A.K. Turner's latest crime fiction series features forensic sleuth Cassie Raven, who was first introduced in two short stories broadcast on BBC Radio 4. She also works as a TV producer and writer making documentaries on a range of subjects from history to true crime. A.K. has lived in East London since its prehipster days and recently qualified as a City of London walks guide so that she can share her passion for the city's 2,000-year history; her specialist subject – crime and punishment!

Also by A.K. Turner
Body Language
Life Sentence

CASE
SENSITIVE

A. K. Turner

ZAFFRE

First published in the UK in 2023 by
ZAFFRE
An imprint of Bonnier Books UK
4th Floor, Victoria House, Bloomsbury Square, London WC1B 4DA
Owned by Bonnier Books
Sveavägen 56, Stockholm, Sweden

A CIP catalogue record for this book is
available from the British Library.

ISBN: 978-1-80418-059-4

Also available as an ebook and an audiobook

1 3 5 7 9 10 8 6 4 2

Typeset by IDSUK (Data Connection) Ltd
Printed and bound in Great Britain by Clays Ltd, Elcograf S.p.A.

Zaffre is an imprint of Bonnier Books UK
www.bonnierbooks.co.uk

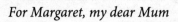

For Margaret, my dear Mum

Chapter One

Cassie woke to the rhythmic *shhh-upp* of water against the timber hull, a comforting sound which, along with the gentle rocking, had been both her lullaby and morning alarm call for the last few months. But today the lazy slap of each wave against the side of the narrowboat was accompanied by an intermittent knocking sound – almost as if someone was tentatively rapping their knuckles on the hull, right beside her ear.

As she drifted up towards consciousness, her brain strained to identify the sound. It wasn't like that caused by the usual flotsam and jetsam which found its way into the canal overnight – bags of rubbish, discarded trainers, once even a plastic cold box which had ended up beating a tattoo against her bows. Judging by the light level it was still before 6 a.m. – three hours till Cassie's shift at the mortuary – so she turned over, trying to stay in the sleep zone and blot out the extraneous noise. But after ten minutes of lying there, just waiting for the next *knock . . . knock-knock . . .* she sat up in her bunk cursing, and pulled a hoodie on over her pyjamas. In her flat she'd always slept naked but after five months living on the boat, with summer fading and the night-time damp starting to penetrate even her fifteen-tog duvet, she'd given in and ordered M&S's hottest flannelette jim-jams and bedsocks.

As she emerged in the tiny cockpit in the aft (she'd learned not to call it 'the back') the chill of a September morning struck her like the flat of a cold hand. She'd always loved the canal in autumn but now as she shivered, peering through the blanket of mist lurking above the black-green water, she felt a stab of nostalgia for summer, even with Camden Town's tourists and trippers who treated her boat like some kind of visitor attraction.

Taking the boathook from the deck, she headed up to the bows of the narrowboat: ten metres long and moored pointing upstream.

Reaching the foredeck on the canal side, she lowered herself down and, keeping one hand firmly around the deck rail, peered down through the shifting skeins of fog that veiled the surface. At that moment a patch cleared in the mist and a wavelet washed something rounded, dark and slick against the hull. A split second later it had retreated out of view, but she didn't need a second look to realise the source of the knocking.

It hadn't been made by a discarded trainer but by the sodden head of a man, face down in the water.

Cassie Raven might only be twenty-six but having spent the last six years working as an advanced pathology technologist – an APT – in Camden Mortuary she'd seen thousands of dead bodies up close. She had sliced through their skin, cracked open their ribs, and extracted their organs ready for post-mortem examination. She'd taken samples of their bodily fluids and could identify the distinctive reek of a decomposed body at twenty paces. But seeing a dead guy floating there, his head

2

inches from where hers had been just moments ago – *cheek to cheek* – gave her the heebie-jeebies. A dead body here, in the real world, was just so . . . out of context.

As she bent to pick up the boathook, which she'd dropped in her shock, she felt her heart beating double-time, pumping oxygen-rich blood to her major muscles, priming them for fight or flight. After taking a couple of steadying breaths, she guided the business end of the boathook into the neck of the guy's puffer jacket, taking her time, knowing how a careless post-mortem injury could make the pathologist's job harder when it came to determining cause of death.

With one hand on the deck rail, she started pulling the body towards the stern. The canal was flat calm today with barely any current and he came through the water easily, as though eager to help. She manoeuvred him around the stern and into the gap between the boat and the canal-side. Even if he sank it was less than a metre deep here and the starboard fender would stop him getting crushed against the black bricks of the side.

As she extracted the hook from his jacket, the guy's body started to turn. He rolled over lazily in the water as if making himself more comfortable in bed, his face breaking the surface. He was in his late twenties, at a guess, broad-shouldered and good-looking in spite of a flurry of acne across his cheekbones. His eyes – a distinctive shade of golden-green – appeared to be gazing up at the sky with a questioning look.

Squatting down, Cassie leaned towards him. 'How did you end up in the canal, then?' she asked gently. Held her breath in the hope of picking up what she had sometimes got from the dead bodies she looked after at work – some clue to their last

3

thoughts, to what had happened to them. But deep down she knew she was just going through the motions.

Green-Eyes remained stony silent: further confirmation that the special bond she had felt all her years working with the dead – the sacred vocation that had given her life meaning – had deserted her.

Chapter Two

After Cassie reported her dawn visitor to Camden nick, a young uniformed female cop was the first to turn up, later followed by two divers wearing dry suits and carrying recovery equipment. Ducking under the police tape strung across the towpath, they approached the boat and peered down at the body.

The older of the two, a bearded guy of about fifty, gave Cassie the once-over, followed by the look she was wearyingly used to getting from older guys. Put into words it would say something like *If you didn't have that weird punk haircut and facial piercings I might have done you the honour of fancying you.* Holding his gaze she widened her eyes briefly, sending him a message of her own – *You should be so lucky, dickhead.*

They didn't bother putting on their breathing apparatus, simply stepped backwards over the canal-side into the metre-deep water. Within minutes they had the body strapped onto an inflatable stretcher and were manoeuvring it out onto the towpath. Cassie crouched to take a last look at Green-Eyes before they covered him up.

Water had started to foam from his nose and mouth and the shoulders of his jacket were festooned with duckweed. She couldn't see any obvious external injuries and from the absence of any decomp smell he'd probably only gone in the previous day. Most likely an accidental drowning.

She got back to her feet to find the older diver staring at her. 'Dead bodies don't bother you then?' – clearly disapproving that she hadn't fainted and needed reviving with smelling salts.

She shrugged. 'Not really. I see about twenty or thirty of them a week' – enjoying his confused expression for a moment before adding, 'I'm a mortuary technician. I'll probably be eviscerating this guy later.' Turning to climb back on the boat she heard him mutter to his mate.

'Weirdo.'

Well, she couldn't argue with that.

Later, not long after they'd left, she was finally getting ready for work when she heard a jaunty knocking on the deck followed by a familiar voice. 'Permission to come aboard, Captain?'

It was her dad, Callum, clutching two takeaway coffees. She greeted him with a kiss, feeling again the conflicting emotions he stirred in her. Love and affection, yes, but exasperation, and even . . . anger. Like today, he'd obviously forgotten she was due at work at 9 a.m. – half an hour's time – so she'd have to neck this coffee uncomfortably fast. Meanwhile his expression showed only uncomplicated happiness at seeing her. So why did she feel like this?

OK, it hadn't exactly been your straightforward father–daughter relationship. From the age of four Cassie had been raised by her grandmother to believe that her mum and dad had been killed in a car crash. It was only recently she had learned the true story – that her father was alive, but had spent seventeen years in jail for murdering her mum Kath.

Now it was clear that Callum had been wrongfully convicted and his official exoneration was working its way through the legal system.

They drank their coffees in the cockpit: the sun had broken through and was burning the layer of mist off the canal.

'You should have got yourself a bacon roll,' she said, eyeing him. He was good-looking – in an ageing rock star kind of way – but far too skinny for his height and frame. 'It's not good to be underweight at your age, you know.' Callum was only forty-nine but his long stretch, part of it spent sharing a cell with a heavy smoker, had left him prematurely aged and suffering from emphysema.

She handed him a paper bag she'd brought up with her.

'More pills?' he asked with a doleful look.

'Just some zinc for your immune system. Are you taking the other supplements?' She heard the nagging note in her voice but Callum's diet was a horror story, consisting almost entirely of beans on toast interspersed with takeaway junk food.

He gave her a mock salute and pulled his lopsided grin. 'Yes, Captain. I even ate an apple the other day.'

They watched a mother moorhen bustle by, her chicks peeping frantically in her wake. Sensing that he was about to mention her mum, Cassie headed him off. 'How's the hostel working out? Have they found any work for you yet?' Callum had relocated from his family's hometown in Northern Ireland to start a new life closer to his daughter.

'Oh, you know, the usual, there's a FTSE 100 company looking for a CEO, Arsenal need a striker, but I think I'm leaning towards the record deal with Sony . . .' He laughed, revealing a gap where a pre-molar should be, and she made a mental note to find him a dentist.

'I'm still not keen on your living here on your own,' said Callum, shaking his head. 'You know there was a stabbing up by the lock last week? I mean anyone could just waltz on board at night.'

Cassie was glad she hadn't mentioned her floating visitor. 'Look, I was lucky to get it,' she told him. 'The average rent in Camden is two grand a month. And all the council could offer me was a place in Enfield.' Just as her council block further east had been due to fall to the developers' wrecking ball, an old mate from her squatting days had gone off to live in Goa for the foreseeable and lent her his narrowboat, *Dreamcatcher*.

'Camden used to be for ordinary folk,' said Callum, shaking his head. 'But now . . . The tourists! And all these coffee shops and trendy takeaways. I nearly ordered a vegan kebab by mistake the other day!' – looking genuinely shocked that such a thing could exist.

Out of the corner of her eye, she took in his stooped frame and grey-sprinkled hair, once near black like hers. She still found it tough, having to swap the big strong daddy of her early childhood memory for the reality. Maybe twenty-six was too old to be acquiring an unforeseen parent – a thought which made her gut twist with guilt.

She reached out and took his bony hand, feeling the grateful returning pressure. *What was wrong with her?* Why couldn't she just be happy that after more than two decades believing she was an orphan she had a father again?

FLYTE

The grainy black and white CCTV footage projected on the screen of the conference room showed a young man making his way down a deserted night-time alleyway with the exaggerated care of the seriously inebriated. From the rain-wet cobbles illuminated by the streetlight, Detective Sergeant Phyllida Flyte knew the guy was in the labyrinth of alleys and Victorian warehouses around Camden Lock, which housed the area's hipster bars and music venues. He paused and turned, unsteady on his feet, as an older man, tall and heavy-set, hove into view, holding out what must be a cigarette, clearly asking for a light. They appeared to chat amicably as the first guy groped drunkenly in his pocket for a lighter before handing it to the bigger man.

Then, a sudden blur of bodies. When the image came back into focus the big man had the drunk in a headlock, his forearm wrapped around his throat, half lifting him off the ground. The victim's mouth gaped, just a black hole at this distance. He made a few pathetic attempts to bat at the restraining arm, but after thirty seconds his knees buckled and his attacker lowered him to the ground. The big guy scoped the street, left, right, before bending to rifle through his pockets. Seconds later, he strolled off, without a backward glance at his victim left crumpled on the cobbles like a pile of dirty washing.

DCI Mike Steadman reached out to his laptop and rewound the CCTV footage to the moment of the attack.

'This lad, Harry Poppleton, got unlucky,' he told the members of Camden's Major Crimes Unit gathered around the long table. 'The compression of his neck did some serious damage. He wasn't found for another ten minutes and he's been in a coma in Camden General for the past week. Dean, what's the latest?'

DS Dean Willets said, 'Yeah, guv. According to the MRI scan, the headlock fractured a bone in his throat . . . the er . . .'

'Hyoid.' Flyte didn't realise she'd spoken out loud until she got a death stare from Willets. Her cheeks flamed and she heard her mother's scolding voice 'I think we've heard enough from you, Clever Clogs.' As the new girl on the team she had to remember to watch her step.

'As I was about to say,' Willets went on, 'the hyoid bone. According to the medics, the fracture caused swelling that closed his airway, starving him of oxygen. His brain scans show barely any activity and the family have been told not to expect recovery. So it's already attempted murder and once they've' – he flicked an imaginary switch upwards – 'it'll be murder one.'

Flyte resisted the urge to roll her eyes: Dean Willets watched too many American crime dramas.

'Thanks, Dean.' Steadman sent a searching gaze around the table, pausing to meet everyone's eyes individually. 'This Hugger Mugger, as the press are inevitably calling him, is a menace. Has he used this tactic before? The CCTV only gives us a partial facial to work with but he looks to be about my size.' Steadman glanced down at his own frame with a wry smile. Standing over six foot tall and wide-shouldered, he was big all over without being fat. 'Dean, come here a minute. You're what five eight?'

'Five nine, boss,' said Willets in a mock-aggrieved voice, going over to him.

'It's the extra inch that counts,' said DC Nathan Cassidy – Willets' most loyal sidekick – to general sniggering.

'OK, enough of that.' Steadman frowned, getting to his feet. 'Anyway, you're more or less the same height as the victim.'

Willets turned his back to Steadman, allowing him to put his beefy forearm loosely around his neck and make as if to lift him off the floor. 'So the guy we're looking for is someone around my height – six foot two,' said Steadman, releasing Willets and nodding towards the CCTV image. 'His build makes him fairly distinctive. Phyllida, could you handle the press on this? Give the *Gazette* the best image of this guy, see if we can raise any witnesses.'

Willets was made the investigating officer on the case which was officially dubbed Operation Palmerston – Steadman liked to name ops after former prime ministers.

After everyone stood to head back to their desks, Steadman caught Flyte at the doorway.

'Phyllida, I'm sorry I've been so busy lately. I've been meaning to ask how you're settling in?' He held the door into the corridor open for her – an old-fashioned gesture that might make some women bridle, but one of which she approved.

'Oh fine, thanks,' she said, thinking this a more politic response than the truth. She was the lone female detective on the team that comprised four fellow DSs and three DCs; the only other female being a civilian officer. The atmosphere she'd encountered in her first few weeks here had been mostly polite suspicion with a dash of borderline hostility.

He sent her a perceptive look. 'It can't be easy joining a team who've been working together as long as these guys have. You do know that was a big factor in favour of hiring you? I wanted to break up the boys' club . . . not that you weren't eminently qualified regardless. Two murder cases sewn up in less than a year over at CID!' He sent her an admiring look. 'That's quite a record.'

'Thanks, boss' – feeling a warmth climbing her cheeks at the praise. Steadman was in his fifties but unlike some male cops of that vintage he managed to be friendly without ever behaving unprofessionally. He had never asked whether she had a boyfriend, gone on about her 'looking nice today', or ever directed his conversation at her chest.

He paused outside the door to the main office before lowering his voice. 'Listen, Phyllida, I'm well aware they can be a somewhat . . . unreconstructed bunch, but it's ninety-five per cent bravado. You'll soon find out they're all good coppers.' He paused. 'Anyway, I need you to pop over to Camden Mortuary, take a look at an unidentified floater pulled out of the canal this morning. I got a call from your old boss over at CID. He's two detectives down since you left so he had no one available to attend the scene. There are no suspicious circs – probably an unlucky drunk who fell in – but I said we'd help out, so that he can say a detective attended.'

'Of course.' She pulled a can-do smile to hide her irritation: she hadn't joined Major Crimes to cover CID's back on a routine non-sus death.

'It'll only take you half an hour and you can hand it straight back to them afterwards,' he said kindly before turning to go. 'Don't worry, you'll get your own murder case soon enough.'

She realised she'd probably be seeing Cassie Raven again, for the first time in months. And her new job would doubtless present many more opportunities to attend the mortuary. The thought stirred up a muddle of emotions. And although muddle was something that Flyte abhorred, she had to admit that the prospect of seeing the tattooed morgue girl prompted a buzz of anticipation.

Chapter Three

At work, after changing into scrubs, Cassie headed into the autopsy suite where her fellow APT Jason was already prepping one of their guests for the post-mortem list. That meant the pathologist had already done his external examination of the body and would be on the clean side checking his emails. Was Archie doing the list today? She couldn't ask Jason – for the last few months she and Archie Cuff had been occasional lovers/boyfriend–girlfriend/friends with benefits . . . ? – she wasn't really sure what to call it, but they had agreed to keep work colleagues in the dark about their affair.

Going over to Jason's autopsy station she saw the body of a middle-aged woman, who was already open from the suprasternal notch at the base of the throat to the pubis, her ribs butterflied to expose her heart and lungs. From the central line still taped in place under her right collarbone – all catheters and cannulas were left in situ for the PM – she'd clearly died in the hospital, to which the mortuary was linked by an underground walkway.

'You don't get many of them to the pound,' said Jason, with a nod and a sly grin.

There was no mistaking his meaning: either side of the midline incision the woman's breasts stood unnaturally upright, like upended flowerpots. Cassie could see the tell-tale silvery scars, several years old, under each breast where she'd had silicone implants inserted. As the senior technician she could tear Jason off a strip, remind him of their duty to treat their guests with respect, but he was fifty-one, and she knew it couldn't be easy for him, taking orders from someone half his age.

In any case, since Cassie's bond with the dead had deserted her, she had to admit to feeling less emotionally invested in her work. Her old conviction that she'd been able to pick up the last thoughts of her 'guests' hanging in the air like unspent electrical activity seemed like a child's fairy tale. It was obvious to her now that her occasional insights into why someone had died had just been a matter of clues she'd picked up either from the bodies or from her dealings with their loved ones.

She watched Jason fitting a new scalpel blade, whistling along to a cheesy track on the radio. He had once summed up their job for her in three brutal words: 'cut and shut'. Maybe she would end up a cynical old lag like him, treating the bodies like cars on an assembly line.

'Have you made a note of the augmentation?' she asked. Although vanishingly unlikely to have contributed to her death, the lady's breast implant surgery should still be recorded.

Jason nodded towards the body chart on his bench. It was pre-printed with two basic outlines of a body – front and back view – which the technicians marked up to alert the pathologist to anything out of the ordinary. Usually, the location of the implants would have been marked with a simple cross in the chest area but instead Jason had added comically outsized breasts.

Twat.

15

'Do it again, Jason. Minus the hilarious artwork,' she snapped, unable to conceal her irritation this time. 'So, what is this lady's story?'

'Came into A&E with a bad headache, kicked the bucket a couple of hours later.'

Shrugging, he leaned against the body and started filleting out the neck structures, blood frothing out of the severed jugular vein. 'I'd put a tenner on a stroke.'

Although Cassie no longer got the same buzz she once had from looking after the dead, she still felt a duty to those left behind to find answers.

'Can I see her notes?' she asked.

Jason heaved the viscera into a waiting pail. 'Do what you like, I'm going for a smoke.'

The hospital notes said that forty-seven-year-old Becka Bennett had been brought in by her husband Dan at 11.30 the previous night with a severe headache which she had reported as a nine on the pain scale. The red flag was muscular weakness down her left side – a classic sign of stroke. Becka had contrast medium injected prior to an MRI scan of her head – which explained the line in her subclavian vein – but before they'd even got her into the scanner her heart had stopped. With no detectable rhythm there was no point in defibrillating her, and repeated 1 ml doses of adrenaline hadn't brought her back. Ten minutes later, Becka Bennett was declared dead. Since she'd previously been in good health and her death was unexplained, the coroner's office had ordered a routine – i.e. a non-forensic – post-mortem.

The death left Dan Bennett a widower and their two teenage daughters motherless. What must it be like to bring your wife in with a bad headache and an hour later watch her flatline and die despite the frantic efforts of a team of medics?

Cassie noticed the little dancing dolphin tattooed on her left hip. 'Hi, Becka,' she murmured. 'I'm going to get you ready for the doctor so that we can find out what happened to you.'

Nowadays, speaking to the guests was just habit, a reflex: it had been months since she'd experienced the slide into dreaminess, the hyper-heightened senses, the fizz of static in the air that used to foreshadow her moments of communion with the dead.

Putting her hand on Becka's fridge-cold arm, Cassie closed her eyes, straining to feel something.

Nada.

She turned away. Each failure to connect left her feeling a little more hollow inside.

A loud rapping made her jump, pitching her back to the sound of Green-Eyes' skull knocking against her hull. Looking up, she saw the wide cheekbones of DS Phyllida Flyte through the wired glass of the door to the clean side, wearing her default look of borderline impatience.

Great. That was all she needed.

They exchanged greetings, not quite making eye contact. They'd spent a lot of time together during two murder investigations – including the two-decades-old killing of Cassie's own mum, which had found the real perpetrator and absolved her dad of the crime. Yet still there was this awkward vibe between them: the air of something . . . unresolved.

'How's it going with your dad's appeal?' asked Flyte. Cassie always forgot how extraordinary her eyes were: ice blue with a darker limbal ring. *Like an Arctic fox.* She had ditched her go-to pale-pink lipstick in favour a nude matt tone that offset her pale Scandi colouring and wheat-blonde hair, which these days she wore in a choppy bob.

'The hearing should be pretty soon.' Cassie managed a smile. 'The brief says it's a formality – the conviction will be set aside.'

'I'm pleased for you.' Another pause and then her tone returned to its usual brisk, no-nonsense setting. 'Right. I'm here to see the unidentified male pulled out of the canal, to get some photographs for the local paper and mispers database. I hear you were the one to find him?'

'Yeah. Like I don't get enough bodies in the day job.'

Cassie led the way to the body store, struggling with the emotions that Flyte could stir in her. The uptight cop was her polar opposite, but whenever they met Cassie felt the buzz of something intriguing – unfathomable – about her that she had to confess she found appealing. And now and again during their encounters she'd felt that the attraction, although unspoken, might be mutual.

Anyway, it was all academic. Cassie couldn't imagine dating a cop, and Phyllida Flyte was clearly so deep in the closet she could see Narnia.

Cassie pulled out drawer number six of the giant fridge that occupied the whole of one wall. It took more effort than it should do, sticking on its rollers, but then the whole unit was past its sell-by date. Her manager Doug knew about it, but his application for a new refrigeration system had twice been rejected. *Budget cuts.*

The ID tag on the side of the white body bag said simply 'Unknown male', a reference number, and the date and location on the Regent's Canal where he'd been found.

Cassie unzipped the bag down to his chest and Flyte pulled out her phone. 'The officers who attended reported no signs of injury, but said he had no wallet or phone on him?' she said, taking a close-up of his face.

'They're probably at the bottom of the canal.' Cassie shrugged. 'The button fly on his jeans was partly undone, so he probably had a skinful, went to take a leak in the canal and lost his balance. We get a few of these a year. The water's cold at night and if he was drunk . . .'

They fell silent for a moment. The last time they'd stood together over a body recovered from the canal had been the previous winter – and the victim had been the closest Cassie had to a best friend. No hard evidence of foul play had ever been found but Cassie knew he'd been killed in the course of helping her investigate her mother's murder. After his funeral she'd buried the whole episode in a lead-lined mental box, so it was a relief when Flyte didn't drag it all up.

'What was he wearing?' Flyte asked. 'It might help identify him.'

Cassie read from the property inventory. 'Massimo Dutti puffer jacket, Reiss top, Diesel jeans, Nike Air trainers.'

Flyte raised her eyebrows. 'Upmarket labels.'

Cassie shrugged. 'I suppose so.'

Flyte was staring intently at the guy's face. 'What colour are his eyes? For the description.'

Cassie pictured the guy's perplexed stare after he was pulled out of the canal. 'A kind of goldish-green.'

'Any tattoos or birthmarks?'

'Nope.' Cassie glanced at the clock; she didn't have time for this. 'Look are we done here? I've got two customers to eviscerate next door.'

Flyte ignored her, still staring at the guy's face. 'How long do you think he's been dead?'

'I don't know!' Cassie burst out. 'I'm not a pathologist.'

Flyte glared at her. 'Don't you care about finding out who this poor chap was? Letting his family know as soon as possible?'

Cassie felt a jolt of guilt. 'Sure I do,' she snapped. 'But I forgot to bring my Ouija board in today. If you're that interested I suggest you come back for the PM on Monday.' Knowing that a detective would rarely – if ever – attend the post-mortem on a non-suspicious death.

'I might just do that,' retorted Flyte.

FLYTE

Flyte didn't know what to make of that morning's encounter with Cassie Raven.

When they'd first met about a year earlier Flyte had taken an instant, visceral dislike to the girl which she recognised now had largely been a reaction to her challenging look – albeit a commonplace in 'alternative' Camden Town. Flyte still couldn't understand why such a pretty girl would go out of her way to make herself look so *unfeminine*: that half-shaved black-dyed hair, the tattoos, the cruel-looking bolts and rings piercing the soft skin of her lip and eyebrow. All topped off with the regulation black nail varnish and workman's boots – and the bolshy attitude to match.

But as she had got to know her, Flyte had discovered that beneath the 'screw you' facade was someone who not only possessed unusually acute observational skills but also looked after the dead with profound care and respect – almost as if they were still alive. Her knee-jerk impression had finally evaporated with the discovery that Cassie had once slept on the mortuary floor alongside a dead child because his mum said he was afraid of the dark.

That had struck home because three years earlier Flyte had suffered her own loss when her baby girl had arrived stillborn.

21

The cause was a rare syndrome in which the umbilical cord didn't properly attach to the placenta during Flyte's only pregnancy. The rupture of the umbilical vessels during labour caused Poppy, as she had unofficially named her, to bleed out her tiny volume of blood within minutes.

When Flyte had finally felt able to face reading the medical report it had been Cassie who'd helped her to understand the jargon and to explain why her ultrasound scans hadn't picked up the condition, prompting a C-section that might have averted tragedy. The explanation had helped her to accept that no one was to blame for Poppy's death – including herself.

Now and again she had wondered whether the two of them might become friends. *Or more . . .* A rogue thought she was quick to stifle.

So it had come as a shock seeing her again. Flyte had always viewed her as a troubled soul who drank too much, smoked cannabis – and doubtless worse – but she'd been expecting to find her happier, more settled, now that her father was back in her life. The old Cassie would have been far more engaged with the guy pulled from the canal and driven to find out who he was. Today, she'd come across as detached and impatient.

Picturing his face, with its heartbreaking scatter of acne, she imagined his parents, girlfriend . . . surely someone would be starting to worry that they couldn't raise him?

She'd been weaving her way through the human traffic jam along Camden High Street but now she ducked out of the throng into a shop doorway. She pulled out her phone and clicked on the photos she'd taken of the dead guy. There was something about his face that had been niggling at her – almost as if he looked familiar? But after flicking through all the images, she gave up, unable to say who he reminded her of.

Whoever he was, the thought of having to hand him back to CID made her feel guilty but she reassured herself: it could only be a matter of time before someone called the police to report him missing.

Chapter Four

Returning to the autopsy suite, Cassie found Archie stood at the dissection bench snapping on his nitrile gloves. It was a good sign that the sight of his broad back and rugby player's shoulders still gave her a buzz. His gingery hair was curling over the neck of his scrubs she noticed; time for a bit of gentle nagging. He took stuff like that with good humour.

Jason was back at his station and had just fired up the electric bone saw in readiness to take off Becka Bennett's calvarium – the top of the skull.

'Morning, Cassie,' said Archie, with a casual glance over his shoulder.

She was about to retrieve the next guest out of the body store but instead something made her go over to his bench where he was just severing the respiratory block from the trachea in order to dissect Becka's heart and lungs.

'Stop,' she said, but Archie didn't hear her over the insolent whine of Jason's bone saw.

'Stop!'

Archie paused, his scalpel poised in mid-air.

'Look,' she said, speaking more quietly now that Jason had stilled the saw, and fully aware he might be earwigging. 'It's probably nothing but maybe you should consider an air embolism?'

He raised a questioning eyebrow.

'I'm serious.' She showed him Becka's notes. 'Look, she had a central line inserted to inject contrast medium ahead of an MRI scan. If something went wrong when they were inserting it, can't that cause air to get into the vein?' She recalled hearing about such a case a few years back.

Archie read over her shoulder, frowning. 'The scan didn't happen.'

Cassie pointed out the times recorded by the medical team. 'Because she went into cardiac arrest right after the line was inserted.'

'A fatal air embo is pretty rare,' Archie mused. 'But her heart rhythm did look normal up till then.'

They both knew that if a large enough bolus of air had entered Becka's vein it would have reached the right ventricle in half a second. The heart muscles would be unable to pump the resulting froth of blood and air, resulting in cardiac arrest.

'Ideally, I'd request a scan of the heart,' said Archie, frowning.

'Good luck with getting the coroner to stump up for that,' said Cassie. If it had been Professor Arculus demanding a non-standard procedure then maybe, but Archie was still a new boy.

'True,' he said. 'Right then. I guess we'll have to go old-school.' He rubbed his hands in anticipation. 'Get me your biggest bowl would you?'

Archie used the flexible hose at his bench to half fill the bowl with water. He fully submerged the still-intact heart and lungs and then, taking a pair of scissors, carefully opened the thin white pericardial sac to expose the smooth red curve of the heart. Cassie was gripped: she'd read about this in autopsy handbooks but never seen it in real life.

25

Archie picked up a scalpel with a magician's flourish. 'Here goes!'

Holding the submerged heart in his left hand he used his right to make a cut in the tissue above the right ventricle. A string of silvery air bubbles rose to the surface. Air that shouldn't be inside the heart.

'Geronimo!' he cried, planting a swift kiss on Cassie's forehead.

Jason had just brought the brain over in a plastic bowl and dumped it on Archie's dissection bench. His gaze flitted between the two of them. Then his eyes met Cassie's and his raised eyebrow and smirk told her that he knew that she and Archie were more than work colleagues.

Bollocks.

Chapter Five

'It was bound to happen eventually.' Archie looked unconcerned as he raised a spoon loaded with noodles and fragrant broth from his bowl of pho. They'd met for lunch in a little cafe off the beaten track, having left the mortuary five minutes apart. 'I mean there's no rule against it, is there.'

'I know. It's just . . . embarrassing. He already hates having a twenty-six-year-old female as a boss and now he's going to be giving me his "sex face" all the time . . .' She mimicked a speculative leer.

'Well played today.' He beamed at her. 'If I'd gone ahead and dissected the heart as normal the air would simply have dissipated and we'd have no evidence of the embolism. Shame we didn't film it.'

'What, to put on TikTok?'

'On what?' Archie looked genuinely puzzled. 'I mean I could've used it when I get onto the lecture circuit.' Since he was only a couple of years out of med school this was clearly a decade or more in the future but he looked so artlessly pleased with himself it was impossible to dislike him. Where did the posh get their confidence? Cassie wondered. Was it dished out at Harrow along with the breakfast porridge? It certainly hadn't been on the menu at her school – or she might have ended up studying harder, might even have tried for med school herself.

'Thank Christ it wasn't Curzon doing the list today,' said Cassie. 'He'd have slapped me down, or complained to Doug about the uppity minion at it again.' It wasn't long since Cassie had narrowly escaped a disciplinary for daring to go looking for a deep vein thrombosis in a body without Dr Curzon's express permission.

An alert sounded on Archie's phone and he frowned down at the screen. 'Aha! The radiographer got back to me, and he confirms that Becka Bennett sat up suddenly, feeling sick, just as the doctor was putting in the line.' He dispatched another mouthful of broth. 'If the patient is sitting up, it lowers their venous pressure, which is why we're taught to have them supine during insertion.'

'So if the pressure in the vein is lower than the outside pressure, it sucks air in around the needle?'

He nodded.

Cassie pushed her bowl away. Becka might have gone on to live another forty or fifty years, but the laws of physics had sealed her fate in less than a second. Lately, she'd started to wonder what the point of life was when it could end so randomly.

'Are you OK?' Archie asked, his eyes clouded.

'I'm fine.' She faked a smile. 'Will the doctor get into trouble?'

'I doubt it,' he said. 'It was a busy night and apparently he was an A & E newbie. The coroner will probably call it a tragic accident, nobody to blame.'

Becka's cause of death would go down as air embolism, but as for what had caused the symptoms that had brought her into hospital – the severe headache and muscular weakness – that was likely to remain a mystery. Archie hadn't found any signs of

28

stroke in her brain and the rest of her organs appeared healthy too. Cassie imagined what it would be like for Becka's husband to discover that his wife's death had stemmed from a misdiagnosis followed by a terrible accident.

Iatrogenic death. Iatro- from the Ancient Greek for 'doctor'. Death caused by medical treatment.

Maybe it would have been better to leave Becka's family in ignorance of what had killed her.

'What made you think of air embolism anyway?' Archie sent her a cheeky look. 'Should I mention your sixth sense in my report?'

'I just saw some froth in a severed vein,' she said, shaking her head. 'No psychic powers involved.' The spurt of satisfaction she'd got from her hunch being proved right had been short-lived. The frothy blood she'd glimpsed while Jason was eviscerating Becka was just further proof that her occasional insights were down not to some 'special bond' with the dead but the result of straightforward observation.

Watching him scarf down the last of his noodles before lifting the bowl to drain the last of the soup, Cassie felt a wave of affection. Archie was one of the good guys, he was uncomplicated, amusing company – and the sex worked. So why couldn't she see them getting to the next stage, i.e. living together? On the other hand, why did that have to be the inevitable next step? The only person she'd ever lived with was Rachel, a trainee psychotherapist who had packed her bags and her umbrella palm into an Uber after five months, blaming the break-up on Cassie's inability to 'express herself emotionally'. . . At least she never got any of that sort of chat with Archie.

Uncomplicated. What could possibly be wrong with that?

FLYTE

That afternoon, as those not on lates were packing up for the day, DCI Steadman swung by the office, wearing his coat, to ask Dean Willets for the latest on what everyone was calling the Hugger Mugger case.

Willets jumped to his feet, his stance mirroring Steadman's body language, feet planted apart. 'We're putting together a file of all recent muggers per your suggestion, see if anyone has used the tactic before, and cross-checking descriptions against our suspect.' It made Flyte want to gag, the way Willets sucked up to him. Apparently, they'd worked together for years, with Willets following his old boss to Major Crimes. Still, at least Steadman played a straight bat – always at pains to treat all the DSs the same.

After updating Steadman, Willets said, 'A few of us are going for payday drinks down the BrewShack. Fancy joining us, guv? We could toast your promotion.'

Steadman looked embarrassed. 'Well, I'm only acting up while the DCI chair is empty.' The regular DCI of Major Crimes was on a placement with the National Crime Agency and Steadman had been bumped up to run the unit in his absence. He looked at his watch. 'Maybe just a swift pint.' He smiled over at Flyte. 'Are you joining these reprobates?'

Willets flashed her a look tinged with anxiety; she'd overheard him arranging drinks earlier with his little cabal but she hadn't been invited.

Flyte hesitated, about to cover for Willets. But Steadman had clocked it immediately – he was perceptive like that. His gaze went back to Flyte. 'Will you join us?'

Although she wasn't keen, she appreciated his efforts. 'Sure,' she said. 'Just a quick one.'

The pub – an old backstreet boozer that had been made over into a craft beer place – was Flyte's idea of hell on earth. A football match commentary was blasting out from a giant screen that kept catching her unwilling eye. Despite there being free tables, Willets and co chose to stand, and as she clutched a glass of sub-standard Sauvignon – the only acceptable option on the stunted wine list – she felt her blood pressure surge every time someone pushed past her to the bar.

'Thank you, Sebastian,' she said, with a smile at DS Coles, who'd just bought her a drink. He was the friendliest of her colleagues, probably a few years younger than her, in his early thirties. At around forty-five, Dean Willets was the oldest of the group, Steadman aside, which might help explain why all the others seemed to defer to him. He was standing nearby in a group with the boss, and from what she could hear above the din the chat was all Arsenal this, West Ham that.

'You're welcome, but call me Seb, would you?' He crinkled his eyes at her. 'The only person who calls me "Sebastian" is my mum, when she's telling me off.' His gaze lingered on her and she wondered if he was just being friendly or something more. Having been in the Job what, fifteen years, she was accustomed to being viewed by male officers as a sexual challenge or someone to be mistrusted by virtue of her sex – or both. Still, he was good-looking.

Her gaze fell on Dean Willets in the midst of the neighbouring group, telling some story, although it was clear the only audience he cared about was Steadman.

'How long have Dean and the boss worked together?' she asked.

'More than ten years,' said Sebastian – *Seb*. 'Dean's always going on about the good old days at Hackney nick when he was a uniform in a squad car and the boss was patrol sergeant. This was back in the Jurassic era.'

Recognising that he'd made a joke, Flyte smiled obligingly.

'I hear Dean even dragged him along on one of his shooting expeditions a couple of times,' Seb went on.

'Shooting?!'

Seb laughed at her expression. 'It's all above board. Dean likes going out to Essex to shoot bunnies at weekends – vermin control for the farmers. He's always on at me to go with.'

'And have you? Gone shooting?' She widened her eyes.

He shook his head. 'Slaying innocent wildlife isn't really my cuppa, to be honest.' He leaned in, and she got a sour gust of his beery breath. 'I hear Dean goes a bit Rambo, you know, camo jacket and all.'

'But Steadman doesn't go anymore?'

'No, not for years. He hasn't socialised outside work since he became a DI – except occasionally this kind of thing.' He tipped his beer bottle towards the group. 'Apparently, he could have retired on full pension six years ago but he stayed on.'

'Why?' The biggest perk of the job for someone in their fifties like Steadman was the right to retire on a full pension after thirty years' service.

'His daughter is doing a four-year degree at uni.' Seb rubbed his fingers together to indicate how much that would be costing. 'In any case, I think he genuinely loves the Job.'

Steadman was making his way over to them, carrying his coat. 'I have to be off. My daughter Emily has been up in Cambridge today checking out her new digs and the wife is cooking some fancy meal.' He chuckled. 'More than my life's worth to be late for those two.'

'What's your daughter studying?' Flyte asked.

'Anthropology, at Trinity College. Nothing that will get her a proper job, in other words.' Steadman rolled his eyes, failing entirely to disguise the pride on his face. 'How did it go at the mortuary today, Phyllida?'

'Oh fine, boss. I've sorted the paperwork and taken some photographs.'

'Sorry to lump you with CID's housekeeping. But you can punt it back into their in-tray now.' He checked his watch. 'I'll leave you youngsters to enjoy yourselves.'

Flyte had been thinking of leaving herself but she knew the protocol was to buy a round, getting a mineral water for herself this time. Seb had joined the rest of the group and she got there just in time to hear Dean Willets telling the end of an anecdote which she gathered was about two gay men he'd caught having sex in public. '. . . So, I said to him, "Didn't your mother teach you not to talk with your mouth full?"'

Hell's bells.

Nathan Cassidy, Willets' chief acolyte, spat some beer; the two other DSs laughed; only Seb looked embarrassed. Most uncomfortable of all was the way Willets and the rest of them all looked to Flyte for her reaction. She felt a blush flood her face – a reaction she never could control.

'Of course, this was all back in the Stone Age,' said Willets in a pseudo-disapproving tone. 'Nowadays we positively celebrate *al fresco* gay love.' A pause. 'Personally, I've got no problem with it – I'd just rather it was girl-on-girl action.' Earning another noisy snort from Nathan. 'Don't you agree, Phyllida?'

The implication was clear: that she was a lesbian. It wasn't the first time she'd faced the allegation. Did her efficiency and no-nonsense demeanour play into certain tired stereotypes?

Flyte knew that someone like Cassie Raven, who openly dated both men and women, would have a smart comeback to this kind of homophobic remark, something that would put Willets back in his box and raise a laugh. But she wasn't Cassie Raven.

'Very funny,' she said tightly into the waiting silence. 'Well, I want to catch *Newsnight* so I'd better . . .' And feeling like a fool she grabbed her coat and headed out, hearing the suppressed laughter that broke out in her wake. *Flaming fishcakes* – why on earth had she mentioned *Newsnight*?

Bants, 'canteen culture' . . . It was worse here than in CID, where there had been other female officers on the team. Flyte understood where it came from. The gallows humour and off-colour 'jokes' were a way of blowing off steam, a reaction to the constant diet of random death and violence you were exposed to in the Job. The trouble was, the humour always came from the same standpoint – that of a white heterosexual guy. Gay people, women, anyone of colour, or from a different culture? They were the Other.

The Met could send its police officers on diversity training courses every week from now until Doomsday but nothing would change until the police started to look a bit more like the people they were supposed to serve.

Of course, if she were to report Willets' comments up the chain of command he'd be in big trouble. And what would that achieve? They would both spend the next few months mired in an investigative process which would leave him with a slapped wrist and her relationship with her new team damaged beyond repair.

She pictured her darling pops, heard him saying in cod Latin, '*Noli illegitimi carborundum.*'

Don't let the bastards grind you down.

Chapter Six

'Do you remember your mum's flapjacks, Catkin?' Eyes alight with nostalgia, Callum smiled the lopsided smile that always tweaked Cassie's heart. 'With her secret ingredient of dried apricots?'

Dried figs, actually. But she shook her head, taking a tiny forkful of kremowka, a puff pastry tart with a baked cream filling that her gran had made.

They were at Weronika's flat, Cassie's childhood home, for Sunday dinner, which she'd only rarely missed since leaving home at seventeen to live in a squat. They'd already had a rib-busting main course of bigos – except today, as well as a vegetarian version for Cassie, Weronika had made one with pork and Polish sausage, because, in her words, 'men need meat'.

Cassie knew it was thoughtful of her, and a ton of extra work, but still she couldn't help feeling edged out, like she was no longer the sole focus of her gran's attention.

Childish and *selfish. Double bubble*, as Jason would say.

Since Callum's return to Camden he'd been joining them most Sundays. Her grandmother naturally felt guilty over his wrongful conviction for her daughter's murder, having told the court he'd given her a black eye when Katherine had actually hurt herself falling over drunk.

'Fantastic meal, Babcia,' said Cassie, using her napkin to hide the uneaten portion of kremowka and pushing her plate away.

'You didn't finish it! And you hardly ate any bigos.' Nothing escaped those beady eyes, as Cassie had learned from living here through childhood and teenage years, before she'd mounted the great escape.

'Your mama always ate like a sparrow,' said the old lady. 'The trouble I had getting her to eat a proper meal!'

'Except when she was pregnant with you,' Callum told Cassie. 'I remember her having some really weird cravings.'

'Yes!' Weronika put a hand on his arm. 'Remember the time when all she would eat was banana and bacon sandwiches?!'

The two of them chuckled together and Cassie dredged up a smile.

She understood their desire to keep Kath's memory alive, and also to forge the three of them into a family unit, but since she barely remembered her mum it sometimes felt like they were discussing a stranger.

A few fresh memories had floated to the surface when Cassie had been digging into her mum's murder, and now and again she had even sensed her presence. But once the real murderer had been charged, those feelings had evaporated.

It was less painful just to stop thinking about her.

Callum slapped his skinny ribs with both hands, making a hollow sound. 'That was a grand spread, Weronika.' Getting to his feet, he said, 'I'll clear the table. And then we could take a look at those school reports?'

Christ on a bike. Cassie's gran had mentioned she still had her daughter's school reports which meant the rest of the evening was going to be another Kath-nostalgia-fest.

Cassie surreptitiously scratched the back of her right hand; she'd developed some kind of a rash. 'Can't we just watch telly or play cards like normal people?' she asked tetchily.

Seeing her grandmother's face fall was like a gut punch. 'Oh, I don't mean to be grumpy, Babcia – it's just I've had a tough day at work.'

'Oh, I'm sorry to hear that, *tygrysek*.' Looking concerned, she reached out to touch her granddaughter's arm. 'Are you still seeing that nice Dr Archie?'

'Uh-huh.' As Cassie stood to help clear the table, she cursed herself for letting Archie pick her up from the flat a couple of weeks back. He'd charmed the pants off her gran, naturally, interrogating her about life in fifties Poland, including her six months in a Warsaw jail for organising a student protest against the Stalinist regime.

When she returned from the kitchen, Weronika was telling Callum, 'He went to Harlow you know. It's a fancy private school.'

'Is that right?' said Callum, sending Cassie a surreptitious wink.

Cassie rolled her eyes.

Even after she'd discovered her gran's surprisingly laid-back attitude to her unconventional love life, Cassie hardly ever talked about boyfriends or girlfriends. Why? Because having reached the conclusion she'd never settle down with anyone she didn't want to get her gran's hopes up.

When she sat down again, she saw Weronika looking at the rash on the backs of her hands – and caught the tail end of the look that passed between her and Callum.

'Cassandra, darling,' she said, 'you've not been yourself these last few months. You know you can talk to us about anything that's bothering you.'

Yikes.

'I'm fine, Babcia.'

'You have had some terrible shocks recently,' Weronika went on. 'Finding out about your poor mama, then your friend drowning.'

Ducking their worried looks, she started to collect the used napkins.

'We know you're a tough cookie, Catkin,' her dad chipped in, 'but you know, anyone would find this . . . stuff hard.'

'I'm fine. Really I am,' she parroted, folding one of the napkins into a tiny neat square. All she could think about was the cigarette she'd have the moment she was out on the walkway.

She stood and leaned over to kiss her grandmother's cheek. 'Thanks for a lovely dinner, Babcia, but I really have to go: I've got an early start tomorrow.'

Going to get her jacket from the hook by the front door, she found Callum reaching over her for his.

'Dad, I really don't need walking home,' trying not to sound impatient.

'It's getting dark and I don't like you walking down that towpath on your own' – shaking his head like he couldn't be talked out of it.

The freaking patriarch routine made her snap.

'I managed to survive without you for twenty-one years,' she told him under her breath. 'I don't need a big daddy to look after me now.'

He looked crushed but still Cassie had to resist slamming the door behind her.

FLYTE

After having the weekend off, Flyte knew that she had no business returning to the mortuary for the canal guy's post-mortem. A detective wouldn't normally attend a routine PM on a non-sus death, especially since she'd been told to hand the case back to CID. But since she was on lates, not starting until 2 p.m., she told herself that she'd be doing it on her own time.

The PM list was starting at the crack of dawn so here she was pitching up to the mortuary on a chilly morning at 0700 hours. And the first person she saw was Cassie Raven, leaning against the wall, one leg up behind her, a coffee in one hand, a cigarette in the other, looking for all the world like a truanting teenager.

'I must say I'm astonished to see you, of all people, smoking,' said Flyte.

'Don't start,' the girl snapped. 'And what do you mean, me of all people?'

'Because you see what smoking does to people's lungs, all the early deaths it causes!'

'I only do it occasionally' – sounding surly. But she dropped the half-smoked cigarette and ground it out with the heel of a boot that would look more appropriate on a hod carrier. 'So, you here for Green-Eyes?' she said over her shoulder as she headed inside.

Cassie didn't ask why she was attending a routine PM, which was just as well. Flyte couldn't really nail the reason herself, beyond a feeling that she needed to see the guy's face again. She'd checked the recent reports of missing persons received by the Met and found nobody matching the description of the dark-haired young man. Why was his absence still unnoticed by his workplace, his friends and family?

Once Flyte returned wearing PPE, Cassie introduced her to the pathologist. 'Dr Curzon, this is Detective Sergeant Flyte.' She gleaned from Cassie's polite neutrality that the two of them weren't exactly bosom buddies.

'How delightful to meet you, Sergeant.' Curzon gave her an appreciative once-over which he probably thought of as 'chivalric admiration' but which actually came across as 'handsy uncle'. 'Welcome to the house of mirth. I would shake hands but . . .' He waggled gloved hands that were gore- and blood-stained.

'Thanks for having me. I'm here to see the unidentified male?'

Curzon frowned, but the older technician – a big middle-aged guy with a red face – had just arrived at the bench carrying a pail full of what looked like offal.

'You here for Freddie?' Even this guy, who must be fifty, had a diamond stud in his ear and an ace of spades with a skull inside tattooed on the side of his neck. Why were all mortuary folk so . . . peculiar?

'Freddie the Floater,' he clarified. 'This is him.' Tipping the bucket so that a deep red organ sprawled onto Curzon's bench.

Curzon chuckled at Flyte's expression as the meat-faced guy returned to his bench whistling. 'Technician humour I'm afraid. Jason calls all bodies recovered from water Freddie.'

'What if they're female?'

41

'Fergie.'

'Right.' Tamping down her distaste.

As Curzon started to slice into what Flyte now recognised as a liver with workmanlike strokes, the smell triggered a childhood memory: the sting of a slapped wrist, her mother's mouth an angry lipsticked gash ... 'Eat your liver, Phyllida! I don't cook perfectly good food simply to throw it in the bin!' *Why would anyone serve a child something she hated?*

'Are there any clues yet, as to cause of death?' she asked.

'There are no ante-mortem injuries to suggest foul play, so the COD is almost certainly going to be drowning. Toxicology will confirm whether he was drunk or on drugs.'

'It's clear-cut then?'

'Drowning is never clear-cut.' There was amusement in his voice at her ignorance. 'Death in water is a multifaceted issue. The water in this chap's lungs could equally easily have found its way there post-mortem. He appears to be physically fit and healthy, and in the absence of any other obvious cause of death we can only deduce from the circumstances that he drowned.' He looked at her. 'Unless you have a line of enquiry suggesting otherwise ...?'

'No, no. I just wanted to ensure we've covered all the bases.' The rusty-iron smell coming off the liver was making her want to gag. 'How long has he been dead?'

'Difficult to say. Immersion in cold water delays the decomposition process which makes time of death harder to calculate. But there is already some putrefaction. If I had to hazard a guess I would say he'd been dead around thirty-six to forty-eight hours when he was found.'

Enough time for the decomposition gases to build up in his gut and cause the body to float back to the surface. 'How old would you say he was?' she asked.

42

'Late twenties or early thirties? As you will know, estimating the age of a dead adult is not an exact science.'

'I'd like to take a look at the body.'

'Of course!' But Curzon's mask of chivalry had slipped to reveal a grimace of impatience. 'Jason has popped out for a nicotine fix, I suspect, but I am sure Ms Raven would be happy to assist. I would usually accompany you myself but I have a lunch to discuss a paper I'm giving at a conference. In Dubai.' Unable to resist the brag.

Cassie led her to the autopsy station where the shell of the drowned man's body lay. The pallor of his skin was tinged blue now, in startling contrast to the Malbec-red chasm from throat to groin where his organs had been. Discoloured patches, which she knew were signs of decomposition, had started to surface on his torso.

Flyte had been coping all right up until now, but now her knees threatened to fold.

Cassie touched her arm, looking concerned. 'Are you OK? Do you want to sit down for a minute?'

'I'm fine. It's just I haven't been to a post-mortem in ages.' Although Cassie had taken her hand away, Flyte could still feel the touch of her fingers on her upper arm.

Out of nowhere, she got an image of Eleanor, who'd been her best friend at boarding school – at least until Flyte had blurted out a declaration of love over a private midnight feast. She pushed the memory away. A schoolgirl crush didn't make you a lesbian.

The dead guy wasn't especially tall, and now she could see his whole body his shoulders and biceps struck her as out of pro-portion for his frame. 'Is this post-mortem swelling?' she asked, indicating his top half.

Cassie shook her head. Pointing to the wedge-shaped muscle between his neck and shoulder. 'From the humped trapezius, looks like he was a gym bunny.'

A gym bunny who couldn't swim. Flyte lowered her voice. 'So, do you think he drowned?'

'Looks that way.' Cassie shrugged.

'Is there really no way to confirm it? I mean microscopically or something?' Flyte persisted.

'You can try aspirating the sphenoid sinus behind the nose to see if he breathed in any water. You can run tests for diatoms – waterborne organisms, which, if they're breathed in, can reach the bone marrow . . .'

'But . . . ?'

'It all costs money and nothing gives a hundred per cent confirmation.' She pulled a face. 'So it ain't gonna happen.'

Cassie appeared to be making more of an effort this time, but she still showed little of her previous curiosity or engagement. Flyte bent to peer at the underside of the body which was a painful-looking bright red at his shoulders, back, calves and heels. 'Didn't you say you found him face down in the water? Yet the blood has pooled to the back.'

Cassie nodded. 'Yeah, you do usually get lividity on the front of the body and in the fingers and toes in drownings. But when he sank initially he might have ended up on his back. By the time he re-floated and rolled over the blood would have coagulated and stayed put.' She sent her an enquiring look. 'What is it about this guy that has you so interested?'

Flyte hesitated, unsure whether to admit the reason. Since taking the photos of Green-Eyes, as Cassie called him, she'd found herself going back to the images several times, feeling the mental itch of recognition.

'I can't shake the feeling that I've met him,' she admitted. 'But I have no idea why or where.'

Cassie considered this. 'Maybe he just has one of those faces. You know, regular features, dark brown hair, good-looking but nothing too memorable?'

She was probably right. Apart from the acne, Green-Eyes had the generically handsome look of a Z-list American actor you might see on some obscure cable channel.

Flyte straightened. 'I expect someone will report him missing soon enough. You'll be keeping him here for the time being? We'll need to take fingerprints and run a DNA test in case he's already on the system.'

'Sure. But if no one claims him within thirty days he'll go into the deep freeze.'

'And after that?' – although she already knew the answer.

'He'll get a public health funeral.'

The fate of an unclaimed body; what used to be called a pauper's funeral, with only an officiant presiding. And that saddest of all ends to a life: an unmarked grave. Their eyes met, sharing for an unspoken moment Flyte's own loss.

Giving into a sudden impulse, she asked, 'Can I look at his eyes?' Leaning forward, Cassie gently lifted one eyelid. His eyes had dimmed, the corneas clouding, but their colour was still discernible: a distinctive goldish-green.

Flyte stared at them, once again feeling that nagging flicker of recognition. But his eyes, hair, jawline, they were like a fiendishly complicated jigsaw puzzle that defied reassembly.

45

Chapter Seven

Cassie woke to the shush and slap of water on wood, accompanied by a more urgent sound – a loud purring in her ear and the dead weight of Macavity on her chest.

'Oh, you're back, are you?' She stroked his black silken fur. 'Good of you to show your face.'

Macavity was a rescue cat she'd adopted when she'd lived in the flat. The cat shelter had advised her to keep him indoors as he'd been a lifelong house cat. After the move to the boat he'd spent weeks sulking below deck, staring moodily out of the portholes before finally venturing out into the cockpit. Nowadays, he was king of the towpath, jumping on and off neighbouring boats and sometimes disappearing for twenty-four hours.

'You're only here for breakfast, am I right?' His unwinking green eyes stared back at her. 'You treat this place like a hotel.'

Yawning convulsively, she dragged herself out of bed. She dimly remembered a looping nightmare in which she'd had repeatedly tried to fish her dad's body out of the canal, failing every time. Eventually his face had disappeared beneath the bubbling black water. Remembering the unkind words she'd flung at him on Sunday night – about how she'd done fine without him all these years – she cringed. It wasn't his fault that he'd spent half his adult life banged up for a crime he didn't commit.

She knew she ought to make an effort to join in the conversation about her mum, start processing her death ... *yada, yada* ... But the more Callum and her gran shoved it down her throat the more it made her dig her heels in.

She reached for her phone and tapped out an apologetic message to him, signing off with 'love Catkin' and adding a string of guilty 'x's. The rash on the backs of her hands had got worse – angry red, the skin broken in places – presumably from scratching it in the night. She should get something for it.

After pulling her leather jacket on over her pyjamas, Cassie took her coffee up on deck. It was dry but cloudy out, the wind-ruffled water a dull jade green today. She loved the canal's chameleon trickery – its shifts from near black through every shade of battleship grey and khaki to a reflective silver blue.

She remembered hearing Green-Eyes' skull knocking against her bows, and how fresh his body had seemed when the cops pulled him out of the water, like he'd only gone in the night before. But yesterday, while showing him to Flyte, she'd been puzzled to notice the signs and smells of decomposition. Decomp didn't usually progress that fast.

'All right, Cassie?' She turned to see Gaz, the bloke who owned the neighbouring narrowboat, on deck and smoking his first joint of the day. 'Want some?' He gestured with it.

'I'd love to, but I'm working today,' she said with a grimace.

'Yeah, we don't want you cutting your 'and off.' Gaz laughed, triggered a wheezing cough.

Cassie had instantly warmed to the boat folk she'd met on the canal. An alternative breed of vagabonds and eccentrics, stoners and loners, they reminded her of the people she'd once squatted with when she was seventeen – before she'd got her science A levels at evening classes and rejoined the straight world.

Gaz had to be in his late sixties, but he seemed to thrive on boat life. Despite consuming his own bodyweight in drugs as a roadie in a rock band back in the day he looked to be in good nick, jumping on and off his boat like someone twenty years younger. Maybe it was the yoga: now and again she spotted him in some improbable positions out on deck.

'I see you got the wood burner fired up last night,' he said.

'Yeah, just like you said, it draws better when it's windy.'

Gaz had been a fund of boaty intel. It was him who'd drilled her in port and starboard, stern and bows, and where she'd need to take the 'cassette' or Elsan toilet when it needed emptying – a task she wasn't looking forward to.

'Water level's low,' said Gaz, frowning at the canal surface. 'We could do with some proper rain soon. You should let me rig you up a harvester.'

Lashed to the deck of Gaz's boat was a rain collection apparatus cobbled together out of two black plastic drums jaggedly split lengthways which fed rainwater via a hosepipe to the tank. It wasn't pretty, but it spun out his water supplies.

'I hear you found some poor pisshead who went for a swim in the canal?' he asked.

She nodded. News travelled fast among boat folk.

'I saw a dead guy the lock-keeper pulled out once, years ago.' He gestured upstream with his spliff. 'I'll never forget the state of his hands when they laid him on the towpath. They were covered in scratches and gouges, his fingernails bloody stumps from trying to claw his way up over the side.' He gave a graphic shiver. 'Was your one the same?'

'No, nothing like that.' Cassie couldn't recall seeing any damage to Green-Eyes' hands when she'd shown Flyte the body. But then if he couldn't swim or he panicked in the cold water then he might never have made it back to the edge.

She stood up. 'Gotta go. See ya, Gaz.'

'No peace for a working stiff, eh?' he said with a rusty chuckle. 'I remember it well.'

At work she donned clean scrubs, but whereas once that routine had filled her with a sense of purpose and anticipation, now each layer felt like a lead blanket, and the day ahead something to be endured.

Checking the time, she stifled a sigh. Becka Bennett's husband, Dan, was coming in to view her body, which meant it was time to put on her game face.

Ten minutes later, she was leading him into the viewing room. He was probably only in his early fifties, but shock and grief had aged him by a decade. Gaunt and zombie-like, only nominally present, it was clear that he'd barely started to process his wife's death. The room was bisected by glass doors covered with a curtain behind which Becka's body was laid out on a trolley.

He stood still and silent, preoccupied with his thoughts, as Cassie went through the script intended to prepare him for the sight of his dead wife: that there might be visible stitching, even describing the red coverlet covering her. One step at a time towards the new reality.

'Red to hide the bloodstains. Practical.' It was the first thing he'd said. 'When you see it on the telly everything's all white and pristine.'

'Becka might look quite different from how she did in life,' Cassie said gently. 'Living faces are a record of a lifetime of expressions, smiles and frowns. When we die the facial muscles slacken.' It was surprisingly common for the bereaved to deny that the body they were being shown belonged to the person they'd lost.

'Shall I?' At his nod, Cassie pulled the curtain cord to reveal Becka in profile on the other side of the glass, the coverlet pulled up to her chin to cover the stitching of the midline incision. Seeing his frown she wondered if she'd need to show him his wife's dolphin tattoo to persuade him it was her.

But after a moment he said, 'That's my girl,' his voice shaky.

Taking her cue from him, she opened the door and they went through. He stroked his wife's hair, becoming chatty. 'She was a true original, my wife. Gave up a good job in insurance a few years ago to start a dog grooming business which she absolutely loved.'

Cassie adopted an encouraging expression; some people needed to share with whoever was present.

A mystified look crossed his face. 'She was always so *healthy*. Do they know yet what was wrong with her?' He turned a questioning gaze on Cassie.

She shook her head. 'There are still tests that need running on Becka's blood and tissue before we'll know for sure.' Which was technically true. Anyway, it was up to the coroner to drop the bombshell: that Becka's death had come in the shape of an air bubble injected into her vein – that if Dan hadn't brought her into A & E she might still be alive. Worse still, that whatever had caused her stroke-like symptoms in the first place was likely to remain a mystery.

'Becka's hospital notes said she didn't have a GP?' asked Cassie.

'She hated doctors.' He grinned. 'She always said a doctor was as likely to kill as cure you.'

Oh Jesus.

'But she took good care of herself, you know, ate well, exercised, and went to a homeopath.'

Cassie's ears pricked up. 'What did she go to the homeopath for?'

Dan looked awkward. 'Oh, women's things. Her age, you know . . .'

She'd been forty-seven, Cassie recalled. 'Was Becka starting to experience menopause?'

He shrugged, embarrassed. 'Yes, she had those hot flushes, trouble sleeping.'

'No headaches before?'

'Just occasionally I think. But I'm a long-distance lorry driver so I'm away a lot, and maybe she didn't want to worry me? It was lucky I was home that night when she got really sick.'

'Do you mind telling me what happened that evening?'

He furrowed his brow, remembering. 'It started like a normal headache, you know, but it just gradually got worse and worse.'

'And the weakness on her left side? Was that a sudden thing?'

'No, that came on bit by bit as well.'

A distant bell was sounding in Cassie's head but she didn't know why.

'Let's hope that the tests get to the bottom of her symptoms,' she told him. 'Once the coroner has the full report he'll release the body, and you can make arrangements for the funeral.'

After Dan had left, Cassie went online, trying to nail what was bugging her about Dan's report of his wife's symptoms. An hour later, she put in a call to Archie.

'Hello, beautiful,' he said.

He had a way with him, that was undeniable.

'Listen, remember Becka Bennett?'

'The air embolism?'

'*The lady* with the air embolism, yes.' It pissed her off, pathologists' habit of referring to the deceased not by name but by cause of death. 'So I was wondering. Could she have been suffering a hemiplegic migraine?' From the Greek *hemi-* for half; *-plegia* from the verb 'to strike'. Hemiplegic migraine was an extreme version of the condition that could cause muscular weakness on one side, mimicking symptoms of stroke.

'Hmm.' Archie mused. 'It's rare of course.'

'But she did present with severe headache and unilateral weakness.'

'True,' said Archie. 'What made you think of it?'

'Becka's husband said that her symptoms got worse gradually.'

'While the effects of stroke are usually sudden. In any case there was nothing in the brain to account for her symptoms.'

'A hemiplegic migraine would leave no trace, right?'

'Right,' he mused. 'I'll look into it. The ante-mortem diagnosis isn't really my bailiwick, but if it stands up I'll put it in the PM report. The coroner will want to know what brought the unfortunate lady into hospital in the first place.'

FLYTE

When the alarm woke her at seven o'clock the following morning, Flyte started the day as she always did. Turning to the framed photo on her bedside table, she put her fingers first to her lips and then to the face of Poppy, the daughter she had given birth to three years ago.

Stillborn – but still born.

The photo, which a kind nurse had encouraged her to take in the final hour she spent with her, showed a wise little face, eyes closed and one doll-like hand curled beneath her chin like a question mark. For more than two years after it happened Flyte hadn't even been able to look at the image – had literally refused to look her loss in the face – but nowadays it made her feel as if her daughter was still with her. Her early feelings of near-unhinged grief and fury had gradually subsided, giving way to an ever-present sense of loss – but also a profound gratitude for her daughter's brief existence.

Her marriage hadn't survived the tragedy, not helped by the fact that her ex-husband Matt had been focused on 'moving on' from the loss – as if that were possible. While Flyte had still been deranged with grief and drugs, he had allowed Poppy to be cremated with two other stillborn babies, their mingled ashes scattered in the hospital memorial garden. *An unmarked grave.*

Her thoughts drifted to Green-Eyes, the young man fished out of the canal, lying in his cold drawer at the mortuary, unclaimed and unidentified. It was five days since he'd been found and still nobody had reported anyone of his description missing. Was it simply the anonymous nature of inner-city London? So many people seemed to drift here before moving on, often leaving little trace.

Before heading into work there was a call that she'd been putting off.

'Hello, Mother. It's Phyllida.' Introducing herself averted an embarrassing silence while Sylvia worked out who she was.

'Oh, hello, dear. How are you? Is it getting cold there?'

'It's only September, Mother.' Her parents had moved to Cyprus for her father's army posting, sending the thirteen-year-old Flyte to a girls' boarding school in Northumbria. After her darling pops had died seventeen years ago, Sylvia had stayed on, later marrying another expat called Ralph.

What a crying shame her father had died first. These days, Flyte felt no guilt at this emotion. Sylvia was a cold fish, simply not cut out for motherhood; all her childhood memories of affection and fun emanated from Pops. 'How's Colditz?' he would whisper to her, twinkly-eyed, when she came to Cyprus for the school holidays. 'Have you built the glider yet?' Clearly, he'd have taken her with them rather than exiling her to that chilly dump on Hadrian's Wall peopled with dull-witted teachers and even dimmer classmates.

'I've got a date for the ceremony.'

She could almost hear Sylvia racking her brains.

'The memorial and naming ceremony for baby Poppy, your granddaughter?' said Flyte.

'Of course, darling. They are doing it in a church, you said?'

'Yes, the local C. of E. priest has been really helpful.'

'Oh, not a real church?' Disappointment in her voice. Sylvia Ferrers had been born into a grand Catholic family who could trace their roots back to before the Reformation. 'Do you know the family seat in Norfolk had a priest hole?' she asked for at least the hundredth time. 'Such a rich history.' These reminders of Sylvia's glittering forebears were always edged with bitterness, underlined by the unspoken reminder that she had 'married down' in choosing Flyte's father, who had never risen higher than the rank of major. In marrying Ralph, she had at least traded up to a brigadier.

'As you know, I don't have a faith per se but it's important to me to mark the fact she existed,' said Flyte, digging her nails into her palms. The only way to do that was to hear Poppy Flyte-Howard named in church. Matt hadn't entered a name on the stillbirth certificate and when Flyte tried to rectify that later she discovered that – for some cruel and unaccountable reason – giving a stillborn baby a name retrospectively wasn't permitted.

'Poor Phyllida,' said Sylvia awkwardly.

'So, I was hoping you might attend the service. Matt will be there, so it would be just the three of us.'

'You mean fly to the UK?' From Sylvia's tone you'd think she'd been asked to board a rocket to Mars. 'You know how I loathe flying, darling. And it's so expensive.'

Flyte was determined to keep her temper. Sylvia's attitude could be summed up by her astonishing response when she'd learned of Poppy's death: 'You could always have another baby.' Her continuing insensitivity had recently caused the polite détente that characterised their relationship to crack open into outright conflict.

'It's less than five hours and you can afford to fly club class,' Flyte pointed out. 'You're welcome to stay in the flat; I can take the sofa bed.'

'Oh, no, no.' Horror in her voice. 'That's so kind of you, darling, but I couldn't put you to that trouble.' Sylvia sighed. 'I suppose I could stay at the Pelham, and visit your great-aunt in Kensington afterwards. Two birds with one stone as it were. All right, darling, send me the date and I'll look into it.'

'I appreciate it, Mother.'

'And now I must rush because the man who cleans the pool is coming and Ralph is out playing golf. Chin-chin, darling.'

Flyte decided to call CID Camden, where she'd worked till recently, to hand back the drowned guy before heading into the office – she didn't want Dean Willets finding out she still had the case. She had a feeling he'd leap at the chance to drop her in it.

'Hey, Josh . . . Yes, all good, thanks. Listen, I helped out filing the report on a Cat 2 death, a John Doe fished out of the canal when you lot were busy last week.'

'Oh, great. So I'm the lucky winner of an unidentified floater?' he asked. In anyone else she might have objected to his tone but she liked Josh. He was the brightest of the younger DCs, and they'd had a good working relationship.

'An artist's impression has gone to the mispers database,' she told him. 'Nobody has reported him missing yet.'

'Down and out?'

She pictured the upmarket brands listed on the inventory. 'No. He had clothes worth six or seven hundred quid on his back. You'll need to send a CSI to the mortuary to take a deadset from him.' A deadset: aka fingerprints taken from a body.

'Hmm. Sounds to me like the poor old taxpayer will be shelling out for his funeral.' Josh sounded sceptical.

Flyte knew that Josh would do a competent job, but no more. She was gripped by a sudden impulse; she couldn't let Green-Eyes go, not yet.

'I tell you what,' she said. 'I'm seeing a reporter at the *Gazette* later about another case. Why don't I give them the details, see if we can get his pic in the next edition?'

'OK great, thanks for that, Sarge.' Josh sounded delighted.

'I'll need to give your name as contact obviously, since technically it's back with CID.'

'Technically?' Josh didn't miss much. 'The post-mortem didn't find anything, did it?'

'No, no, but I wouldn't mind keeping a watching brief on it. I suppose I'd just like to know whether the guy gets reunited with his family.'

Josh was probably tempted to take the mickey out of her for such a sentimental admission but instead he just said, 'Understood, Sarge.'

After hanging up, she bit her lip. It wasn't like her to expose herself like that.

Of course she was risking a rocket from DCI Steadman, and before she'd even had a chance to prove herself, but she simply couldn't abandon Green-Eyes. And not because of the feeling that he looked familiar. No. She simply couldn't bear the idea of him being laid to rest with no one to mourn him, just as Poppy's ashes had been scattered to the wind with nobody there who had loved her.

Chapter Eight

As it was her day off Cassie spent her morning at the launderette – with no washing machine or tumble dryer on the boat it was a necessary weekly chore.

While her stuff was drying, she killed time doing some online research into why Green-Eyes' body seemed to be decomposing faster than she'd expect. She waded through a couple of papers on post-mortem processes but by the time her clothes were dry she was none the wiser. None of the common factors that could speed up putrefaction applied: he hadn't been wrapped in plastic, there had been no insect activity and he definitely wasn't carrying excessive body fat. The only other possibility was a malfunction of the body store refrigeration.

Returning to the boat, she saw her grandmother coming the other way and rushed to help her climb on board. 'Babcia! What are you doing here?' Trying to take her arm.

'I still have the full use of my legs, thank you,' said Weronika with a beady look, pushing aside her outstretched hand. Following her granddaughter below deck she squeezed herself into the bench seat at the table before pulling a Tupperware box out of her carrier bag.

'What's all this, then?' Cassie asked as she took the seat opposite.

'Oh, just a few pierogi. I made too many and I didn't want them to go to waste. The filling is ceps and twaróg.' The mushroom and curd cheese version of the dumplings: the vegetarian kind she only ever made for Cassie. 'They will keep fresh for a week in the fridge.' She cast a sceptical look around the narrow cabin. 'You do have a fridge?' Making as if to get up.

'Of course I do. Here, let me.' She didn't want her grandmother seeing the contents of the mini-fridge – a tin of cat food, beer, vodka and the remnants of last night's pizza.

As Cassie stowed away the food, Weronika pinned her searching gaze on her granddaughter. 'You know I'm worried about you, *tygrysek*. And your father is too.'

'You've seen him?'

'He pops round for coffee occasionally.'

Imagining them talking about her brought a spurt of irritation. As Cassie's surrogate parent, her grandmother might have earned that right, but Callum? He'd only turned up in their lives five minutes ago.

'Really, Babcia, I'm fine. Work's been difficult lately and I guess I'm still getting used to living on a boat.'

'It's more than that, I can tell.'

Cassie blew out a breath. 'Babcia, I don't want you worrying about me.'

'You can only put your feelings in the deep freeze for so long you know. Sooner or later you need to talk about your mama.' Taking both Cassie's hands in hers, Babcia turned them palm down and nodded at the raised welts, weeping here and there. She made a sympathetic tutting sound. 'I saw this when you came to dinner. This is what happens when you bottle things up,' she said, reaching into the carrier bag. 'I brought you some calamine lotion. Use it every day, and at night, *dobrze*?'

'All right. Thanks.'

Fixing Cassie with an entreating gaze, she went on. 'Your father and I, we were wondering whether you would consider talking to a doctor.'

'You mean a head doctor?!' Cassie stared at her. 'Even when I brought dead animals home as a kid you didn't send me to a shrink.'

Shortly after being told that her parents had died, Cassie had developed an obsession with dead things, starting with a fox cub she found by the kerbside. Stroking its ginger fur, she got a vivid image of the cub as it had been in life; she could still recall now the intensity of that moment and sometimes wondered if that was what had sparked her now-lost 'special bond' with the dead.

A dead magpie had become the first guest in her earliest mortuary – a shoebox under her bed. Her grandmother had handled it calmly, only suggesting a funeral once the stink had started to permeate the flat.

'I know you're strong,' her grandmother was saying. 'But all the grief you've had to deal with recently, and your father coming back, it's too much for anyone to cope with alone. I can pay for a doctor. I have savings and nothing else to spend it on.'

Cassie shook her head. 'Save your money, Babcia. Months of navel gazing? It's just not me.'

'Think about it, *tygrysek*. For my sake.' Hearing her voice break on the last two words, Cassie felt a catch in her own throat.

'OK.'

Weronika captured Cassie's hand in her own, warm and papery-feeling, and looked her in the eye. 'Promise me.'

'I promise'. *Thinking* about it was an easy promise.

'Ahoy there!' A voice from the towpath.

Poking her head out of the cockpit, Cassie found Archie climbing aboard with a bottle of champagne in one hand.

It was six already and she'd totally forgotten they'd talked about going out for dinner. The only thing she felt like snuggling up to at the moment was a chilled bottle of vodka.

Babcia came out of the cabin behind her, doing up her coat.

'Oh, hello, Mrs Janek! I do hope you're not leaving on my account?' Archie said.

'No, no, I must get home.'

After putting the bottle aside, he jumped off the boat and took both her hands to help her down onto the towpath – she didn't refuse *his* assistance, Cassie noticed.

She beamed up at him approvingly. 'Such a tall young man!' she said, before refusing his offers to walk her home.

As Cassie turned to go below deck, she saw her gran take Archie's forearm again and him bending his head towards hers.

'What was she saying to you just now?' asked Cassie once she'd disappeared.

'She asked me to cheer you up.' But the pink tinge she caught suffusing his pale complexion suggested a fib.

Below deck, Archie could barely stand upright so he sat down to uncork the bottle.

'What are we celebrating anyway?' she asked, tipping some elderly crisps into a bowl.

Archie poured the champagne into two cheap wine glasses and avoided her eye.

Uh-oh.

'Do we need an excuse to drink fizz?' he said, raising his glass. 'Here's to us.'

'Cheers,' she said, downing a third of it in one. 'What did my gran say, really?'

He looked crestfallen. 'Am I that bad a liar?'

'Yes. It's one of the nicest things about you.' It was true. She couldn't imagine Archie ever being unfaithful: he was Mr Reliable. He'd make someone a lovely husband.

'She told me to give you a good seeing-to.' He raised his eyebrows.

'Yikes!'

'Yes, it was, er, unexpected. She said she was a bit worried about your . . . state of mind.' Seeing his agonised expression Cassie's annoyance swiftly gave way to amused sympathy. Psychological chit-chat was *terra incognita* to him.

'You don't think I'm crazy, do you?' she demanded.

'No, of course not. Super-sane. Too sane if anything.'

'But . . . ?'

'Well, I suppose you have seemed a bit down lately, not your usual cheery self.' As Archie topped up their glasses, Macavity appeared, jumping up onto the bench beside him. 'But I've got an idea that might help.'

'Mmmm?'

'Hear me out. OK?' Macavity presented his head to be stroked and Archie obliged. 'My mortuaries are all up in town and the travelling is a real pain, so I need to move out of Guildford. I'm on decent money now so I could afford something pretty nice around here' – sounding like he'd practised the little speech.

As Macavity gazed up at Archie adoringly, his purr getting louder, Cassie felt a building sense of panic as she guessed what was coming.

'Wouldn't you prefer to live somewhere a bit more . . . comfortable?' He cast an eye around the tiny cabin.

'Are you saying we should shack up together?'

'Well, I'd be inclined to put it a bit more romantically than that.' He cleared his throat. 'Listen, Cassie, I think you're a great girl. The best. And I think that maybe you and I, we could make . . . a good match.' The tips of his ears had gone pink during this little speech.

Fuck.

Archie was fun, uncomplicated, reliable – a good catch. He looked so sweet and hopeful that she almost said yes, let's do it.

Almost.

Cassie took some crisps, playing for time, and remembered her brief period of living with Rachel, an experience that would surely be replayed with Archie. She would start to resent the emotional demands, the forced closeness, and react by staying out more, becoming more uncommunicative at home, causing more and more friction – until the inevitable happened. Archie would dump her – just as Rachel had – and she'd be left amid the wreckage feeling . . . *abandoned.* It was something she'd come to accept: she just wasn't cut out for that kind of closeness. Not with the living at least.

'I'm flattered,' she said.

Archie's face fell – he was no fool. 'Too soon?'

She took a glug of fizz. 'Look, Archie, I'm glad you brought it up because we probably should think about where we are, what we both want, *yada, yada.*'

'And?'

'I am very fond of you, Archie. Really I am. But living together, playing house, all that malarkey. I'm crap at it.'

'That could change though, right?' The hopeful look on his face made her want to cry.

'I'm not sure it will, no.' She touched his hand. 'Look, I'm really happy with things as they are. We have a great time together. Can't we just . . . jog along?'

'Jog along?' Archie blinked, disbelieving. 'No, I'm sorry, Cassie, but that's not going to work for me. You see, I'm nuts about you and if we carry on seeing each other, I'll just get in even deeper.'

Whoa! This was spinning out of control. 'But, Archie, I love spending time with you—'

Then he was extracting his hand from underneath hers. Getting to his feet, he reached for his jacket. 'Good luck with everything,' he said, with a tight smile and for a horrible moment she thought he was going to shake her hand.

When he jumped off onto the towpath, the boat seemed to rock for a long time. Cassie felt like she was in free fall. *What the fuck?* Why had he reacted like that? She didn't want to break up with him – she just knew the whole living together thing would end in tears. *Her tears.*

Macavity had stopped purring and now he fixed her with an accusatory look.

'You're supposed to be on my side,' she told him miserably, emptying the last of the bottle into her glass before reaching for her phone. 'Hey, Jerome . . . You got any Molly?'

Chapter Nine

It was a novel experience, the relief Cassie felt on seeing Dr Curzon's name on the PM list the following morning, but today she'd prefer seeing even him to Archie. She'd spent a sleepless night replaying the evening's encounter and how it had ended, constantly picturing Archie's face closing down as he got up to leave.

She felt wrecked today – but not because of the MDMA. Jerome had delivered her pills within thirty minutes of her call. But before she'd had a chance to take any, her neighbour Gaz had come knocking with a bottle of Jameson's. Gaz had got seriously messed up on heroin when he was a roadie, so it didn't feel right doing Class As in front of him. Instead they'd ended up rolling a few spliffs and putting away the best part of the bottle.

Now, she reflected that if she'd stuck to the pills she probably wouldn't be feeling quite so rough this morning. In the loos, she pulled a comb through her hair, which was showing an inch of lighter-coloured roots, and realised she hadn't even washed it for what, four, five days?

The prospect of not having Archie in her life hurt more than she could have imagined. But she told herself it was better to hurt now than suffer worse – far worse – down the line. Because deep down she knew that she'd never be able to hack a settled relationship. She remembered something her ex had once thrown at her: *You give so much of yourself to the dead, there isn't much left over for the living.*

Except now even the dead weren't speaking to her.

The face that stared back at her from the mirror was pale and waxy, like it belonged to one of the bodies. *Which one day it would.* It struck her that the average human heart beat around two and half billion times in a lifetime. Maybe life was just a matter of counting the beats.

Going into the autopsy suite, she started marking up the big whiteboard attached to one wall with the names and d.o.b.s of the deceased on one side, adding columns headed 'heart', 'lungs', 'liver' and so on, ready to record the weight of each organ – an abnormal weight could indicate disease and require further microscopic analysis. With six bodies on the PM list it was going to be one of those days.

Jason surveyed the board, shaking his head. 'No peace for the wicked, eh? Can I grab a ciggie before we start?'

'There's no time for that. Let's get the first two out.' Judging by the surly look on his face, she'd spoken too bluntly, but in her current mood she couldn't give a toss.

She and Jason eviscerated their bodies more or less simultaneously at their tables, before delivering the viscera from each to Dr Curzon's bench for separation. Then they took the individual organs over to be weighed on a set of hanging scales, before returning them for dissection, and recording their weights on the whiteboard. The final step of the process was collecting the dissected viscera from Dr C's bench and packing them into a blue plastic bag to be repatriated to their owner before closing the midline incision as neatly as possible.

They made good time and less than three hours later they were on the last two bodies – Cassie taking Lily Peck, a lady in her sixties who'd been knocked down by a car on the high street, leaving Jason with Michael Kavanagh, an obese middle-aged man who'd suffered a cardiac arrest after post-operative complications.

Cassie managed to plod through it, working like an automaton, and was now cleaning up Mrs Peck's eviscerated body, washing away the blood with the flexible hose, the water gurgling down the drain at the foot of the steel tray.

Curzon called out 'Service!' – a joke he never tired of – and she went to collect Mrs P's dissected organs from his bench. A minute later, she was manipulating the bag containing the organs back into Mrs P's body cavity. It was a bit of a squeeze, but then viscera always seemed to expand with dissection. After finally getting the bag in, she took the curved needle, ready-threaded with linen twine, and started sewing her back up.

Ten minutes later she was wheeling Mrs P back to the body store when something struck her. Lily Peck had been a slender woman, but now her abdomen seemed out of proportion to the rest of her, almost as if she were pregnant.

Cassie felt a sickening chill run up her neck. Turning the trolley around she went back to the autopsy suite before going over to Jason's table where he was about to sew up Mr Kavanagh.

'Jason, don't close him up just yet.'

Going to the whiteboard, she cast an eye over the organ weights, feeling nauseous, her heart beating double time. Michael Kavanagh – liver weight 1610 grams; Lily Peck – liver weight 1350 grams, which was just as she'd expect – women's organs weighing significantly less than men's.

Back at Jason's table, she told him, 'We need to weigh Mr Kavanagh's organs before you sew him up. I think I might have put his viscera back into Mrs Peck.'

Wordlessly, Jason reached into the body cavity, pulled out the bulging blue bag and handed it to her.

Please, please, please, she muttered to herself, nursing the fervent hope that she was fretting about nothing. But as soon as she put what was supposed to be Mr Kavanagh's viscera on the pan beneath the scales she knew. They didn't weigh nearly enough for an overweight guy in his forties.

Dr Curzon had already disappeared to get changed so she pieced together what had happened with Jason. It turned out that Dr C had dissected Mr Kavanagh's organs before Mrs Peck's, so when he'd called for 'Service', Cassie took the pile at the end of his bench without thinking, not realising they were the wrong organs.

'I got ahead of you, remember? When you had to go change your blade?' Jason said, eyeing her – clearly enjoying the know-it-all girlie getting her comeuppance.

She nodded grimly. Putting the wrong organs back in a body? You heard about it happening, of course, but never to her, not even on her watch. How could she have made such a terrible error? The fact that they were working under pressure was no excuse.

'Listen' – Jason threw a conspiratorial look over his shoulder – 'nobody needs to know about it. I close this guy up and we both keep schtum. What the family don't know can't hurt them, right?'

She looked at Jason's moon-like face with its ill-concealed expression of Schadenfreude. But that wasn't the worst thing. The idea of delivering any of her charges to their families with a stranger's heart, liver, brain – that was unthinkable.

She shook her head. 'No, I'm going to reinstate the organs into the right bodies. You go off home. I'll close them both up.'

'Fine, if you want to waste your time, it's your funeral,' he said with a surly shrug, starting to strip off his gloves.

Half an hour later, she was closing up Lily Peck for the second time. 'I don't know what's wrong with me, Mrs P,' she said, cutting the thread on the last stitch. 'I'm so sorry I let you down. Right now, if I could swap places with you I would.'

FLYTE

'It's good of you to meet me,' said Luke, eyeing her with a hint of curiosity. 'Usually we just do this by email.'

Flyte had chosen a backstreet cafe for her meeting with Luke Lawless – the aptly named crime reporter of the *Camden Gazette*. She didn't want anyone in the office earwigging on a telephone call, because although she had a legitimate reason to talk to him about the Hugger Mugger suspect she also wanted to tack on a request regarding Green-Eyes.

'I'm out and about a lot at the moment, interviewing witnesses and tracking down CCTV so this was the best way to talk properly,' she lied smoothly. 'And I know you guys don't have a local office anymore.'

Luke shrugged regretfully. 'True. I work from home mostly – just as well now the regional office is in Enfield.'

'And you cover Camden and Kentish Town?'

'I wish. I cover everything from Finchley over to Finsbury Park, and Kentish Town down to Regent's Park. One crime reporter for three local papers, all of them covering crime hotspots.'

'That's a pretty huge beat, right?' Having only lived in London just over a year her mental map of its boroughs was still patchy.

'Yep. It means I get most of my stories from press releases. The older journos never tire of telling me that back in the day they were out on the streets, following up stories, interviewing witnesses – you know, proper investigative stuff.' He sounded exercised about it, regretful that the job had changed.

Flyte nodded, trying to look sympathetic. Truthfully, the last thing the police needed was some frustrated hack trampling all over an investigation in his size nines. Luke couldn't be much older than thirty but he was dressed like an old-school PI – sand-coloured trench coat over a rumpled button-down shirt and narrow tie. He was probably aiming for Philip Marlowe as played by Bogart, but with his weedy build and hair that needed a cut the overall impression was more early Columbo.

'So, this Hugger Mugger is now a murder inquiry?' Luke adopted a professional frown but shifted in his chair, clearly thrilled to be covering a juicy non-domestic murder case. Flyte didn't approve of the nickname but it was inevitable and it would help raise the profile of the story.

'Not yet. But doctors believe the victim, Harry Poppleton, has no chance of meaningful recovery so life support will probably be withdrawn once the family give the go-ahead. As it stands we're looking at an attempted murder.'

'And I can use that?' His pen poised over his tan-coloured Moleskine notebook – another PI prop.

She nodded; Harry's mother and father had agreed to release the medical details in the hope of getting witnesses to come forward.

'I've sourced the best still from the CCTV to help us ID the suspect.' She showed him the image on her phone. 'Obviously, we've pixellated Harry's face.'

He squinted at it, clearly fascinated. 'Not much to go on facially, is it? But the perp is a big guy. Over six foot? Unless the vic was really short?' Luke was clearly loving the chance to use jargon he'd picked up from true-crime box sets.

'No, I checked. Harry was five foot nine so we calculate the attacker to be at least six two' – remembering Steadman's and Willets' unscientific yet effective demonstration.

'Who's the IO?'

Aka investigating officer.

'DS Dean Willets. And the SIO is acting DCI Mike Steadman.'

He made a note. 'So any promising leads?'

'It's early days. There are calls coming into the incident room – thanks for getting the number up online so quickly. A few people saw Harry stagger out of the Underworld club in the direction of Middle Yard but we've yet to find any eyewitnesses who saw the mugger. If we can trace his movements it might give us better CCTV of him from elsewhere in the area.'

They agreed a wording for the appeal for witnesses and the level of detail Luke could put in the story. He grinned at her. 'I can have it online by this evening and in the next print edition. We are getting this ahead of the nationals, right?'

Flyte put her head on one side and pulled a little frown. 'Well, strictly speaking we can't play favourites like that. I know the press office would like to get it out to everyone as soon as possible.'

'But as the local paper we're the ones who can deliver witnesses.' A hint of the steel that any journalist needed surfacing in his voice.

'I agree. What you offer as a local paper isn't just news but a valuable public service. In fact, I also need your help identifying a body . . .' She showed him the artist's image of Green-Eyes based on the photos she'd taken of the body.

After a few minutes of horse trading, Flyte had extracted a promise that the pic, plus description and details of what he was wearing, would get a prominent spot in the online and print editions appealing for information. 'The unidentified male is being dealt with by Camden CID,' she told him. 'But if you get anything, update me direct on my mobile and I'll pass it along, OK?'

'Nothing fishy about it?' he asked hopefully.

'No, not at all. A straight drowning according to the pathologist. He was probably inebriated – we'll know when the tox report comes back.'

Flyte thought she'd been convincingly casual about it but as they got up to leave she caught Luke's sideways look and cursed inwardly. The wannabe private eye had scented her interest in the case.

Chapter Ten

After reconstituting the bodies of Lily Peck and Michael Kavanagh, correctly this time, Cassie went to clean up and change. Then she went in to see Doug, the mortuary manager.

After her little speech, he sat back in his chair, frowning, surveying her face. 'You really want to make this official?'

'It's a HATARI, so it should be reported,' she said flatly.

The acronym stood for Human Tissue Authority Reportable Incident. The body that oversaw mortuary procedure, the HTA, required every body part and organ to be recorded, tracked, and accounted for. Putting the wrong organs back in a body was most definitely a HATARI, even if she had spotted it in time. Cassie was the mortuary's 'designated individual' responsible for reporting any breaches of the protocol – an irony that wasn't lost on her.

'But you rectified the error?' Doug asked, his habitual worried expression deepening. 'So everything has been squared away?'

She lifted her chin. 'Yes, but we should still report it. It's a near-miss. I've mailed you my report to send to the HTA.'

'Cassie, I know you take your responsibilities very seriously – that's why you're so good at your job.' Ignoring the soft scoffing sound she made, he went on, 'But I think you're being overzealous. A mistake like that, which was immediately put right, doesn't warrant reporting, in my opinion.'

'Look, Doug, your loyalty has meant a lot to me over the years.' She shook her head slowly. 'But I think it's time I did something different with my life. I'm just . . . I just don't have the gift for this job anymore.' Leaning forward, she put her mortuary key card on the desk between them.

Now Doug's face creased in distress and coming round her side of the desk, he perched on the edge. 'You've reported this so-called incident to me and it's up to me to pass it on or not. I'm worried about you, Cassie. I'm no medic but anyone can see that you're not yourself. It's not the right moment to go making big decisions.'

His eye fell on the rash that had now spread across the backs of both her hands and up the wrists, the weals bleeding here and there. 'That's contact dermatitis, from the nitrile gloves. I've seen it before.'

'So now I'm allergic to the job.' She laughed mirthlessly. 'Perfect.'

He waved his hand. 'We can get you some hypo-allergenic gloves, that's no problem. But allergies like that can be a sign of other . . . issues. Look, I know you don't like asking for help, but I think you need to speak to someone.' Turning his laptop round he scrolled through his emails. 'Here, I got this yesterday. The head of psychiatric services at the hospital is looking for NHS workers "vulnerable to psychological consequences from their day-to-day duties" to be part of a pilot programme.'

Vulnerable. Not a word she'd ever thought to apply to herself. It was her job to look after other people.

'You would need to work a month's notice in any case. Let me arrange for you to talk to someone in the meantime, and if you still feel the same a few weeks down the line, I won't try to talk you out of it.' Doug sent her a kind smile. 'How does that sound?'

Cassie pictured the faces of her guests backed up in the body store. Of course there was no way she could just walk out and leave them in the lurch.

Staring down at the bloodied backs of her hands, she recalled the promise she'd made to her gran. Maybe the only way to get both Babcia – and now Doug – off her back was to play along. 'OK,' she said, 'but I still want to give a month's notice.'

'Deal!' Doug's relief was palpable, which only made her feel guilty. In a month's time she'd be out of here.

FLYTE

Flyte spent the rest of the day working the Hugger Mugger case from her desk, calling back potential witnesses who'd phoned into the incident line since it went up online.

'So you think you saw a drunken man falling out of Underworld. When exactly?' . . . 'So was this on the Thursday or Friday night?'. . . 'Yes, it's important.' *For crying out loud.* 'You'd have to ask Bez . . . Right. Why don't you call back when you've done that. Thanks.'

She hung up, her face stiff with the effort of dealing with the general public.

Her mobile buzzed and seeing that it was Luke Lawless, the crime reporter from the *Gazette*, she took it out into the hallway.

'I've got a lead on your floater,' said Luke, trying, but failing, to sound cool.

'Oh yes, go ahead?' She felt her own pulse quicken.

'A security guard called Ezekiel Drew who works at a wine and spirits warehouse up in Kentish Town just called. He reckons the pic that went live last night is a guy he used to see working out at a local gym.'

'Hang on,' she said. 'Why did he call you and not the police number we gave out?'

A micro-pause.

'We printed the newspaper number as well, just as backup. As you know, not everyone likes talking to the police round here.'

She emitted a sharp sigh. 'I hope you haven't been contaminating our witness?'

'Not at all! I said he should really to talk to you. Anyway, he didn't give me a name for the guy or any more details really.'

So Luke *had* given this Ezekiel guy the third degree . . . 'I explained that you were struggling to ID the body, and laid it on thick about the poor family, you know.' His voice had become conspiratorial, as if they were fellow detectives co-working the case.

'Did he say when he saw him last?'

'Eight or nine years ago.'

Her heart sank. 'Not exactly fresh meat, is it? He's probably an attention-seeker.'

'I don't think so,' said Luke defensively, 'he sounded pretty sure about it.'

'Well, Luke, if he tells me that aliens dropped our guy into the canal from a spaceship it'll be the end of a promising collaboration.'

As she hung up, she saw Dean Willets coming out of an interview room down the hall, holding the door open for a young woman, probably only in her late twenties, although impeccably made-up in a way that made her look ten years older. She thanked him, with a little coquettish look up at him, fiddling with her long blonde hair. He grinned down at her, lapping it up.

Yecch.

He nodded to Flyte as they went past, and she heard him saying, 'Thanks, Ashley. I'll be in touch.' Did she detect something more than professional politeness in his tone?

When he came back into the office a few minutes later, he was greeted by catcalls from some of the guys. He did a little swagger and waved his phone. 'She's WhatsApped me already.'

'He shoots . . . and he scores!' intoned Nathan Cassidy.

Willets caught Flyte's eye. 'Of course any contact will remain strictly within the bounds of rules and regs.'

Raising his arms, Willets did a little hip-swivel gesture which brought more jeering. Then she noticed that they'd all fallen silent.

Unseen by Willets, DCI Steadman had come in behind him. He didn't say anything, just went over to have a word with one of the other detectives.

But on the way out he said, 'Have you got five minutes, Dean?'

It was all Flyte could do to keep a straight face: Steadman had a famously low tolerance of off-colour banter so Willets was in for a good talking-to. Slipping out of the office, she took the stairs and waited till she was outside before calling the security guard who claimed to recognise Green-Eyes.

She had arranged to meet him after her shift. As she approached the Kentish Town greasy spoon that he'd named for their rendezvous, she wondered again what she was doing, taking on the task of ID-ing a non-sus death. Hadn't she joined Major Crimes to get away from the routine CID work?

From the biblical name, she'd been expecting somebody older but Ezekiel Drew couldn't be much more than forty, tall and broad-shouldered, although judging by the remains of the fry-up on his plate and the little paunch protruding through his open security guard jacket, he didn't spend much time at the gym these days. He'd taken a table by the window, and as she sat down opposite him, his gaze flickered past her, doing a quick scan of the place. Since policing Camden, she'd become accustomed to this cagey response, especially from people of colour.

After ordering a tea – the place was run by Turks so the waiter wasn't fazed by her request for lemon, no milk – she introduced herself with her most winning smile. Ezekiel didn't respond.

Her only previous posting had been in leafy Winchester – which was more her natural habitat – and she still struggled some-times to navigate Camden's various cultures and sub-cultures. As a north London black guy, Ezekiel probably had good reason to be wary of the police, having no doubt been stopped and searched dozens of times by officers like Dean Willets. She found herself wondering how Cassie would approach this.

After the waiter brought her tea, she squeezed the lemon against the side of the cup. 'Ezekiel. He was an Old Testament prophet, yes?'

Ezekiel pulled a guarded smile. 'Yeah. My mum's a big churchgoer. Pentecostal. Church of the Sinner Redeemed. They wear long white robes, there's healing, speaking in tongues, the whole charismatic thing . . .' He flapped a tolerant hand.

'And you, do you go?'

'No way! My mum's Nigerian but my dad's from round here and he thinks it's all rubbish. So us kids didn't have to go to church, but we all got names from Scripture.'

Noticing how he'd started physically to loosen up during this exchange, Flyte leaned in and said, 'Go on.'

Counting on his fingers he said, 'So there's my oldest sister, Abiyah, then Bathsheba, then my brothers, Caleb and Daniel . . .'

'I'm sensing an alphabetical system?'

'Right. I'm the youngest and I got the "E"s. I swear to God, if my dad hadn't put his foot down, my mum would have had me christened Enoch.' He looked at her, seeing if she got the reference.

'Enoch as in Enoch Powell?!' She widened her eyes.

He laughed then – a big laugh. 'Yeah. "Rivers of blood" man. Y'see, in my mum's book, Enoch was Noah's great-grand-daddy.'

She tipped her head on one side. 'Ezekiel suits you.' It did, too: he was over six foot tall and there was something of the Old Testament prophet about his face – high cheekbones and wide-set eyes – that gave him an austere grace. 'Got any kids?' He wore a chunky white-gold wedding band.

He nodded, a proud smile creeping along his lips. 'Two girls. Eleven and nine.'

'Did you keep the biblical theme going?'

He chuckled, shaking his head.

'Did you get grief for the name at school?'

Those wide dark eyes hardened for a moment 'Nah. I knew how to look after myself. Anyway, everyone calls me Zeke.'

'May I? Call you Zeke, I mean?'

'Sure.' With a graceful tip of his head.

Having prepared the ground, she said, 'So you think you recognise the picture of the man we found, from a gym that you both attended?'

'Uh-huh.' Ezekiel stirred more sugar into his tea. 'It was near Gospel Oak station.'

'The name of the place?' Her pen poised over her notebook.

He screwed up his eyes. 'It was called Pump something. Like Pump Action, or Pump It. Then it changed its name but I couldn't tell you what to. Anyway, it shut down a few years back.'

'And the man's name?'

'Shane.'

'And his last name?'

'I don't know. I don't remember.' He dropped his eyes.

'Didn't ever know or don't remember now?' Trying to keep the testiness out of her voice.

'Never knew it.' Ezekiel shrugged, frowning into his tea. 'He was just, like, someone I would nod to in passing. We weren't mates or nothing.'

Flyte sat back in her seat. 'So you didn't know his actual name, you only knew him to nod to, and the last time you laid eyes on him was at least eight years ago. What makes you so sure it's him in the photo?' Suppressing a sigh, she started a mental inventory of what she had at home that might provide the makings of an easy supper. A jar of pesto. Some pasta. A few green beans, elderly but not beyond the hope of resurrection. Was there any parmesan left or should she stop off at Sainsbury's?

'I've got a good head for faces,' said Ezekiel. 'When I saw the photo online I was ninety-nine per cent sure it was him. I can't stop thinking, you know, somebody must be wondering where he's at? What's happened to him.' He sounded quite upset at the idea. 'And all the time he's dead. Drowned.'

'Did he ever talk about family, a wife, girlfriend – or boyfriend?'

He dropped his gaze, shaking his head.

'Anything else that might help us find out who he is, anybody he hung out with, where he lived, where he worked?'

Raising his eyes to hers, Ezekiel said, 'I did overhear some-body pass comment on his job once.'

'And?'

He folded his lips over his teeth, as if making a decision.

It was warm in the cafe but Flyte felt a shiver go through her.

'From what I heard,' said Ezekiel, meeting her eye, 'he was in the Feds.'

Chapter Eleven

A hefty dose of Polish vodka had got Cassie off to sleep, but the following morning she had surfaced still half entangled in a vivid nightmare. She was at Lily Peck's funeral, which, in the weird logic of dreams, was taking place in the fruit and veg aisle of Sainsbury's. As Cassie approached the open coffin to pay her respects, she recognised Mrs P's slender form but when she got closer she reeled back. The face belonged to a young man with acne-sprinkled cheeks. He opened his golden-green eyes and shook his head sadly, as if reproaching her.

She was woken properly from the dream by her phone ringing. Scrabbled for it, half hoping it might be Archie; half hoping it wasn't.

It was Doug. The hospital's psych department had called to say they'd had a cancellation and he'd pencilled her in for an appointment with a shrink that afternoon.

'So soon?' she asked weakly.

He ignored that, instead saying, 'There's no PM list today so you can take the day off, take it easy.'

Cassie didn't argue, staying in bed until gone ten, thinking idly about what she might do when she left the mortuary. She felt hollow, not quite present, like she was already in transit to somewhere else, whatever shape that might take. Maybe just bar work for a while. She'd done the odd casual shift during her squatting days and right now it felt like the least demanding and most attractive option. Not seeing Archie routinely would also help her get over him quicker.

Later that day, she got a call from Phyllida Flyte.

'I might have a lead on Green-Eyes' identity,' she said – her clipped tones not quite disguising an undertow of excitement.

'Oh yeah?'

'I'm just checking he's still with you?'

'He hadn't gone anywhere last time I looked,' said Cassie. 'So, what's the story?'

'I don't know yet, but I just wanted to say, call me if there's any move to freeze him or anything,' said Flyte.

'Sure.'

Then another pause before Flyte asked in a softer voice, 'How are you doing?'

'Fine, why?'

'I don't know, you've seemed different, lately.' She spoke with the warmth that Cassie had occasionally seen break through her default chilliness.

Suddenly unable to trust her voice, Cassie made a non-committal sound.

Flyte went on, 'If ever you wanted to talk about anything, I'm here, OK? I won't ever forget how you helped me understand the medical report into Poppy's death.'

'I'm Pauline Martinez. I'm the lead psychologist on the pro-gramme for NHS workers who might face distressing situations in the course of their work. The idea is to see what we can offer that might help, whether that's short term or long term.'

Cassie nodded, trying to look engaged. They were sitting opposite each other in a therapy room on the third floor of the hospital. An effort had been made to make the room welcoming, soothing, *or whatever*, but the pastel paintwork, sub-Cath Kidston floral curtains, and the kitsch artwork – a poster of the sun setting over the sea *for Chrissake* – just got on her nerves.

'Would you like to take your jacket off?' asked the shrink.

Cassie shook her head, folded her arms. 'No, I'm fine, thanks.'

Pauline glanced down at her notepad. 'Your boss doesn't think you're fine. Why do you think that is?'

Having decided it would make sense to play along, Cassie trotted out her story: being brought up as an 'orphan', the discovery of her mum's murder, her dad turning up, two of her close friends dying in the last year, *yada, yada*.

Pauline just put her head on one side, nodding, her kind eyes resting on Cassie. As the silence grew in the room she said nothing.

Finally, Cassie said, 'I used to live with a trainee shrink – sorry, psychotherapist. *She* said I was suffering from "unresolved grief",' giving the phrase a mocking edge.

'And what do you think?'

Cassie shifted irritably in her seat. 'Isn't that your job? To find out what's wrong with me?'

Pauline pulled a rueful smile. 'I'm here to help *you* discover what might underlie any difficulties you're experiencing.'

The silence yawned between them. 'I think I managed fine growing up,' said Cassie. 'I had my grandmother and I didn't really think about my parents. Now my dad has turned up . . .'

Pauline tipped her head.

'It's just, sometimes, he talks like he's got all these parental rights. I'm twenty-six for Christ's sake. I don't need a daddy.'

The whine of a drill somewhere in the building split the silence.

'You've had a very challenging time recently,' said Pauline. 'But what is it that's troubling you at the moment?'

A long pause before she replied. 'This probably sounds nuts, but hey, at least I'm in the right place. I used to talk to the dead people I look after – as if they were still alive.'

Pauline did the head tipping thing again.

'And sometimes I felt as if . . . they spoke back to me? I mean their lips didn't move, or anything, but I could *sense* things from them, about what happened to them? But now' – she looked up at the ceiling – 'that feeling has gone.'

'That must feel like a loss.'

'It makes my job meaningless. I mean if they're just dead meat I might as well be working in an abattoir.'

Pauline appeared unfazed.

'Look, I don't believe in ghosts, and I get that I probably just . . . notice stuff? But it used to feel so *real* . . . So there's this dead guy who got fished out of the canal – it was me who found him actually. And normally I'd be pulling out all the stops to find out who he is, so we can let his family know. But he's just not giving me anything.' Her eye fell on the twee sunset poster. 'Anyway, we're all going to die, aren't we? Maybe the how and the why really isn't that important.'

Pauline looked at the notes she'd taken earlier. 'This young man who drowned in the canal . . . you mentioned that one of the close friends you lost died in exactly the same way quite recently. I imagine that must make this case especially difficult for you?'

Cassie shrugged again. She had no desire to rake over the terrible events of last winter.

All the same, forty minutes later it dawned on Cassie how much Pauline had dragged out of her by doing little more than tilting her head and looking kind. Which pretty much summed up her own strategy when she sensed that a bereaved relative needed to talk.

Pauline glanced at the clock. 'We're out of time, but I would like to offer you further sessions if you feel it might help?'

Cassie jiggled her crossed leg. 'How long would it be for?'

'That's up to you. Until you are feeling better, but if we decide together that you might benefit from longer-term therapy, I would refer you to another colleague. In the meantime I'd suggest you think about taking antidepressants to help you through this difficult period?'

Cassie made a scoffing sound. 'I'm not taking any drugs!'

'No?' The amused set of Pauline's lips reminded Cassie that she'd admitted during the Q and A at the start of the session that she smoked weed, drank a litre of vodka a week, and took the occasional pill.

'I'll arrange a prescription for Sertraline,' Pauline went on. 'It's an SSRI, which—'

'A selective serotonin re-uptake receptor inhibitor. Yeah, I know.'

The theory was that SSRIs stopped the feel-good hormone getting hoovered out of the brain too quickly.

'If you decide to take them, be aware it can take a week or two before you feel the effects.'

Heading down the towpath to the boat, Cassie tried to gauge her mood.

Worse and better, she decided. Her darkest thoughts seemed to have retreated to a more manageable distance. But she also

88

felt flayed – as if the session had peeled back her epidermis to expose nerves, tendons and muscles – like a pathologist would sometimes do during a forensic post-mortem to find any damage hidden beneath the skin.

Then she spotted it on the side of the towpath, amid the scabby grass and discarded takeaway containers, bottles and cans. A dead magpie, one of its wings bent upwards and fluttering in the breeze as if beckoning her.

Engulfed by a wave of sadness so strong it made her sway, she dropped to a crouch and stroked its plumage – smooth but not soft, an iridescent blue-black. Not yet fully grown, but otherwise almost identical to that first dead bird she'd brought home as a kid. One keen little eye, not yet clouded, looked up at the sky. 'I'm sorry you didn't get as much life as you deserved,' she murmured to it, vaguely registering rain falling on the back of her hand. *Warm rain?* Touching her face, she found it wet with tears.

She couldn't remember the last time she'd cried.

Rooting in her bag, she found a pack of tissues. She opened two of them out on the grass, gently picked up the bird and placed it on top.

'There,' she told it, enfolding it in its makeshift shroud. 'You're safe now.'

Chapter Twelve

Cassie had ignored Doug's injunction to take the rest of the day off. With the deterioration of Green-Eyes' body still nagging at her, she'd called out a refrigeration engineer to check the body store was working properly.

When she pulled out one of the drawers, the engineer, a young guy called Sufian, physically recoiled at the sight of the white-shrouded body inside.

'Come on, then,' she said, eyeing his aghast expression. 'You just gave me a lecture about opening the drawers for as short a time as possible.'

He hastily stuck a digital thermometer on the inside wall of the fridge before pulling his hand out and wiping it on his overalls.

'First mortuary visit?' she asked, re-closing the drawer.

He nodded. 'I usually do food cold stores, supermarket fridges, that kind of thing.'

They moved up the fridge and he repeated the thermometer placement.

After the third, Sufian had recovered his composure. 'Working with dead bodies is a funny job for a girl, isn't it?' he asked her.

Cassie was so weary of this question that she had to check a momentary but shocking impulse to slap him.

'Not really,' she said. 'Caring for the dead has always fallen to women traditionally. Not that long ago the female relatives would wash the body, put pennies on the eyes to stop them opening, plug the body's orifices to prevent leakage . . .' Seeing the growing look of horror on his face she relented. 'So . . . do you think there's a problem with the fridge?'

He grasped gratefully at this change of subject. 'Nothing obvious. The compressors are clean and the vents are clear. If these readings are too high then I'll run a check on the thermostat.' He nodded to the digital temperature display, showing 3.6 °C. 'What made you think the indicator might be wrong anyway?'

Because a supposedly fresh corpse is starting to smell like kimchi, she thought. Pulling a wry smile, she said, 'I wouldn't ask if I were you.'

Half an hour later, Sufian came to find her. 'It's all working fine, no hotspots,' he told her, pulling on his jacket as she signed the paperwork. 'You've got one door seal coming loose that'll need replacing at the next service but that's it.' Grabbing the paperwork from her hands, he sent her a nervous smile and scuttled off, probably keen to avert any more talk about plugging orifices.

By the time she'd caught up on her admin it was gone seven and she was alone in the mortuary. Dusk was turning the sky through the windows cobalt blue as she performed a final circuit of the empty mortuary: her evening ritual.

If it wasn't a faulty fridge making Green-Eyes decompose faster than expected, he must have been in the water longer than she'd originally thought. She ought to call Flyte to tell her that he might have gone in earlier than Curzon's estimate, although it felt like an enormous effort.

In the body store, as she reached up to turn off the lights, her eye fell on the drawer containing Green-Eyes, the words 'Unknown Male' written there in marker pen, and she noticed it was open a crack. Had Sufian failed to close it properly?

She saw her hand reach for the handle of the drawer as if in slow motion. A crackling hum filled the air, and she found herself slip-sliding, helter-skelter, into the dreamlike state she hadn't experienced in months. The burble of the giant fridge had grown to a rushing roar, and the suddenly fierce light made her narrow her eyes.

After unzipping the body bag to reveal Green-Eyes' face, she bent her head towards his pale-blue lips, like a priest hearing confession and murmured, 'Is there something you want to tell me?'

Silence, and then a hoarse and plaintive whisper.

'*Cold. So cold.*'

FLYTE

Flyte had done her best to conceal her shock when Zeke had suggested that his fellow gym-goer 'Shane' had been a police officer – presumably in the Met.

If Zeke was right, then it could explain her feeling that she recognised Green-Eyes. She might have met him in a work context – although not in Winchester and she felt sure not recently either. Which left one other option – the thirteen-week basic training course at Hendon Police College which she'd attended straight out of uni.

When she got home that evening, she opened her barely used Facebook account and searched for the private group for her intake, which she hadn't visited since qualifying some fifteen years previously.

The group photo showed them lined up in their spanking new uniforms after the passing-out parade. Flyte found her own image – the only woman standing in the back row, surrounded by men. The photographer had wanted to have all the 'ladies' in the front row, but she had refused to be the passive eye candy while the guys stood, ready for action. Zooming in, she saw that the camera had captured her irritation after the little spat. She went along the row, scanning the faces of the men intently.

At the end of her row her eye snagged on a good-looking guy with dark hair and she felt her pulse bumping in her throat.

That itch of recognition hadn't just been her imagination: the dead man in the mortuary and this guy really were the same person. Now she saw him as he'd been in life she remembered his open, uncomplicated smile.

Reaching for his name. Not Shane.

Sean.

Scrolling to the end of the post beneath the image, she found him tagged as 'SeanQKavanagh', although clicking it his Facebook profile no longer existed.

As Cassie often said, the inanimate faces of the dead sometimes seemed only distantly related to the living version, which was probably why Flyte had taken a while to place him. He was a bit younger than her – probably one of those who joined up at eighteen – and they'd only been on nodding terms, but now she'd made the connection she remembered seeing him in class, in the canteen. And hadn't he brought a glamorous woman to their passing-out party? Flyte dimly recalled a fabulous frock and a cloud of strawberry-blonde hair.

Some of the other faces in the group posts reminded Flyte how much she'd hated her time at Hendon. After three years studying for her degree in criminology, it had come as a brutal shock to encounter attitudes among some of her fellow probationers which she'd assumed had died out in the eighties. These guys – a small but noisy minority – kept schtum during the diversity lectures but outside class they snapped right back to their default sexist and gay 'jokes'. She hadn't been alone in finding the atmosphere toxic, but anyone who dared to challenge the dickheads inevitably got labelled as a snowflake.

Discovering that Sean Kavanagh had been a police officer threw up a new mystery. Since nobody had reported him missing she'd assumed he must be a recent arrival in Camden, possibly doing casual shifts in a bar, say – the kind of place where if someone stopped turning up it wouldn't necessarily ring alarm bells.

But a police officer? How was it possible that no hue and cry had been raised when he'd vanished? Had he left the Job at some point before ending up in the canal?

There was nothing to stop her identifying him herself – except it would mean confessing to DCI Steadman that she'd ignored his explicit instruction to get shot of the case. Better that she track down his next of kin and let them confirm to CID that Green-Eyes had been a policeman called Sean Kavanagh.

Chapter Thirteen

Saturday was one of those balmy late September days, the sky a soft blue, and that afternoon Cassie took her coffee up on deck and gazed out over the canal, replaying what she'd heard rising from Green-Eyes' motionless lips.

Cold, so cold.

It didn't matter whether he really had 'spoken' or whether it was just her subconscious working overtime: either way, the words shed no new light on his final moments since obviously the canal would have been cold. All that mattered was that after months of silence her bond with the dead had been rekindled.

Her gaze drifted across the canal towards the derelict concrete hulk of an old seventies housing estate a little way upstream. A new hoarding had gone up on the canal embankment trumpeting, *Canalside Quarter: luxury apartments with waterfront views.*

Long marked for demolition, its facade was pitted with broken windows through which ragged curtains flapped like the flags of a beaten army. The developers would make a packet while no doubt offering the fewest 'affordable' dwellings they could get away with.

It was the kind of place Archie might live – *where both of us might have lived if you hadn't blown it* noted her disapproving internal voice – a thought she pushed away.

Macavity jumped up beside her. Cassie pulled out the packet she'd got at the pharmacy, pressed a torpedo-shaped pill out of the foil, and knocked it back with the last of her coffee. 'I'll try anything once,' she said, shrugging at his sceptical gaze. 'At least Babcia will be pleased.'

She'd promised to pop over to her gran's that evening to help defrost her fridge-freezer which was apparently so iced up the door would no longer close properly, although that was no doubt just a thinly veiled excuse to check up on her granddaughter.

Cassie was expecting her dad to be at the flat, and was bracing herself for the inevitable *Do you remember . . . ?* Kath-fest but there was no sign of him.

'No Callum this eve?' she asked casually after stepping into the toasty-warm interior with its perennial background hum of cinnamon.

'Just us girls!' said Babcia, heading into the kitchen. Cassie's spirits rose – a feeling that instantly morphed to guilt. 'And I've made your favourite for dinner.' She opened the oven door to show a baking dish bubbling with melted cheese, releasing a mouth-watering gust of savouriness.

'Kopytka? Yum.' The Polish version of gnocchi, baked with lashings of cheese and bacon – the vegan variety obvs – had been her go-to comfort food since her teenage years.

While her grandmother prepped the veg for dinner, Cassie used a bread knife to dislodge the worst of the icebergs in the freezer compartment and by the time they sat down to eat, their conversation was punctuated by the periodic clunk of falling ice as steaming bowls of boiled water hastened the defrosting.

As Cassie tucked into her kopytka, she noticed Babcia smiling at her.

'You've got your appetite back,' she said approvingly.

After taking a swig of beer, Cassie said, 'So ... I am seeing someone at the hospital about stress and stuff.' Adding hastily, 'But I don't want to talk about it.'

Weronika just took Cassie's hand in hers and gave it a squeeze. 'This is nice, just the two of us,' she said. 'It is good being able to talk to someone who knew your mama, but you know, you're still the centre of my world.'

'How is Callum?' Cassie still didn't feel comfortable calling him dad.

'He's had a bit of a cold, but it hasn't stopped him looking for work.' She waved her fork. 'He would love to see you, but I told him, don't chase her. It has to go at your pace.' Her tone was matter of fact, not criticising.

The irony was that Callum had been the most attentive parent when Cassie was small and her handful of early memories were mostly of him rather than her mum – who she now knew had been wrestling with depression and alcohol abuse. *Riding on his shoulders in the park, going to see* Toy Story *at the cinema, playing monsters around the flat . . .* So why did it stress her out, spending time with him?

After dinner, she went back to work on the freezer, excavating a solid bag of peas and a heel of bread interred in a wall of ice on the back wall. 'I'm going to chuck this stuff, Babcia, it's ancient.'

'Oh, I never take any notice of the dates they put on everything these days.' She made a scoffing sound. 'And it hasn't killed me yet!'

'You go and watch the news,' said Cassie. 'I'll make the coffee after I'm done here.'

She used the bread knife to free a styrofoam tray trapped in the ice: a shrink-wrapped chicken breast dated over a year earlier, and something came surging back to her from one of her A-level biology lessons. They'd been discussing microbiology in the context of food hygiene and her teacher Mrs Edwards had explained what happened when you froze and defrosted food.

Cassie felt a shiver so strong it made her back teeth clack together and the bread knife clattered to the floor.

FLYTE

That morning, Flyte had met up with her ex-husband, Matt, for the first time in months. Although it was a Saturday he'd had to go into work and so they'd arranged to meet in a cafe in Islington, halfway between Camden and the City yet not ideal for either of them. *An analogy of our marriage*, thought Flyte.

'Sorry I'm a bit late. Popping into the office always takes longer than it's supposed to.' Matt rolled his eyes self-importantly, as he set down his briefcase – actually one of those satchel-style bags that even City types seemed to favour these days.

'That's fine, I'm off today.' She squeezed lemon into her tea.

As he folded his coat carefully onto an empty chair, she noticed he'd lost weight since they'd last met, making him look more like the cute, boyish guy who'd chased her on the (reassuringly expensive) online dating site where they'd met. She remembered convincing herself that a white wedding, marriage and children would deliver the feeling of normality that had eluded her all her life. But although married life had been pleasant enough she'd sometimes been overcome by the dislocating sensation that she was performing in a play. And the sex had been more duty than desire on her part.

Still, she would never regret a marriage that had given her Poppy, however briefly. After they'd lost her, the marriage had melted down pretty fast.

After a bit of chit-chat about work, she brought up Poppy's memorial service, which Matt had seemed set on boycotting – until recently. 'I'm so pleased you're coming. Mother will be there too, but don't let that put you off.' They exchanged a rueful look – Sylvia had always tried to recruit Matt as an ally against her 'difficult' daughter but he'd once admitted to Flyte that he found her mother 'terrifying'.

'The priest is lovely – and he knows we're agnostic.'

'Atheist,' said Matt staunchly.

Flyte shrugged. She'd hardly been a diligent churchgoer, having only attended the occasional Christmas or Remembrance Sunday service with her father, whenever they'd been in the same country. But she had still called herself a believer – until the moment Poppy had been taken from them. Recently she'd found herself nursing a glimmer of hope that she might see her daughter again after all, a feeling she pictured as a tiny candle flame that needed shielding from the wind.

Matt played with his teaspoon before clearing his throat. 'I've been thinking of her – of Poppy – more, recently.' It was the first time he'd used the name Flyte had given her. 'I'm sorry I've been such a dick about it all.' He blinked fast. 'I suppose it was easier just to try to blank it out.'

Flyte touched his arm. 'I did the same for two years. I know how hard it is, but once you let the grief in, it actually gets easier.'

'That's exactly what Caroline said.'

Caroline?

101

'Sorry,' he said, a smile curling one corner of his mouth, 'I thought I'd mentioned her. She's a girl – well, woman – at work. We work on the same account.'

'Oh right! Are you . . . an item, then?'– taking her hand from his arm she lifted her cup.

'Not really, not yet.' Still with that irritating private-happiness smile.

Why did this news enrage her? She had not one iota of desire to get back with Matt. Was she envious of him, wearing that sappy 'in love' grin? No. It was the idea of him discussing Poppy with someone else, sharing her precious memory with a stranger.

After Matt left, Flyte checked to see whether any of her fellow Hendon probationers had replied to her Facebook messages asking after Sean Kavanagh. Her cover story: that she was planning a class reunion. *As if.*

There was one message from a guy called Darren who she dimly remembered. He said he'd played five-a-side football with Sean at college and for a while afterwards. But apparently Sean had left the police around eight years ago, and moved abroad – a timescale that would fit with the last time Zeke had seen him at the gym.

Seeing Darren was online, Flyte pinged him a message: *Could you call me?*

A couple of minutes later, she was swiping to accept an incoming call.

'So, Sean emigrated? Wow! Where to?' asked Flyte, acting as though she knew him better than she had.

'Canada, the lucky bastard,' said Darren.

'You say you didn't see much of him after Hendon?'

'Yeah, Sean went to Finsbury Park nick and I was posted to Lewisham, so . . .'

It always amused Flyte how a forty-minute journey was enough to deter Londoners from meeting – especially if it involved crossing the Thames, which seemed to operate as some kind of psychic barrier. When she'd lived in Winchester she'd thought nothing of driving twenty miles or more to see friends – until Poppy died, after which she couldn't bear to see anybody from her old life.

'So he was at Finsbury Park for what, seven years? Before he went to Canada?'

'Yeah. He got a job in a private security firm looking after billionaires.' Darren chuckled. 'From the pic he posted on Facebook of his gaff out there – Vancouver? – I'd say he was minted.'

'Did you ever hear anyone call him Shane?' The only name he was known by at the gym according to Zeke.

'No.' A pause. 'So this is just you wanting to organise a reunion, is it?' Doubt creeping into his voice. Flyte knew she wasn't the obvious cheerleader for a drunken reunion, having once overheard a fellow trainee describe her as 'a stuck-up cow'.

'Yes! It's been too long, right?' Injecting some enthusiasm into her voice. Then, picturing again the glamorous woman on Sean's arm at the passing-out party, she took a punt. 'What about Sean's girlfriend?'

'Which one?' chuckled Darren.

'The good-looking one with the long hair?' she improvised. 'He brought her to the end-of-term party?'

'Oh yeah . . . Bethany something – she was a model. I'd have . . .' He stopped, thinking better of whatever sexist drivel

103

was about to come out of his mouth. 'Did you know they got engaged after Hendon?'

'Really?'

'Yeah, but it didn't work out. No surprises there, given his previous.'

Sean had evidently been a player.

Darren hadn't heard anything about Sean returning to the UK, but promised to check back on Facebook.

An hour later, he messaged to say that Sean must have deleted his account and with it all his old posts. But he did forward a screen-grab of Sean's ex-girlfriend.

It was an ad for a well-known brand of hair colourant, featuring a striking young woman who appeared, presumably by computer-generated trickery, to be riding a snarling tiger. Forehead lowered, she glared into the camera, her long hair flying out behind her – the same tawny colour as the tiger's pelt.

The ad had been posted nine years earlier under the handle Bethany Violet Locke.

Chapter Fourteen

Stupidly early Sunday morning, mist still shrouding the canal, Cassie strode along the towpath, a new sense of purpose lengthening her stride. What she had to do at the mortuary couldn't wait till Monday.

Cold, so cold.

After coming home from her gran's, she'd barely slept, unable to quiet her buzzing brain, consumed by her sudden intuition of what Green-Eyes' words might mean.

The sun was breaking through and for the first time in ages she was aware of the sights and sounds of the early morning canal – a pair of squabbling moorhens, the breeze ruffling the water, and the cheerful whistling of a fellow boat dweller.

Macavity had to go at a trot to keep up with her. It was his usual routine to accompany her as far as the stairway up to the street, which always made her feel like a drunk being escorted off the premises by a bouncer – an image cemented by his black coat and laconic gaze.

In the silent mortuary, she pulled on full scrubs and gloves before making a beeline for the body store.

Ignoring the waft of putrefaction that billowed from Green-Eyes' drawer, she unzipped the body bag over his face and leaned in. 'Listen, I have an idea what happened to you and I need to take a tiny sample of tissue to confirm it. It'll only be the size of a fingernail. If it turns out I'm wrong, I'm really sorry, but if we're going to find out who you are and how you died, it's a risk I have to take.'

And what a risk. It made the mixing up of viscera from two bodies seem like a minor oversight. Taking an unauthorised sample, however minute, was in direct contravention of HTA rules, and if it was discovered she would never work in a mortuary again – might even end up in court.

But Cassie was in no mood to be dissuaded. Green-Eyes had spoken to her and if she didn't follow her hunch, his fate would be a local authority funeral – and the people who loved him would be left forever wondering why he had disappeared from their lives.

After unzipping the body bag, Cassie took up a scalpel.

'*Alea iacta est*,' she murmured. *The die is cast.* It wasn't the first time she'd invoked Julius Caesar's do-or-die crossing of the Rubicon. Hopefully his ultimate fate wouldn't prove to be a bad omen.

It had been difficult calling Archie, obviously, but there really wasn't anyone else she could ask. She had kept her tone friendly but brisk – making it clear that the 'favour' she needed doing was professional in nature. They met in a bar in Waterloo station, on his way to a rugby match: him in his full posh-boy gear – Barbour jacket, cords and rugby shirt.

'Hello, you,' he said, his deep-grey long-lashed eyes searching hers.

Trying to ignore the flutter in her stomach, she said, 'I wanted to ask you something.' Adding swiftly, 'It's a work thing.'

She passed a Jiffy bag across the table. 'I need you to take a look at a tissue sample. Microscopically.'

He blinked at the bag before staring at her. 'Is this an official request for histo?'

She pulled an apologetic smile. 'Curzon did the PM on this chap and put the COD down as a straight drowning so . . . there was no request for further investigation.'

Leaning back in his chair, Archie rolled his eyes.

'Look, Archie, I know it's a big ask, but it's all in a good cause. I just *know* there's more to this case than meets the eye.'

He stared at the package as if it were radioactive. 'Cassie, look, this is off the scale in HTA terms. This could get both of us in really serious trouble.'

But when he lifted his eyes to meet hers she knew he couldn't say no to her. She quelled her pangs of conscience by imagining Green-Eyes' loved ones, desperate for news of him. 'If it ever comes out – which it won't – I'll say that I gave you the sample and a histo form, and told you it was an official request.'

'And if I find some evidence of foul play? Then what?' He ran a hand through his copper-coloured mop. 'I can't inform the coroner this chap needs a forensic without dropping us both in it up to our armpits.'

'Don't worry about that for now. The less you know the better, but I've got a plan.'

She pictured Flyte's face bent over Green-Eyes' body, an intent expression on her severely beautiful face: she clearly had her own doubts about Curzon's verdict of a bog-standard accidental drowning.

'Please?' She pushed the package across the table to Archie. 'Could you do it today?'

With a gloomy nod, he took it, his fingers brushing hers. A blush flooded his cheeks and he cleared his throat. 'So what exactly am I looking for?'

She shook her head. 'I don't want to sway you either way. Just tell me what you see ASAP, would you?'

He nodded.

'I owe you drinks,' she said lightly.

'You owe me a bit more than a drink,' he said, just as lightly.

Their eyes met before skittering apart. She'd found it tough, seeing him without being able to touch him, but she had to stay strong.

It was evening by the time Archie got back to her. On seeing the incoming call, Cassie felt her mouth go dry, suddenly fearful that she might have desecrated a body for nothing.

'Well? What did you find?' she asked.

'I think you know exactly what I found.' He didn't sound very happy.

Chapter Fifteen

Cassie paced the length of her cabin, a journey of five steps one way then five back the other, Macavity's eyes following her from his perch on the sideboard as if watching a tennis match. She checked her phone again. *Where the hell was she?*

Archie's microscopy had confirmed her hunch, which was gratifying, but also posed a conundrum: how to follow up on the revelation, without dropping either Archie – or herself – in it.

At last, she felt the tell-tale tilt of the boat as someone climbed on board and heard Flyte's voice calling her name.

'What's with all the cloak and dagger then?' Her amused look edged with wariness.

It was the first time Cassie had seen her in anything other than her plainclothes detective 'uniform' – a boring, dark trouser-and-jacket get-up. Her Sunday gear was indigo jeans, and an ice-blue cashmere jumper under her classy parka-type jacket that echoed her eyes and set off her Scandi colouring. Noticing she'd applied fresh lipstick, Cassie wondered what she'd be like to kiss.

'It's a bit delicate,' she said. She waved Flyte into the bench seat next to her and opened her laptop on the fold-down table. 'What do you see?'

Leaning in to the screen, Flyte narrowed her eyes. 'Two microscopic samples?'

'Right. They're actually both samples of muscle tissue.'

'Really? They look totally different.' Flyte touched the screen. 'This one has a more even pattern, while this one is more ... random and looks like it's full of holes, like a Swiss cheese.'

They were sitting so close that Cassie could feel Flyte's breath on her cheek.

'This one with the regular pattern is a standard post-mortem sample,' said Cassie. 'But this one' – indicating the splotchy-looking image – 'is from Green-Eyes.'

The sliver of tissue had come from the psoas muscle in his lower back. One of the densest muscles in the body, it was the slowest to decompose and since it was accessible from inside the body cavity Cassie's sample-taking had left no external trace.

'And?'

Luckily, Flyte appeared to have forgotten that no histopathology had been requested on Green-Eyes' body.

Zooming up the slide, Cassie said, 'You see these jagged holes? They're ruptured cells.' She shifted excitedly in her seat, her thigh accidentally brushing Flyte's.

Flyte gave her a gimlet stare. 'Do I have to play twenty questions? Or are you going to tell me what that means?'

Cassie took a deep breath. 'This kind of cell damage only happens at sub-zero temperatures.'

Flyte's head whipped round and her eyes widened. 'What are you saying ... ?'

'Before it turned up in the canal, Green-Eyes' body was frozen.' *Cold, so cold.*

Cassie's light-bulb moment had come when she'd unearthed the chicken breast in Babcia's freezer compartment and suddenly recalled her biology teacher's passing comment about food hygiene in a lesson on microbiology.

Meat which has been frozen and defrosted goes off faster than fresh.

'It's been bothering me for days: why his body was decomposing so fast, and this explains it.'

Flyte looked incredulous. 'Could he have got accidentally frozen in the mortuary fridge?' Cassie shook her head. 'Is there nothing else that could cause this kind of damage?' She gestured at the sample.

'Freezing preserves tissue very well, but the ice crystals take up more room inside the cells.' Cassie traced the holes in the sample. 'When it starts to thaw the cell walls rupture, which speeds up decomposition.'

Flyte's usually pale cheeks were tinged with pink. 'Somebody kept his body frozen before dumping it in the canal.'

'Yep.' Since Archie's call, Cassie had been berating herself for leaving Green-Eyes' evisceration to Jason. If she'd done it herself, who knows, she might have spotted the last traces of ice crystals inside the body cavity.

'How long had he been frozen for? Days? Weeks?'

'Over to you, I'm afraid,' she said. 'Once tissue has been frozen there's really no reliable way of estimating a time of death.' She'd seen a documentary once about a body uncovered by melting ice in the high Alps. At first the man was thought to be a missing climber, until specialist dating revealed that he'd died five thousand years ago.

'Hang on.' Flyte sent Cassie a penetrating look. 'You said that the pathologist wouldn't be performing any microscopic analysis – that it was expensive and inconclusive.'

'That's why I need your help.' Cassie pulled an apologetic grimace. 'This is what you might call a bit of freelance histopathology? To make it official and find out how he died we really need a forensic post-mortem.'

Flyte gaped in disbelief. 'How do you expect me to deliver that? Do you think I can just . . . *swan in* to my boss's office and ask him to sign off four grand for a forensic PM on a random floater?! The guy isn't even officially my case.'

'I dunno.' Cassie shrugged. 'Couldn't you say that you've come up with a new line of enquiry?'

'Oh, sure.' Flyte cheeks were getting redder by the minute. 'Why don't I just tell him an unhinged mortuary technician has just performed her own post-mortem.'

'Look, I get that it's tricky,' said Cassie. 'I suppose I just thought that by now you might have found something that suggested foul play . . .' She trailed off.

Seeing Flyte reach for her handbag, Cassie gave it one last try. 'I thought you really cared about identifying this guy, finding out how he ended up in the canal.'

'I did,' snapped Flyte. 'I do. But I care more about keeping my job – something in which you display very little interest.'

And with that, she swept out of the cabin without a backward glance.

FLYTE

Flyte stalked off down the towpath.

Flaming fishcakes! The girl was the absolute limit!

After she'd calmed down a bit she had to acknowledge that her exasperation with Cassie was partly anger at herself. She should have been the one to uncover evidence that Green-Eyes' – aka Sean Kavanagh's – death was suspicious – especially as he'd been a cop. Now she was in a worse position than before: she couldn't tell anyone about Cassie's discovery and she still had nothing to go on. No motive, no weapon, and no clue regarding Kavanagh's last movements or recent contacts.

She slept badly that night and woke with a headache and a sense of the inevitable: now she knew that this was no accidental drowning, walking away from the case simply wasn't an option – which, of course, Cassie must have known. Flyte had to find some *aboveboard* evidence that would demand a forensic PM – and fast.

Sure, Steadman wouldn't be happy to discover she'd been working the case on the QT, as Pops would have said, but the fact that Sean had been a police officer who'd almost certainly been murdered should take the edge off his anger.

She needed to establish exactly when Sean had returned to the UK and her only lead was Sean's ex-fiancée – the tawny-maned Bethany Locke. She'd scoured online social media sites with no luck, but lots of people used different names online. Had she gone to Canada with Sean after all? But if so, why hadn't she raised the alarm over her missing fiancé?

As she was rostered off that day Flyte was able to put in some calls unobserved.

'Hi, Sebastian, it's Phyllida . . . Sorry. Seb . . . I'm fine, thanks. Did I hear that you did a stint in Special Branch? . . . Look, I need a favour. There's a name I need running through flight manifest records for London–Canada . . . No, just helping CID with ID-ing a John Doe.' Which wasn't exactly a lie.

After agreeing to help out, Seb said, 'How about a drink? Tonight, if you're free?'

A micro-pause before she replied, 'Sure, let's do that.' It would be the first time she'd ever gone on a date with anyone from work – with good reason. She'd heard male cops bragging about having 'nailed' a female colleague, while predictably the woman was branded a slut. But it was getting on for two years since she and Matt had parted and high time she dipped her toe in the dating waters. Seb was undeniably good-looking and smart – unlike the other sexist morons in the office – and she was fairly confident she could trust him to be discreet.

Her next call was to Josh at CID to ask him to run a search on the Police National Computer: if Bethany or Sean held driving licences their addresses would be listed.

Ten minutes later, he called her back. 'No joy with Sean Kavanagh,' he said. 'There are hundreds of them in north London alone. But I did find a Bethany Violet Locke about the right age. No criminal record. Last driving licence issued two years ago. She lives in Seddon House, EC2.'

*

Within an hour Flyte was wending her way through the laby-rinth of the Barbican – a sprawling development of brutalist concrete design. She knew that it was popular with wealthy City types who had weekday pieds-à-terre here, before they scuttled off to places like the Cotswolds at the weekend. It was also infamous for its sky-high rents. To her it looked pretty much like any other sixties or seventies council estate – albeit less scruffy and with slightly nicer planting.

Seddon House was one of the low-rise blocks. Not wanting to try Bethany Locke's buzzer – too easy to get brushed off that way – she hovered outside until a youngish, hipsterish-looking guy arrived and used his key to enter the building. As she followed him in, he shot her a curious look, so she said, 'I'm with the police,' ready to pull out her warrant card if necessary. But her businesslike look was clearly enough to deter further questions and he scurried off up the stairs, leav-ing the lift to her.

Bethany opened the flat door swiftly, as if she were expecting a visitor, but looked confused to see Flyte standing there. 'Oh . . . you're not Amazon.' Her voice was unusually low-pitched for a woman, making her working-class London accent sound even harsher.

On seeing Flyte's ID Bethany's expression turned wary. But not before Flyte thought she detected a flicker of another emo-tion: resignation. Almost as though she'd been expecting this visit for a long time.

In the living room, she declined Bethany's offer of coffee and took the only chair with its back to the window, forcing her hostess to take the sofa in the full glare of daylight. Facing the light put people on edge, like those old cop movies where they trained an anglepoise lamp on their interviewee. There was a faintly fruity smell in the air that Flyte couldn't place.

Bethany wore her thick tawny hair in a plait, and she was still striking-looking nearly a decade on from her tiger photoshoot. But her features had a hardness about them and her complexion beneath her make-up had coarsened, perhaps from too much smoking and drinking – or disappointment. As if to confirm the former, Bethany picked up a vaping device from the coffee table. 'How can I help?' she asked, her accent markedly more 'proper' now that she knew she was talking to a police officer.

Luckily, Bethany showed no sign of recognising her.

'Nice place,' said Flyte insincerely, glancing out at the wind-swept piazza. Funny how the architects who had erected these concrete people-silos in the sixties and seventies seemed to prefer living in Georgian townhouses themselves. 'I imagine the rent must be pretty scary?'

'I own it,' said Bethany, a hint of challenge in her uplifted chin. Her lips looked unnaturally pillowy for someone who had to be around Flyte's age – mid to late thirties.

Flyte made a politely impressed expression, filing away the information. 'I'm afraid I'm here in connection with a death,' she said.

Bethany's expression appeared to be frozen in 'helpful mode', but then her lack of facial mobility might be due to an over-enthusiastic use of Botox.

'Can I ask if you are still in contact with Sean Kavanagh?' Flyte had to resist the impulse to wave away the sickly cloud of fruit-fragranced vape.

'Not for years,' said Bethany quickly. No hesitation, no '*Why do you ask?*'

Flyte waited a moment, but Bethany said nothing more. 'We recovered the body of a man from the canal last week. I'm sorry to say we have reason to believe that it might be Sean's.'

Bethany's hand, the nails long and French-polished went to her mouth. But the expression in her eyes seemed more guarded than surprised.

'Would you be happy to look at an artist's impression?' Flyte asked.

Bethany shrugged her assent and Flyte reached for the phone to pull up the image that Luke Lawless had put in the *Camden Gazette*, pushing it across the coffee table between them.

After taking a deep draw on her vape, Bethany took a long look at the image – conflicting emotions playing out across her face. 'I think so. We split up eight years ago. And he looks . . . different.' She pushed the phone back across the table.

'We know that he was a police officer before emigrating to Canada but his colleagues are no longer in touch with him, so we're trying to find out when he came back to the UK and whom he might have been in contact with.'

'Sorry, but I have no idea. Like I say, I haven't seen or heard from him in years.'

'What about his next of kin? Parents, siblings?'

'He didn't have any brothers or sisters, and his dad died when he was young.' Bethany's foot, crossed at the ankles, jigged up and down. 'His mother was Irish. Lived in London but I couldn't tell you where. They weren't close, so I never met her.'

'I understand you were engaged? Did you live together?'

'Yeah, for almost a year, in my tiny flat off the Holloway Road.'

Halfway between Sean's nick at Finsbury Park and the gym he and Zeke had attended.

'Can I ask why you two broke up?'

Bethany's carapace of make-up couldn't hide a flash of anger. 'He was cheating on me. And more than once, as it turned out. So I dumped him. A few weeks later, I heard he'd gone to Canada. Emigrated.' She shrugged. In spite of her bravado it was clear to Flyte that the betrayal still hurt. And she would bet that it was Sean who had done the 'dumping'.

'Did you have any further contact?'

She dropped her eyes to fiddle with her vaping device. 'No. That was the last I heard of him.'

'How long were you engaged?' Flyte pulled a sympathetic smile.

'Five months.' She lifted a shoulder 'It wasn't meant to be.'

'If I can't find a next of kin, would you be prepared to officially confirm his identity?'

A complicated series of emotions – wariness, regret, something else Flyte couldn't name – flitted across Bethany's face. 'Would I have to go see him?'

'No, you could do it from a photograph.' Television dramas loved to portray the grieving relative bending over a body in a starkly lit mortuary, but, in real life, it was common practice to ID the dead from a post-mortem photo, especially if the body was decomposed.

'I'll think about it,' she said. 'It was all a long time ago.'

Flyte had no power to insist on a formal ID. She put her notebook away. 'If you think of anyone at all he might have been in contact with when he came back from Canada, would you let me know?'

As they swapped numbers, Bethany asked, 'Where is he, now? Who is going to bury him?' From her look, the unspoken bit being *Not me, I hope?*

118

'For the time being he's in the general mortuary attached to Camden Hospital. If I can't track down a next of kin, the local authority will have him cremated.'

Flyte got up to go. 'I saw that ad you were in, with the tiger, on Facebook? Are you still modelling?'

A look of pride crossed Bethany's face. 'That was fun while it lasted. I've got my own beauty salon now.'

At the door, Flyte paused and turned back to her. 'Oh, by the way, did you ever hear Sean mention someone called Zeke?'

'No,' said Bethany, shaking her head, but her improbably lashed eyes had blinked a few times.

As Flyte took the stairs down she replayed Bethany's reaction. It was no more than a hunch but she would swear that the name Zeke had meant something to her.

Back out on the concourse, she ran an online check on the history of property prices in the Barbican. Eight years ago, a flat in Seddon House would have changed hands for a little over £400,000, which raised an interesting question. Even allowing for the proceeds of her 'tiny flat', how had Bethany been able to go ahead with the purchase without Sean around to contribute?

Chapter Sixteen

Since Archie had confirmed her hunch that Green-Eyes' body had been frozen, Cassie had been in a state of fizzing, restless excitement. Getting into the mortuary early the next day, she had gone straight to his drawer in the body store. Not wanting to open it and let warm air in, she leaned close to the brushed steel surface and murmured, 'Don't worry, I'm on the case.'

Cold, so cold . . .

Part of her believed that it was the words she'd 'heard' from Green-Eyes which had given her the crucial clue, but she was well aware of an alternative – rational – explanation. The speed of his decomposition had bothered her – to the point of having a refrigeration engineer check out the body store. Then defrosting her gran's freezer had simply helped her retrieve the memory of how the freeze-thaw cycle could speed up decomposition.

In a few weeks' time – sooner if they ran out of body-store space – Green-Eyes would go into the mortuary's long-stay deep freeze, destroying forever any chance of proving his body had been frozen *before* being dumped in the canal.

But for the coroner to authorise a new, forensic post-mortem, the police would need to find evidence to suggest that the death might be suspicious after all.

120

Flyte was her only hope. Despite her furious exit the previous evening, Cassie had a strong hunch that she'd be redoubling her efforts to investigate the death. The two of them were worlds apart in practically every way, but if they had one thing in common it was a single-minded determination to get to the truth.

Right now, Cassie had to prepare for a family viewing: two sisters coming in to see their elderly mum who had died after collapsing at home the previous night.

In the loo, she freed her hair from its topknot and let it down to cover her shaved undercut before removing her piercings, three from the left eyebrow, one from her upper lip, and stowing them in the trouser pocket of her scrubs. She did this ahead of family viewings – partly because people already fragile with grief might find her look a bit hard core, but also to mark the fact that she was stepping out of the world of the recently dead – the 'red side' in mortuary jargon – to care for those they had left behind.

After draping the body of seventy-eight-year-old Dido Smythe with a coverlet, she wheeled her through to the viewing room and locked the wheels before casting an eye over her. She didn't look bad, and since the cause of death had been signed off by her hospital doctor there was no post-mortem stitching to worry about.

Dido was a widow living alone in Primrose Hill – the poshest corner of the borough – when she'd been rushed into A & E the previous evening after her neighbour found her collapsed and unconscious on the kitchen floor. An MRI scan of her head showed she'd suffered a massive CVA, or cerebrovascular accident, aka a stroke, and a little over an hour later she had died without regaining consciousness.

Cassie took a comb to Dido's luxuriant and expertly cut silver hair, before arranging it round her face – fine-boned and with an aquiline nose like the prow of a galleon. 'There,' she told her, 'we want you to look your best, Mrs S. It's been a terrible shock for your girls, losing you so suddenly, but seeing you will help.' She put a rolled towel under Dido's neck to angle the head back slightly, to prevent her mouth falling open.

Dido's silence didn't dent Cassie's upbeat mood. The spark of connection she'd sometimes felt with her guests had always been sporadic and since hearing Green-Eyes 'speak' she was confident that her gift had come back.

Ten minutes later, she was standing the other side of the curtained glass doors that bisected the viewing room alongside Dido's daughters, Acantha and Persephone. The two women, both striking-looking and with noses inherited from their mum, were in their mid to late forties and both wore smart dark suits as if they were already on the way to her funeral. The air was thick with the smell of expensive scent.

The younger sister, Acantha, was shorter than Persephone – and chattier. *The people-pleaser.* 'Thank you for letting us see her. We couldn't get to the hospital in time last night. We both live miles away, you see. I'm in darkest Wiltshire and Seffy is in the Cotswolds.'

When a loved one died out of the blue, like Dido, family members who hadn't witnessed their last moments often felt the urgent need to see them. Public health regulations had ended the tradition of laying out the dead in the front room, but for most people, the desire to view the body of a loved one was still a powerful human impulse. Cassie had to push away a sudden image of her dad's skinny body, stretched out on an autopsy table.

122

Acantha went on, talking about how unexpected their mum's death was given how fit she was, how only recently she'd laid on a buffet supper for friends to watch the broadcast of the *Last Night of the Proms*.

'Oh, do shut up, Acantha!' snapped Persephone in an accent even more cut-glass than her sister's. 'We're not at a cocktail party.' She was clearly used to pulling rank as the older sister.

Acantha didn't respond but Cassie saw the mulish look that came over her face. The just-bereaved were emotionally frayed and fallings-out at a viewing weren't uncommon. After her usual spiel to prepare them for the sight of their mum, she pulled the cord to open the drapes, a moment that always reminded her of the stage curtain going up in the theatre. Beneath the coverlet, Dido's body was sunken-chested, touchingly frail, although her beaky profile gave her an undaunted look.

The sisters' reactions were quite different. Putting both hands to her face, Acantha gasped and started weeping noisily. Persephone just stared at her mother through the glass, pale-faced but stoical. 'Let's go in,' she said testily.

Inside, Acantha immediately reached for her mother's covered arm, before recoiling. Cassie had already warned them that the body would feel different. Dido's muscles were in full rigor, as pliant to the touch as a wooden chopping board. Acantha stroked Dido's silver hair instead, murmuring through tears, 'Oh, Mummy, where have you gone?'

Persephone stood stiffly, saying nothing. Her first words, addressed to Cassie, were: 'Was she wearing earrings?'

Cassie checked the document that had come over from the hospital. 'She wasn't wearing any jewellery according to the nurses who looked after her,' she spoke carefully, meeting Persephone's

123

eye. 'Every personal item is removed, logged, and kept safe.' Was there going to be trouble? The jewellery and clothes someone had been wearing when they died could assume the importance of a religious icon to the bereaved.

'Oh, just shut up about the sodding earrings!' Acantha burst out tearfully. 'Is her jewellery all that matters to you?'

Persephone gasped. 'How *dare* you? She was the centre of my life.'

'And mine!'

'Really. Last time I looked you were busy with your husband and the children. I was there every fortnight without fail.'

It was Acantha's turn to gasp.

Here we go, thought Cassie. She'd seen it before, how sudden death could tear down the polite fictions constructed over the decades to paper over familial cracks.

'Listen.' She set a tentative hand on each woman's shoulder. 'You've both had an awful shock—'

'I didn't take the precious bloody earrings, OK?' Cassie felt Acantha's shoulder muscles tense under her hand as she hurled the bitter words at her sister.

'I'm not staying here to be sworn at and . . . and . . . abused.' Persephone's voice wavered for the first time. 'I'm sorry, Mummy,' she said, resting a hand on Dido's hair for a moment before sweeping out.

Cassie got Acantha a chair and a box of tissues and let her cry for a bit.

When the weeping had died away to sniffles, Cassie said, 'You can tell me to mind my own business, of course, but if you did want to tell me what that was about . . . ?'

Acantha took a deep breath and nodded. 'Mummy used to have these sweet little gold earrings in the shape of roses – they were a gift from Daddy when they were first married. She only wore them on special occasions but when we were little she would let us get them out, just to look at. Anyway, at the house this morning we started bagging up her clothes for Oxfam.' She lifted a shoulder. 'It was just a way of keeping busy. Then Seffy stormed in saying the earrings were missing from Mummy's jewellery box and more or less accused me of stealing them!'

'Why would she think you'd done such a thing?'

'We'd already had a bit of a falling-out over them.' Acantha grimaced. 'According to Seffy, Mummy had always said that *she* should have them when she . . . passed. But Mummy had been clear that she was leaving them to me.' She fumbled in her handbag for her phone. She scrolled through her photos and pulled up one of her and Dido, standing in a garden with people in the background. 'She was wearing them at a family christening just a couple of weeks ago and she said it again.' Mother and daughter were beaming into camera, their heads touching. Dido wore a dated but beautifully cut powder-blue Chanel suit and Cassie could just make out the earrings that had stirred up such sibling rivalry.

'It's a lovely picture,' she said. 'You and your mum were obviously very close.'

It was clear as vodka that the conflict had nothing to do with the earrings per se and everything to do with their symbolic value. Cassie had seen it countless times, the way death revived the question that, deep down, every child with siblings wanted to know: who did Mum or Dad love best? Poor prickly Seffy was dealing with what she'd probably known since childhood: that for whatever reason, Acantha had been her mother's favourite.

You didn't need to be a shrink to know that the earrings stood for their mother's love: who had she chosen to leave it to?

'Do you think your mum might have said the same thing to both of you?' said Cassie. 'Obviously not intentionally but . . . she was seventy-eight. Most people that age can be a bit forgetful.'

Acantha gave a little shrug, allowing the possibility.

'Listen, Acantha, feelings are very raw at a time like this . . . but after your mum's funeral you and Seffy will still be sisters, and you'll need to look after each other. The earrings will turn up somewhere.' She eyed Acantha – wondering if she might have taken them in an impulsive moment? 'If and when they do reappear, maybe you could think about letting Seffy have them? They are just earrings, after all.'

And you have something far more precious: you were the favourite child.

Acantha stroked her mum's hair, all the anger gone out of her. 'Maybe I will,' she said. 'If we ever find them.'

FLYTE

She was relieved to find that Seb had suggested the Vine pub for their drink that evening rather than somewhere wallpapered with screens playing football.

For a start, it was a mile away up in Kentish Town where they were unlikely to bump into anyone from work, and refreshingly upmarket, more of a gastropub, aimed at the area's media workers and residents wealthy enough to afford the grand early Victorian properties hereabouts.

She still couldn't get over the fact that for the price of a one-bed flat here you could buy a four-bedroom house in a leafy Winchester suburb. The main shopping street was even shabbier than Camden Town, and was dominated by fast-food joints, betting shops, pound shops and the like. None of that – nor the local crime rate – seemed to deter wealthy north London hipsters. Maybe they thought they were 'keeping it real'.

Sebastian – *Seb* – was already there when she arrived, for which she awarded brownie points. Followed by further points when he helped her out of her jacket and hung it on the back of the chair. Flyte believed in female equality, that was a given, but she viewed traditional gentlemanly gestures as a harmless courtesy and not a slippery slope that ended with spiked drinks and date rape.

He already had a pint of bitter on the table but insisted on ordering a bottle of wine – going with her choice of a Chilean Sauvignon. While he put in the order she checked him out discreetly. Regular features and a clean jawline. From his wide shoulders and the biceps that filled his shirtsleeves, he worked out regularly without overdoing it. And his suit was just right – not the flashy cut and too-shiny fabric favoured by Dean Willets who was always boasting about how he got his suits from a 'guy in Jermyn Street'.

As he poured their wine, she said, 'So tell me more about Willets . . . ? No offence if he's a friend of yours but he can be a bit of a blowhard, can't he?'

Seb looked confused, reminding her that she'd inherited some of her descriptions and phrases directly from Pops, who'd probably inherited them in turn from his father, an army colonel who, incredibly, had been old enough to serve in the First World War. No wonder she sometimes felt as if she were marooned in the wrong era.

'He's fond of the sound of his own voice, I mean,' she clarified.

'Oh, for sure.' Seb chuckled. 'Dean's pretty harmless though.'

'Not to the poor little bunnies in Essex he isn't.'

'Fair point.' Seb laughed.

'And you say the boss used to go on these shooting parties years ago, when he was patrol sarge? He doesn't seem the type.'

'He probably wasn't. Apparently, Dean was always badgering him to go because his old lady – his wife, I mean – knew how to skin and gut the rabbits. She's French, so she made a mean rabbit casserole.'

Flyte made a face and they both laughed, their eyes meeting. Seb was a nice guy and amusing company, she decided – and he looked the part. She had always pictured herself remarrying one day, so now she allowed herself to play fantasy wedding: her in a frock suitable for a second time round wedding, nothing too frou-frou or virginal, Seb at her side, cutting a fine figure in an elegant suit. All silly schoolgirl stuff, of course.

'That was awkward in the pub the other night, when I came in on him talking about nicking those guys having sex in public.' She grimaced. 'I mean fair enough, nobody walking their dog wants to stumble on a gay porno – or a straight one come to that – but the way he talked about it . . . it was pretty homophobic, don't you think?'

Seb made a rueful face. 'Yeah . . . Dean did tell me he ran a sweepstake for the uniforms at his old nick for who could catch the most guys at it in public. They earned points depending on the sex act – you know, five points for a hand job—'

'OK, OK, I get the picture.'

'He called it Blowjob Bingo.' Seb was trying to look disapproving but not entirely succeeding.

'Did none of the brass do anything?'

He drank some of his wine. 'According to the gossip, when Steadman found out about it he came down on Dean like a ton of bricks. It's probably why he hasn't made it past sergeant.'

Seeing her expression, Seb pulled an awkward grin. 'Look, Dean isn't a bad guy. He's a good detective underneath it all. He puts on a bit of an act to wind people like us up, you know, because we came in as graduates while he was out on the beat breaking up pub fights.'

Flyte enjoyed the evening – inevitably it was mostly shop talk because that was their life – and it struck her what a hermit she'd become. Once they'd emptied the bottle, she declined his offer of dinner but he talked her into another glass of wine. Halfway through that and feeling a bit reckless she decided she'd let him kiss her goodnight at the Tube. No more than that mind: she was cautious, had never been one to jump into bed with a man at the first opportunity. In fact, aside from the single fumbled act with another ex-pat sixteen-year-old boy during the school holiday in Cyprus – a deliberate shedding of her virginity endured through gritted teeth – Matt was the only man she'd ever slept with.

She remembered Willets boasting about the witness he'd just interviewed contacting him on WhatsApp, and emboldened by the wine asked Seb, 'Do you think Willets would sleep with a witness?'

'He'd be mad if he did. If Steadman found out . . . he'd have him up before the DPS in a heartbeat.' Three initials to strike fear into any police officer, DPS stood for the Directorate of Professional Standards, which investigated cases of police misconduct.

'Why?' Seb went on. 'Do you think . . . ?'

'No, no, nothing.'

Flyte was aware that the current deluge of stories in the press about sexism, racism, domestic abuse – and even rape – by her fellow cops could be making her over-sensitive to the behaviour of the likes of Willets. She had to keep reminding herself that in a nationwide force of some 150,000 officers there were bound to be some monsters.

They parted outside the Tube, Flyte preferring to walk the mile or so home and declining his offer to accompany her.

'This has been really nice,' said Seb, his brown eyes on hers.

'I agree,' she said, her expression letting him know he could kiss her.

She was grateful to him for keeping the tongue action to a respectable minimum and not pressing his groin against hers, but the kiss tasted of the beer he'd started the night with – something she'd forgotten about men.

As she walked off down Kentish Town High Road, she found herself imagining what it would taste like to kiss Cassie Raven.

FLYTE

Flyte had sometimes wondered what it would be like to get on the wrong side of DCI Steadman. The next day, having been called into his office before she'd even got her coat off, she found out.

'Let me get this straight, Phyllida,' he said, pointing to the chair the other side of his desk, his usual smile absent. 'I instructed you to hand the unidentified floater back to CID without delay, and instead you mount your own private investigation?'

'Well—'

'You brief a local reporter on the case – this Luke something or other – without informing the press office?'

Flaming fishcakes.

Having sniffed her interest in Sean Kavanagh, Luke Lawless must have called the press office, fishing for info and dropped her name. *Idiot.*

'Sir, if I could just . . .'

A curt movement of his hand silenced her.

'Since you got here you've been badgering me to make you IO on a murder case and meanwhile you're doing CID's job for them with some personal crusade, trying to ID a random drunk who fell in the canal while urinating?!'

'He didn't fall in.' Flyte spoke quietly but the confidence in her tone stopped Steadman in his tracks. 'I mean, I have a line of enquiry that his death was not accidental.'

Steadman's expression grew incredulous.

'Look, boss, I'm really sorry. I know it was out of line, but the fact is I recognised the guy.'

Steadman fell silent for a long moment. 'Is this some kind of a joke?'

'No . . . I just wasn't one hundred per cent sure at first.'

'Go on.' Steadman leaned forward, obviously intrigued.

'He was a police officer called Sean Kavanagh.'

Steadman's eyebrows shot up. 'What the . . . ?'

'We were part of the same probie intake at Hendon. Look, I barely knew him but his ex-fiancée has confirmed the ID.'

Steadman could have kicked off but instead he subsided in his seat. One of his detectives wasting time on identifying a random MOP was one thing, but doing it for a fellow cop was a different kettle of fish.

'What makes you think it wasn't accidental?' But from the expression on his face he was hooked.

First thing that morning, Seb had called her. After some warm words about how much he'd enjoyed last night, he told her he'd heard back from his mate in Special Branch who'd run a search on flight manifests.

'Sean Kavanagh's fiancée told me that he left the force and emigrated to Canada eight years ago,' she said.

Steadman frowned. 'So . . . when did he come back to Camden?'

'He didn't "come back", boss.' Flyte left a pause. 'Because he never left the UK in the first place.'

Seb's mate had checked flight manifests going back ten years and had found no record of a Sean Quillan Kavanagh on any flight either to or from Canada. 'There were a couple of posts from Vancouver, supposedly on his Facebook account, but they must have been fictitious. He had no further contact with his friendship group. None. Basically, eight years ago Sean Kavanagh dropped off the face of the earth.'

She was dreading Steadman asking how she'd gained the flight information but instead he said, 'There's no law against fibbing on Facebook. Maybe he just wanted to cut his old ties and start a new life here.'

Flyte hesitated. 'There's something else, boss.'

He raised an eyebrow.

'A senior technician at the mortuary isn't happy about the estimated time of death from the routine post-mortem. Something to do with the rate of decomposition. She's going to ask the pathologist to conduct further tests on the tissue, which will trigger a forensic PM. But I think we should get on it without delay before the body deteriorates any further.'

This was a calculated bluff: Cassie was relying on the request for a forensic PM to come from the police.

Steadman hesitated – understandably, since the bill for a forensic PM would come out of the unit's budget. Finally, he sighed and said, 'This Kavangah was one of ours. I'll get onto the coroner about a forensic, but I want Dean to run the case.' He put his hand up to quell any objection. 'No arguments, Phyllida. You knew the guy, so it's not appropriate for you to be IO, but you can work alongside Dean on it.' He sent her a wry smile. 'In any case, I need to know that you two can work together. It'll be good for you both.'

Hell's bells.

'Who's taking over as IO on the Hugger Mugger?' she asked.

'Didn't Dean tell you?' He turned back to his computer, already onto his next task. 'The victim regained consciousness.

He's brain damaged, probably for life, but it's not our case anymore. Back he goes to CID.

'One last thing, Phyllida,' he said as she reached the door. 'You're a good detective. But if you ever go off-piste like that again, I'll be facilitating your career switch to Traffic.'

Chapter Seventeen

After Flyte called her with the news, Cassie had gone straight to Green-Eyes' drawer. She rubbed out the words 'Unknown male' on the brushed steel surface and printed the name 'Sean (aka Shane) Quillan Kavanagh' in bold black marker pen, including the alias Flyte said he'd used.

'Hello there, Sean,' she murmured, putting her hand flat against the steel surface. 'Nice to meet you properly at last.'

Flyte had been brisk on the phone, saying only that she'd discovered Sean's identity and that she was 'working on' a forensic PM, but Cassie could tell that she was quietly excited at the breakthrough.

Cassie turned to the drawer marked 'Dido Smythe' who the undertakers were coming to collect ahead of her funeral. After transferring the body onto a wheeled trolley, she unzipped the body bag over Dido's face. Her aquiline nose stood even more proud now that the flesh of her face had started to shrink, but the serenity bestowed by death had smoothed her features, revealing what a beauty she must have been in her youth. Cassie recalled the viewing room bust-up between Dido's two daughters, their bottled-up sibling rivalry suddenly laid bare by their mum's death.

'I hope Seffy and Acantha have managed to patch things up,' Cassie murmured to her, checking the details on Dido's ID tag against the paperwork. 'They're going to need each other, now more than ever.' Picturing the image of Dido in her vintage Chanel suit with her younger daughter at the family christening, their heads touching, she leaned closer. 'Do you think Acantha might have . . . taken the earrings?'

Nada.

But Cassie got a strange feeling looking at Dido's face. Her expression seemed to have altered somehow. Although still serene it now seemed to hold an edge of sardonic impatience.

There were no PMs that day but the parents of a young man killed in a motorbike accident the previous night had come in to view his body. After they'd departed, Cassie went into the loo to replace her piercings. She retrieved her eyebrow bolt from the pocket of her scrubs, but couldn't locate the smallest of her lip studs. Finally locating it wedged in the inside seam, she was just about to re-insert it when she felt a chill gust on her neck, as though a drawer of the body store had opened behind her. Her breath seemed to solidify in her throat and she closed her eyes, struck by the sudden sensation that Dido Smythe was standing right behind her.

The feeling was gone in an instant, leaving Cassie still frozen. She looked down at the hand holding the lip stud. But before she could process what just happened she felt her phone vibrating.

It was Deborah, calling from the office. 'I've got a Bethany Locke in reception, wanting to view the unidentified male from the canal?'

Odd that Flyte hadn't mentioned anyone coming in.

In her early thirties, Bethany was made up to the nines, with spidery eyelashes, reddish-blonde wavy hair pumped with extensions ... the Insta-ready cookie-cutter look that men supposedly went gaga for.

'Have you spoken to the coroner's office?' Cassie asked her, already suspecting the answer.

'I ... no. I had some policewoman turn on my doorstep.' From Bethany's lip curl it was clear she and Flyte hadn't exactly hit it off. 'She showed me a picture and told me that Sean's body was here. We were engaged for a while, ages ago.'

Underneath all the slap, Bethany's face had character. Cassie could tell she'd been through a lot in her life.

'I was in the neighbourhood, so I thought ...' she went on, seeming on edge, but then the prospect of viewing the body of an ex-lover, even one you'd split from years ago, couldn't be a relaxing one.

Cassie bit her lip. Technically, requests to view a body should be submitted via the coroner's office, but she'd bent that rule before when a loved one had turned up unannounced.

Bethany sent her an imploring look. 'It would mean a lot to me.'

Cassie wasn't about to take Sean out of his refrigerated drawer so she ushered her through to the body store to view him in situ.

Before pulling out his drawer, she prepped Bethany, but this time adding carefully, 'He's been with us for a while now, so you need to know he's not very ... fresh.'

Bethany nodded, waving a manicured hand.

As Cassie opened the drawer out wafted a smell like over-ripe Camembert, which intensified as she unzipped the bag over his face.

Bethany looked down at him for a long moment. 'You *bastard*,' she said, her words a fierce half-whisper.

Cassie didn't react. It wasn't unusual for the bereaved to express anger at the deceased – now and again, she still got angry herself when she thought about her mother dying. Of course it was irrational, but to those left behind death was the final – the unforgivable – abandonment.

'We were supposed to be having the fairy-tale wedding in Bali,' said Bethany. 'You know, wedding ceremony on the beach, all that crap.' Her voice hardened. 'But you know men, he just couldn't keep his dick in his pants. The worst thing is, he never really wanted me.' She paused, a sad smile creeping across her face. 'He's still a looker, isn't he, even now.'

Cassie agreed before saying gently, 'You say it's been years since you saw him last? You had no contact at all after you broke up?'

Bethany pursed her lips. 'No, not really. It was better that way. A clean break.' She took a last long look at the body before turning away.

Cassie closed Sean's drawer. She was used to seeing the full pick 'n' mix of emotions from the bereaved, and beneath Bethany's tough exterior there was unresolved grief and anger, but she also sensed an undertow of something else. Shame? *Or guilt . . . ?* Which didn't really add up if Sean had been the one who had behaved badly.

Back in reception she told Bethany, 'You know, it can be hard to deal with the death of someone you had a troubled relationship with. I can give you my number if you like? In case you feel like talking anytime.'

Bethany's face crumpled briefly, revealing a sudden vulnerability. 'Thank you,' she said quietly.

FLYTE

'The guv tells me that you're going to be helping out on this Kavanagh case,' said Dean Willets, his tone oiled with patronising mateyness. Word had just come through that a Home Office pathologist had been assigned to conduct a forensic PM on the body the following day.

Helping out?!

Worse, he had perched himself on the edge of Flyte's desk which always set her teeth on edge. She had a visceral reaction to anyone invading her space.

'Fancy you being at Hendon with him! Small world.' Willets sent her a speculative look 'And this mortuary attendant who found the body – wasn't her mother the murder vic in that cold case you worked on?'

'Yes. Coincidentally.'

'She a friend of yours, then?' Did his raised eyebrow imply they were more than friends?

'She's a contact, pure and simple.'

Denying they were friends came easily: Flyte was still irritated that Cassie hadn't notified her when Bethany turned up at the mortuary, only dropping her a text after the event. It was a missed opportunity to gauge Sean's ex-fiancée's reaction to seeing his body.

'If you work in a morgue you probably see murder every-where.' He bent his head to hers and said, 'Look, I know the boss wants us to go the extra mile given this Kavanagh guy was in the Job, but I reckon the whole thing'll turn out to be a storm in a teacup. The original PM report said his flies were open? Sounds like your classic death by urination – he was rat-arsed, he went to take a piss in the canal, overbalanced and drowned.'

'Maybe,' said Flyte, non-committal. She was looking forward to the moment when the official histology proved that Sean Kavanagh's body had been frozen before being dumped in the canal. That should wipe the know-it-all look off Dean Willets' face.

'I hope you don't mind but I've forwarded you the coroner's office forms to fill in,' Willets went on. 'Between you and me, I have a low tolerance threshold for dealing with lazy-arsed civil servants.'

Then his whole demeanour shifted. Removing his backside from her desk, he assumed a serious look. 'So, as I say, I want no stone left unturned.'

She glanced over her shoulder to find Steadman standing there.

'Dean, will you be attending the PM tomorrow?'

'Yes, guv.'

'I'd like to tag along too,' said Flyte.

Steadman seemed to be in two minds for a moment, before looking at Willets. 'Dean? Your shout.'

Willets sucked his teeth, clearly delighted to be given the opportunity to lord it over Flyte. 'To be honest, Phyllida, there's a ton of stuff I need you to be doing here – establishing Kavanagh's recent movements in Camden, for one thing.'

'But, guv, I . . .' Flyte looked to Steadman but his expression told her to suck it up.

Chapter Eighteen

By the end of the afternoon Cassie had learned that Professor Arculus, her favourite pathologist, would be conducting a forensic PM on Sean's body at seven o'clock the following morning.

And there was more good news: just as she was pulling on her jacket she got a call back from Persephone 'Seffy' Smythe, Dido's elder daughter. Cassie had contacted her earlier that day, to tentatively share the flash of intuition she'd had in the loos while replacing her piercings.

'You were right!' Persephone sounded giddy with relief. 'What a marvellous piece of luck that I managed to get hold of someone before they'd had a chance to put it out in the shop.'

The 'someone' would be one of the volunteers at the local charity shop, and the item that might have ended up being sold to a bargain hunter was Dido Smythe's old but much-loved Chanel suit which she'd worn to a family christening a couple of weeks before her death.

'You found them then?'

'Yes! I had checked the pockets before taking it but when I had a proper look, they'd gone down a hole in the lining. That suit was ancient . . . but Mummy did love it.'

It amused Cassie the way Seffy said the word *suit* to rhyme with *newt*, presumably the posh-person pronunciation.

'Wherever did you get the idea?' Seffy asked wonderingly.

'I put my earrings in the pocket of my scrubs sometimes. It occurred to me that your mum might have done the same, you know, after a long day at the christening.'

'Well, I can't thank you enough.' Seffy's words were heartfelt. 'Have you told Acantha?'

A strained pause and when Seffy replied, her discomfort was clear. 'I . . . I didn't behave very well that day, I'm so sorry you got dragged into it. I should have known that Acantha would never stoop . . . Now she's insisting that I have the earrings.'

'That's kind of her,' said Cassie. 'I'd accept if I were you.'

'Perhaps I will. We do love each other you know, in spite of appearances.'

'I could tell,' said Cassie. After hanging up, she was struck by a sudden feeling of melancholy at her lack of a sister – or brother.

Later that afternoon, Cassie was heading back to the boat when she spotted a man in his sixties sitting on a camping stool at the edge of the towpath. He was an eccentric sight: he wore a shabby tweed greatcoat, topped by a clear red plastic mac, and had a bulging leather briefcase beside him. It wasn't the first time she'd seen him: Gaz had told her he was homeless and from the way he talked to himself he probably had mental health issues. Today she noticed he was silent and immobile, with his eyes closed.

She paused beside him. 'Are you OK?'

After opening his eyes cautiously he asked, in a commanding tone, 'What's the time?'

'Umm. It's almost exactly five.'

'One hour and forty-nine minutes to go,' he said. After rooting in his pocket. he pulled out a small black cylinder a bit like a zoom lens.

'Are you waiting for someone?' she asked.

His face twisted in irritation, he pointed downstream. 'It rises *there*.'

'What does?'

'Jupiter of course! It will reach full opposition this evening, next to the moon.'

When he put the gadget to his eye she realised it was a mini-telescope. Squinting eastwards down the canal, a curve of dull silver in the failing light she made out the moon edging over the horizon, its surface surprisingly bright, reflecting the sun's rays directly opposite.

'Three hundred and sixty-seven million miles from Earth.' The guy was flushed with excitement. 'Very close indeed.'

'That's great. Listen, if you ever need some water, a cup of tea or anything, just knock, OK? My boat's just up there. *Dreamcatcher*.'

'Good day to you,' he said distantly, his eye still pinned to the telescope.

Going into her cabin, she immediately got a bad feeling. It was Macavity's dinnertime but he was nowhere to be seen, although he could have scored a sneaky extra feed from one of his boat-dwelling admirers. After checking everything in the galley and the forward cabin where her bed was, she couldn't find anything out of place. It was a while before she realised what was making her nerves jangle.

The hint of an unfamiliar fragrance in the air.

Chapter Nineteen

After her mini freak-out Cassie had passed a restless night, trying and failing to identify whether the faintly citrusy fragrance in the air was aftershave, a female perfume – or something else. Within a couple of minutes, she'd no longer been able to detect it. Had it just been her imagination? Or had some smell from the canal seeped in through the bilges – as sometimes happened? Either way, she ought to get a second lock put on the boat door to back up the old and easily slippable Yale. She even thought of calling Flyte before thinking better of it: her tone had still been frosty the last time they spoke and she could just hear the sarcastic response to her reporting a 'random lemon smell'.

Macavity turned up for breakfast at the crack of dawn as if nothing had happened. 'So was I just being paranoid?' she asked him, yawning – but if he had any intel he wasn't sharing.

In the forensic autopsy suite where Sean Kavanagh's PM was taking place, Cassie laid out the instruments and prepared herself for long periods of boredom, simply because her role was so limited. In a forensic PM the body had to be treated as an exhibit, a piece of evidence, and to preserve its integrity the pathologist would perform the entire evisceration, with the technician's job reduced to handing them the right scalpel and bone saw.

The suite was soon full of people. There was Andy the Crime Scene Manager – a civilian officer with forensics training – an exhibits officer, and a police photographer who would capture images of Sean's body at every stage of its deconstruction.

Still, it was great to be working with Prof Arculus again. He was one of around thirty-five pathologists approved by the Home Office to conduct forensic post-mortems and had only just got back from a sabbatical, researching a book on the Battle of the Somme.

'Your keenest-bladed PM40, please, Cassandra.' The prof twinkled at her over his glasses. Her grandmother aside, he was the only one who ever used her full name. He was wearing new snazzy varifocals in place of his old specs – which had been held together with tape for as long as she could remember – and which he'd occasionally had to retrieve from body cavities. But she noticed that when he wanted to examine something more closely he simply pushed the new glasses up on his head.

'Isn't the investigating officer coming? DS Flyte?' Cassie asked Andy.

Andy told her that the IO was a DS Willets, who had sent a message saying that he was 'unforeseeably detained' at the nick. Cassie raised an eyebrow. It wasn't the first time a lazy detective had left it to the CSM to attend a forensic.

Prof Arculus unzipped the line of stitching that had closed the midline incision on Sean's body and reached inside for the bag containing the organs.

'Cassandra, would you kindly activate my recording apparatus?' He waved a gloved hand at the chunky old-school voice recorder on the bench beside him. The prof had no truck with smartphones, insisting that his circa-2005 Nokia flip-phone fulfilled all his needs. After recording Sean's name and d.o.b., he used the scalpel to peel a flap of skin the colour of a late-stage bruise – motley shades of purple, green and yellow – off his torso before intoning in the direction of the recorder. 'Advanced putrefaction has caused skin slippage and discolouration that impedes accurate identification of any contusions or injuries. Histology should assist us in establishing a time of death.'

Good luck with that, thought Cassie. She couldn't tell the prof that Sean's body had been frozen without dropping Archie in it: that would have to wait until he saw the tissue under a microscope for himself.

After opening the bag of organs onto the dissecting bench, he separated them out. 'The organs show similarly advanced autolysis . . .' He paused, turning an enquiring gaze on Cassie. 'Which means?'

'*Auto-* from the Greek for self; *-lysis* meaning breakdown, disintegration. The self-destruction of cells by the natural action of enzymes.'

'Very good.'

After discovering early on in her job that the roots of all medical and anatomical terms lay in Latin and Greek, Cassie had signed up for her fourth and final evening class, in Classics. It still gave her a buzz discovering how languages last routinely spoken more than a thousand years ago held the keys to human anatomy.

The prof put samples from the organs and tissues into pots and passed them to Andy to label up before they went to the exhibits officer for sealing in bags preprinted with the case reference number.

'And what must we concentrate on in such an advanced state of decomposition, Cassandra?'

The prof had always encouraged her hunger for learning and, unlike Curzon, was respectful of the insights she could bring from the time she spent with the bodies and her contact with relatives.

Cassie frowned. 'The bony structures?'

'The bony and cartilaginous structures.'

He pulled the sternum towards him – a truncheon of bone about a foot long – and bent so close towards its base that Cassie feared his nose might make contact.

'Hmmm.' Narrowing his eyes, the prof carefully filleted the tissue off the bottom end of the sternum, where it protruded beyond the ribs. He beckoned Cassie over and pointed with his scalpel. 'Do you see? A small but distinct fracture of the xiphoid process.'

'No . . . ? Oh *there*!' Making out a crack no thicker than a hair Cassie felt a ripple of excitement.

'So, what does it mean?' Andy the CSM asked.

'As I am sure you know,' said the prof politely, 'the xiphoid process is a small protuberance formed of cartilage that ossifies as we age. It acts as an anchor to the abdominal organs and muscles but it can be vulnerable to fracture.' He turned to the photographer. 'You'll be needing your macro lens.'

'How might it have got broken?' asked Andy.

'Cassandra?' said the prof with a courteous gesture of invitation.

'A xiphoid fracture is usually the result of blunt force trauma,' she explained. 'The most common cause is a sporting injury. Like getting hit in the chest by a rugby ball with great force. Or a violent impact with the steering wheel in a car crash.'

'What about an assault?' asked Andy.

The prof sent him a look of kindly reproach over the top of his glasses. 'That, I'm afraid, is a matter for the police to establish. The body might have been struck by a boat, for instance, while floating in the water. When I put it under the microscope I should at least be able to say whether the injury occurred post- or ante-mortem.'

Andy frowned. 'And a little crack like that could be enough to kill someone?'

'An impact violent enough to break the xiphoid can cause cardiac arrest. A blow of sufficient strength' – he struck his fist against his own sternum with some force – 'if it comes at the wrong moment in the heart's electrical rhythm, can stop it instantly.'

It was called *commotio cordis* – agitation of the heart.

Again, Cassie berated herself for letting Jason eviscerate Sean's body. Mr Cut and Shut wasn't likely to have noticed any tiny bruise over his sternum. Had she spotted one Curzon would have had to call for a forensic PM – when the body had been in a far better condition.

Sean Kavanagh had come knocking on her boat hull. But she'd been too consumed by her own concerns to answer his appeal.

Now she made him a silent promise. *I'll make it up to you.*

After the PM was over and while the samples were being packed away to go to the lab, she discreetly caught the prof's attention. He came over to her workstation and she said quietly, 'Prof, is there any chance you could prioritise the histo on the tissue samples?'

His eyes sparkled with intrigue. 'Has our Cassandra had one of her premonitions?'

'Just a feeling, Prof, about how long he'd been dead when I found him.'

He nodded. Then studying her expression, 'You know, your mythical namesake could see the future but was cursed never to be believed by the powerful.'

FLYTE

DCI Steadman had called a crack of dawn meeting and the conference room was burbling with excitement. As senior investigating officer on the Sean Kavanagh case, he had just told the assembled team – detectives, uniformed PCs and forensics officers – what Flyte had known since Cassie had shown her the microscopic images of his tissue sample.

'Frozen like in a deep freeze?!' said Nathan Cassidy.

'How long for?' asked someone else.

'Dean?' said Steadman, passing the baton to Willets.

'So the HO pathologist says there's no doubt about it. Analysis of Kavanagh's tissues shows he was deep frozen, but, incredible as it sounds, there's no way of telling for how long. Apparently freezing halts all biological processes that would usually give a time of death.'

'So are we talking some kind of industrial freezer?' This from Jethro, one of the uniformed officers.

Willets shook his head. 'An ordinary domestic freezer would have done the job apparently, so long as it had a reliable power supply.' He paused for effect. 'As some of you already know, until eight years ago Sean Kavanagh was a uniformed police officer based at Finsbury Park nick.'

That prompted a flurry of gasps and exchanged looks.

Nodding approvingly over at Flyte, Steadman said, 'Phyllida here has done a sterling job finding his last contacts but nobody has seen hide nor hair of him since then. They believed that he'd emigrated to Canada, but there's zero evidence for that. As our resident technology whizz, Dean will oversee interrogating Kavanagh's digital footprint to try to narrow down a window for his death.' He nodded to Willets.

'Our working hypothesis is that he was killed and his body stored in a freezer for the next eight years,' Dean went on, prompting more muttered gasps. 'His killer sent an email from his address resigning from the Met and put up a couple of Facebook posts – no doubt to prevent anybody raising the alarm over Kavanagh's sudden disappearance.'

'How did the killer access his Facebook and email, Sarge?' asked Nathan.

'Hacking someone's Facebook isn't rocket science – especially if you have access to someone's phone – and Sean's was missing when he was found.'

Or if you were his girlfriend and could guess his password, thought Flyte, picturing Bethany's face. But she didn't want to share what was no more than a niggling feeling: that Bethany knew more about Sean's death than she was letting on.

Steadman nodded towards Andy, the crime scene manager. 'Anything solid yet on cause of death, Andy?'

'Professor Arculus found a hairline crack in a bony protuberance at the base of the sternum. Apparently, a blow hard enough to cause it could have stopped the heart. It's usually associated with contact sports.'

'Which raises the scenario that the injury, although fatal, might have been accidental,' said Steadman, looking around the room. 'Maybe somebody he'd nicked previously spotted him off duty and decided to pick a fight. Kavanagh could have been killed by an unlucky blow, causing the assailant to panic and hide the body.' Turning to Flyte he went on, 'Phyllida, you've met his last known contacts?'

'Yes, boss. There's a security guard who used to attend the same gym as him, no more than a nodding acquaintance,' said Flyte. 'And his ex-fiancée, who broke off their engagement when she discovered he'd been serially unfaithful.'

Steadman nodded. 'It sounds like Sean – or Shane as he sometimes called himself – was a bit of a ladies' man. So a jealous boyfriend or husband getting into a fight with him is a key line of enquiry.'

Willets turned to Seb. 'Didn't you work at Finsbury Park nick a while back?'

'Yeah briefly,' he said. 'I didn't overlap with Kavanagh but there must be some guys still there who would have done.'

'Great, give them a shout, would you, see what you can dig up about him?'

As much as it pained Flyte to admit it, Willets was coming across as sharp and professional, with none of his usual playing to the gallery.

But to her mind no one was addressing the elephant in the room. 'Why would the killer risk keeping the body for eight years and only attempt to dispose of it now?' she asked.

'Maybe he kept it as a trophy,' said Willets. 'You know, the body of his enemy?'

'Or maybe he was moving house so he had no choice but to get shot of it?' offered Flyte. 'And I'm guessing our suspect probably lived alone?'

'That's a good point, Phyllida,' said Steadman. 'I think it's safe to assume a wife or live-in girlfriend might object to a body in the freezer next to the oven chips.' A ripple of laughter.

Willets got up to refer to a map of Camden centred on the canal which was projected onto the wall. 'The estimate is that the body was dumped around two weeks ago. Finding out where it went in is obviously key. Guv, you've fished a few bodies out of the canal in your time?'

'That I have,' said Steadman ruefully. 'I've already spoken to Ray, the lock-keeper.' He looked down at his notebook. 'He said that he'd expect the current to carry an unweighted body at least a hundred and up to two hundred metres. That's a lot of towpath.'

Willets indicated the map. 'So somewhere along this two-hundred-metre stretch between Kentish Town lock in the west and the narrowboat where it was found, here.'

'What about the road bridge?' Flyte pointed to where a minor road crossed the canal roughly halfway between the lock and Cassie's boat. 'Wouldn't that offer the quickest way to get a body out of a car and over the parapet into the canal without being noticed?'

Steadman nodded approvingly. 'Quite right, Phyllida. Why don't you look into that side of things? Check out the CCTV coverage around there.'

He stood to go. 'Dean, I'll leave it with you. Keep me in the loop, OK?' He paused before adding in a quiet voice, 'I want you all to keep in mind that Sean Kavanagh was one of us. That could be you or me lying there in the mortuary, so I expect everyone to give it one hundred and ten per cent. All leave is cancelled for the next month.'

The room was clearing when Willets came over to Flyte and bared his teeth in an insincere smile. 'As IO, I'll take over the key witnesses – Bethany Locke and the one who found the body. This Cassie Raven.'

'Wouldn't it be best if I handled Raven? Since I've worked closely with her—'

'There is such a thing as too closely, don't you think?' Speculation danced in Willets' eyes. 'Let's see what a fresh approach might bring.'

Chapter Twenty

'I'm going to work. Can't we do this later?' Cassie was due on shift at 11 a.m., but truthfully, that wasn't her main concern when she saw the warrant card the shiny-suited middle-aged detective held up from the towpath.

No, the first thing that jumped into her mind was: *that Molly she'd got but had never taken was still in the drawer of the galley.*

Above the guy's practised smile his eyes were as cold as wet pebbles.

'Jethro here can give you a lift to the mortuary afterwards,' he said, nodding to his uniformed sidekick. 'That'll save you a good fifteen-minute walk.'

She caved in and let him into the cabin, leaving Jethro in the cockpit.

'As you know, Sean Kavanagh's death is now a murder investigation so I wanted to speak to you directly since you discovered the body,' said Willets.

She pulled a sigh. 'There's not much to tell. I heard a knocking against the hull, and found him up by the bows. That's the pointy end.' Flashing a mean-girl smile.

He laughed but she caught the flash of hostility in those eyes: DS Willets was surprisingly thin-skinned for an inner-city murder cop.

156

As they talked, she got an all-too-familiar vibe – that he found her piercings, haircut, her whole look, challenging – almost a personal insult. He was probably one of those guys who thought that women's sole purpose in life was to provide a pleasing visual environment to rest their eyes on – *like a fucking footstool.* Back before she'd goth-ed up, barely a day would go by without some random middle-aged bloke in the street telling her, 'Cheer up, it might never happen.' In other words, 'You would be more pleasing to me if you walked around wearing a sappy smile all day.' Her response, without breaking step, was always the same: 'It just has.'

'When you found the body, did you notice anything odd about it?'

'No, nothing.'

'Did you notice that his flies were undone?'

She shook her head, feeling bad that she couldn't remember that detail.

'It was noted in the PM report,' he said. 'As I'm sure you'll appreciate, that helped the story that this was some drunk who overbalanced while urinating from the side of the canal.'

'Which is what somebody wanted you to believe.' Remembering how she too had bought that obvious fiction: something the old Cassie would never have done. 'So where do you think he got chucked in? The towpath is pretty busy this side.'

'Much further up that way, towards the lock.' He thumbed over his shoulder.

'We call it upstream,' she said. 'Can I ask, why isn't DS Flyte here?'

'Now that it's a murder case, I'm the investigating officer,' he told her, his lips thinning into a humourless smile.

'Oh, sorry, I assumed that as she was the only one showing any interest in him *before* it was a murder she'd be the obvious person to run it?' Widening her eyes to drive home the sarcasm.

Flashing her a look of unveiled hostility, he ignored the question. 'You and DS Flyte have spent a lot of time together in the course of her investigations, right?' – his tone insinuating.

She pulled a 'so what?' shrug.

He chuckled. 'I hope you haven't been bumping people off just to tempt our best-looking detective down the mortuary?'

When she stared him out, he raised a hand. 'Sorry, just my little joke.'

'I thought cops had to watch what they say these days' – her tone transmitting just a hint of *I could drop you in it*.

'True enough.' Although he didn't seem especially troubled. 'I understand you were the one who queried how long Sean had been dead, a few days after he was pulled out of the water. What made you question the pathologist's finding?'

Cold, so cold.

'Um, I just noticed he was decomposing faster than he should be.'

'Right.' He sat back and looked at her. 'How long does a pathologist train for?'

'Seven or eight years?'

'But you know better than them?' This with a fake-friendly grin.

'Sometimes, yes' – lifting her chin. Then, regretting her words: 'Look, if we're done here, I need to get to work.'

He sat there looking at her for a moment. 'OK, that's fine for now, but I'm sure we'll talk again. You're not planning a holiday or anything?'

As he left the cabin, she said, 'I'll just be a minute.'

Going to the drawer, she scooped up the paper-fold of pills and emptied them into the sink, using some of her precious water to flush them down, with a silent apology to the fish.

Having declined the lift to work in a panda car – *Er, no thanks*! – she waited until Willets and Jethro were out of sight, before calling Flyte.

'Thanks for warning me!'

'Warning you about what?'

'That I was going to get the third degree from some smarmy cop with a bad haircut. He treated me like a freaking suspect!'

'I'm sorry, but you're a witness in the Sean Kavanagh case and I'm a police detective – you don't seriously expect me to forewarn you of a fellow officer's visit? It's not as though you have anything to hide, is it?'

But Flyte's defensive tone suggested that Willets hadn't told her about his planned visit. *Interesting.*

'So why is it him handling Sean's case and not you?'

'He's the investigating officer, I'm just the bag carrier,' bitterness surfacing in her voice.

'So you've been cut out? That's bang out of order. I told him as much.'

There was a moment of amicable silence.

Feeling like an apology was in order, Cassie gritted her teeth. 'Look, Phyllida, I'm sorry if you felt like I . . . pressurised you, showing you Sean's slides . . .' *Silence.* 'The thing is, once I thought there was something off about his death, I could hardly let them cart him off to a public health funeral. I had to do something.'

'Why not?' She sounded gently curious rather than challenging.

Cassie opened her mouth to give some evasive answer but instead found herself saying, 'It's probably going to sound mad. But out of all the places he could have washed up on the canal, it was my boat he came knocking on.'

'It doesn't sound mad,' said Flyte quietly. 'The dead are quickly forgotten. They need people like you looking out for them.'

Cassie sensed a subtle but tangible shift in the space between them. The sense that although Flyte was a cop to her fingertips, they were on the same side.

'Anyway,' Flyte went on, 'I'm just glad that you're seeming a bit more like your old self.'

'As in pushy, rude, irritating . . . ?'

'All of those things,' she said drily. 'And a bit happier, in general?'

Cassie didn't go in much for navel-gazing, but Flyte was right. She still had the Archie split and the Callum angst to deal with, but the return of her bond with the dead had given her work meaning again. Hard to tell if the antidepressants could've kicked in so quickly but at least she'd suffered no discernible side effects.

'Changing the subject,' said Cassie. 'You know Willets fancies you, don't you?'

Flyte snorted incredulously.

'OK, ignore me, but I'm telling you he does.'

FLYTE

'So you see, darling, it's just not feasible. It would mean getting off one flight and literally straight onto another.'

Flyte stared down at the grey carpet in the corridor outside the incident room, the phone pressed to her ear so tightly it hurt. Sylvia had called to tell her daughter that the date of Poppy's naming ceremony was 'inconvenient' – falling the day after she and her husband returned to Cyprus from a cruise around the Aegean. Poppy's grandma wouldn't be present for her single moment of official recognition.

'Don't be cross with me, darling. I've been suffering with my knees and Ralph thinks I really need this holiday.' Flyte didn't trust herself to say anything. 'But you must come over this Christmas, or in the New Year sometime? The climate is so delightful here in the winter.'

Of course Flyte could move the date she'd agreed with the local vicar for the ceremony, but she knew it wasn't really about a schedule clash. It was about her mother's inability to deal with any emotional situation. The constant refrain she'd heard from an early age: 'Don't make a fuss' . . . 'Least said, soonest mended' . . . the sodding importance of the stiff upper lip. It was the suppression of feelings elevated to a fetish. As a little girl, when she'd needed a comforting cuddle, like the time she trod on a wasp, it had always been Pops to whom she'd turned.

'Phyllida, are you still there?'

'I've got to go, Mother, I'm at work.' She hung up without saying goodbye.

Rather than head back into the incident room, she flew down the stairs, two at a time, borne aloft on a burning fury.

Don't think. Don't think. Her old mantra, the way she'd coped for two years – pressing all thoughts of Poppy, of her loss, out of her mind, until it was a shiny empty place.

Reaching the high street, she headed for the Pret to get a skinny soya mocha coffee, her go-to treat when she needed soothing.

A familiar voice interrupted her thoughts.

'DS Flyte!'

Turning, she saw Luke, the local reporter. *Marvellous.* She didn't slow her pace, but he put on a spurt and caught up with her.

'I've been trying to get hold of you since I heard. So our floater was murdered – and frozen for years! *And* a policeman.' Luke sounded like a man who'd acquired a supermodel girlfriend and won the lottery all in one day.

'Our' floater?!

'Former policeman,' she snapped. 'And it's not actually a murder until we have evidence, a motive, little details like that.'

She saw that he was wearing his beige trench coat and another of those thin ties. *For crying out loud.*

Pulling out a folded copy of the paper from the previous day, he flourished the front-page splash, which read: CANAL MAN: BODY OF EX-COP FROZEN 'FOR YEARS'. And underneath the headline: 'By our crime correspondent Luke Lawless'.

'The news editor at the *Mail* called me today,' he said modestly. 'A case like this, it gets local reporters noticed.'

'Congratulations,' she said.

'You knew there was something funny about it from the start, didn't you?' he said, ignoring her sarcasm. Despite her long stride, he was sticking to her like Velcro. 'That's why you didn't want to let it go.'

'Look, Luke, was there something? I've got to be somewhere.' No way was he getting anything out of her, not after dropping her in it with the press office.

'Could you just . . . ?' He was breathing fast from the exertion. Relenting, she paused. He pulled out his Moleskine notebook and tapped it meaningfully. 'Listen, I doorstepped Sean Kavanagh's ex, Bethany Locke,' he said, scanning her face for a reaction.

Fishcakes.

'It's really not helpful having members of the press interview witnesses,' she said coldly. 'But there's no law against it' – her tone making it clear that were it up to her, there would be.

Luke did a near-comic conspiratorial look over his shoulder. 'I think she knows more than she's saying about what happened to Sean.'

'Really. What did she say, exactly?'

'It wasn't what she said, just a feeling she wasn't being totally upfront.' Luke nodded slowly, pocketing the notebook.

'Right.' Imagining Bethany's response to a pesky reporter turning up asking intrusive questions about her dead ex.

'The press release said that he didn't go to Canada as his contacts believed, so obviously somebody faked the Facebook posts he supposedly did from there.'

'What Facebook posts?' She stared at him; those details hadn't been released.

She remembered that the press release had named Sean's last nick as Finsbury Park – one of the areas that Luke mentioned covering for his newspaper group. Had he tracked down one of Sean's old colleagues there? Perhaps even paid for information? All highly illegal of course, but given the eye-popping stories that were emerging about cops, no longer that surprising.

As if to confirm her hunch, Luke said, 'I've got my contacts.' He lowered his voice. 'You have to ask, who is the person most likely to know Sean's log-in details and be in a position to lay a false trail in Canada after he was already dead?'

She remembered thinking the same thing in the briefing.

Luke wasn't giving up. 'Doesn't it strike you as odd that Bethany, whose modelling career sounds pretty short-lived, was able to go ahead and buy a pricey flat in the Barbican even after she and Sean split up?'

When Flyte had mentioned the same concern to Dean Willets that morning before he'd gone to interview Bethany, he'd been dismissive. He didn't buy her as a suspect as she'd had 'nowhere to store the body' and 'wouldn't have been strong enough to manhandle a body in and out of the boot of a vehicle'.

'Do you see what I'm saying?' Luke persisted.

'Look, you'll have to go through the press office like everyone else. We're not issuing individual briefings. And this time, keep my name out of it.' And with that, she struck out for the coffee shop leaving him standing on the pavement looking like Columbo's younger brother.

Chapter Twenty-One

When Cassie arrived at work she was keen to get an awkward conversation out of the way. Still wearing her civvies, she put her head round the door of Doug's office.

'I'm making tea, Doug, fancy one?'

'Yes, please, and a Hobnob – if Jason hasn't scoffed them all.' He turned back to his computer screen, but then realising she had lingered asked, 'Was there something else?'

She suddenly thought: *Christ, what if he's already lined someone else up for my job?*

'I wanted to say . . . thanks for putting me in touch with the psychology lady.'

'It's no trouble,' he said.

'And, umm, just to say . . . can I still withdraw my notice?'

Doug frowned for a moment before breaking into a smile. 'What notice?'

The sight of Archie in his scrubs coming through from the clean side set off a fusillade of feelings in Cassie's chest. Embarrassment, awkwardness, desire . . . *Snap, crackle and pop.*

The first thing he said was, 'Dr Curzon has food poisoning so I said I'd step in.' Taking care to explain why he was there.

'Sure, no problem,' said Cassie, trying to meet his gaze, to say it was cool, no biggie, but those ginger-lashed eyes slid away from her.

'What have you got for me?'

'Just two on the list, both pretty straightforward.' She nodded over to Jason's workstation, where a body already lay stretched out. 'An elderly gentleman – sudden death at home – and I've got an RTC, a lady hit by a motorbike crossing the high street.'

RTC – Road Traffic Collision: they were discouraged from calling them RTAs, Road Traffic Accidents any more on the basis that it pre-judged a conclusion.

Archie lowered his voice. 'I hear your floater is a murder case now.'

She murmured back, 'All thanks to you.'

But he didn't crack a smile. And things didn't improve during the PM list. Jason noticed the chilly atmosphere – of course he did. Standing alongside her, waiting to weigh organs on the scales, he nodded over to Archie and murmured, 'Somebody's got the hump today,' his tone sly. 'Trouble in paradise?'

After Archie had completed his external examinations and before she immersed herself in blood and viscera, Cassie ducked out into the corridor. Having received Sean's PM report, the coroner's office had agreed to release the body and sent over contact details from his police service record for his mother, who lived in Kilburn. The cops had already informed her of her son's death and the investigation, but Cassie needed to get details of the undertakers who'd be collecting his body.

'My brother is handling the funeral arrangements,' Bridget Kavanagh told her. 'He'll be cremated at Kensal Green. A very small service, just for close family.'

Parents could react in several ways to the death of a child – they could be distraught, angry, numb . . . but Mrs K sounded oddly matter-of-fact, borderline chilly.

'Is that where you held his dad's funeral service?' Cassie knew from the notes that Michael Kavanagh had died when Sean was a teenager.

'No,' she said. 'His father is buried in the Catholic cemetery over at St Mary's. God rest him. At least he doesn't have to hear that his son has gone and got himself murdered.'

Which was a funny way of putting it.

'Can I ask when you last saw Sean?' asked Cassie.

'Oh, it must be ten, twelve years ago?'

So they'd clearly been estranged for a while even before Sean disappeared.

The only time any sign of emotion entered Mrs Kavanagh's voice was when Cassie asked if she wanted to view his body.

'No, no, not at all,' she said, before recovering herself. 'I'd rather remember him as he was. When he was a little lad people said he was the most beautiful child they'd ever seen.'

An hour or so later, with the PM list done and dusted, Cassie was heading out to grab a late lunch when she saw Archie waiting at the end of the lane.

'You shouldn't have asked me to do that histo,' he said, his pale cheeks flushed.

'You could've said no,' she said reasonably, feeling her heart beating double time.

'I never could say no to you' – a bitterness she'd not heard before etching his voice.

'Look, I'm sorry, Archie, you're right. I shouldn't have asked you. It was out of order in the circs. But I had nowhere else to turn.'

Instead of replying, he kissed her. And after a moment she raised her arms as if in surrender and kissed him back.

FLYTE

It was the best medicine for Flyte's troubles, being out and about that afternoon, walking the canal from Kentish Town lock, the furthest point west from which Sean Kavanagh could have gone in the water. Since two weeks or more had passed since Sean's frozen body had been dumped, during which time thousands of people had tramped all over what might laughably be called a crime scene, there was no point taping off two hundred metres of towpath on both sides of the canal.

She took the south bank first – the side opposite Cassie's boat. From the lock, the canal curved gently eastwards, downstream towards where it would finally fall into the arms of the Thames. Sketching a map in her notebook, she started marking the sites of any CCTV cameras on the towpath and canal approach routes.

Reaching the road bridge that she'd identified as a good spot to offload a body into the canal, she crossed halfway and leaned on the parapet, picturing the scene at night. The bridge was one-way, and had only a single carbon light at each end; on one side of it stood an industrial estate, on the other a sprawling scaffolding yard, one of the last survivors of Camden's light industrial past – both of which would be deserted after nightfall. Even now, mid-afternoon, the only traffic crossing the bridge was one lone scooter. And the parapet was barely waist-high: a reasonably fit man – or woman? – could manoeuvre a body over the edge without great effort.

She bent to pick up a twig with a couple of leaves attached out of the gutter and dropped it into the canal upstream, on the lock side, swiftly crossing the bridge to the east. She blinked, wondering if it had got caught up under the bridge, before she finally saw it emerge, drifting slowly downstream.

On the other side, she took a steep stairway down to the canal and headed east towards Cassie's boat, the ten-metre-high black brick embankment to her right making further access to the towpath from street level impossible. Ten minutes later, the crumbling hulk of a derelict housing estate came into view. Here, the towpath was backed by a twelve-foot-high steel mesh security fence topped with razor wire which must encircle the whole estate.

Signs in shouty lettering said: HAZARD! SITE PATROLLED AT ALL TIMES! BEWARE OF THE DOGS! WE ALWAYS PROSECUTE TRESPASSERS!

If Flyte had her way it would be the developers who'd be prosecuted – for excessive use of exclamation marks.

Here, the towpath was overgrown and strewn with junk, and blocked by a waist-height steel barrier. It would have been easy to climb over but Flyte didn't bother; she could see that the path dead-ended in more mesh fence ten metres further on which bore a more recent poster bearing the name of a demolition firm. The developers weren't going to risk squatters holding up their schedule – and the payback on their investment.

In any case, why would anyone drag a body all the way here from the stairway up to the street when there were far easier places to dump it further upstream?

Shading her eyes, she looked across the water to the north bank and Cassie's narrowboat. The access all along that side was nigh on impossible: there too, the towpath was backed by a cliff of black brickwork as far as the eye could see, and since it led to the pubs and clubs of central Camden, it would never be truly deserted, even late at night. Far too risky a site for body disposal. Anyway, if Sean's body had been dumped this far east then according to the lock-keeper's report the current would have carried it much further downstream towards King's Cross. No, the road bridge further west had to be the stand-out candidate.

Her eye drifted over the boat again. She could make out Cassie's black cat lying on deck assiduously cleaning itself.

It made her shiver. *Dreamcatcher*? Nightmare-catcher more like, sleeping with only a flimsy wooden door between you and the rapists, junkies, and assorted scumbags of Camden.

After retracing her steps, she took the stairs up to the street and, noticing a lone pub on a corner one street back from the canal, made a note to check that the DCs were including it in their door-to-door checks for witnesses. Realising she was thirsty, she strode towards it.

Inside, she blinked in the gloom. The Wharf was one of Camden's few surviving old-school pubs, all dark Victorian wood, with a dartboard and a near-visible fug of stale beer. A gaggle of old guys at the bar were talking about football, pausing in their chat to survey her with polite suspicion. She felt as if she'd fallen through a wormhole into the eighties.

Five minutes later, she was standing at the bar finishing her mineral water when she froze with the glass at her lips. One of the old guys had left his barstool, clearing a visual corridor through to an old-fashioned snug bar on the other side of the pub. The only occupants were a man and a woman, who from their body language, were clearly on a date. The woman, who was more or less facing her, was the witness with the long blond hair Willets had interviewed in the office – the one he'd boasted had contacted him on WhatsApp.

The man raised a flute of what looked like Prosecco and the two of them clinked glasses. Even from the rear he was instantly recognisable as Dean Willets.

Chapter Twenty-Two

As the bus trundled north to Gospel Oak that evening, Cassie couldn't stop herself smiling as she replayed the unplanned snog with Archie. They had arranged to meet the following evening.

Was it a good idea? *Who knew.*

Tonight she had to pay a duty call – her first visit to the charity-run hostel where her dad was staying.

She'd put off visiting for too long, scared of it being a downer, but in reality the place came as a pleasant surprise: a tidy low-rise block framed by greenery and with a freshly painted reception area.

After the receptionist had buzzed her through to the cafe, she scanned the room, her eye sliding over a stooped old man at the drinks machine, before realising it was Callum. When he turned and saw her, the joyful look that broke over his face made her give him a longer hug than usual.

'You look thinner,' she said, looking him up and down. It still made her weirdly angry, how crap he was at looking after himself.

'This is a nice surprise!' he said, still scanning her face with eyes that looked watery and red-rimmed.

'Oh, I was in the area,' she lied. In truth, her grandmother had called to tell Cassie that she was worried about him. 'How are you?' Making it clear this was more than a polite enquiry.

'I'm not so bad, Catkin,' he said, before covering his mouth to cough. 'But I just can't seem to shake this cold.'

'Gran said you threw up after dinner at her place the other evening.'

'Oh, she told you that, did she?' He lifted one shoulder rue-fully. 'I reckon I'm still not used to her cooking, after years of prison food, you know. It's so good but it's all pretty rich, the Polish stuff, isn't it?'

Cassie couldn't argue with that. Babcia never saw a recipe that wouldn't benefit from an extra dose of cream and butter. 'Do you have any other symptoms?'

'I'm fine. Just a bit run-down is all.' He touched her hand tentatively, and she resisted the reflex to withdraw it. 'Listen, Catkin, I don't want you fretting about me. I should be the one looking after you. That's my job as a father.'

It was when I was a little girl that needed you. Irrational, of course. He couldn't be blamed for his wrongful imprisonment, but still, there wasn't any way to make up for those missing years.

Remembering the smell of perfume – or aftershave – on the boat, she wondered if he'd gone there to check up on her. He knew where the spare key was hidden in the cockpit.

'You didn't pop by the boat a couple of days back, by any chance?'

'No, why?' He frowned, shaking his head.

'Oh, nothing. I just thought I might have seen you.'

Taking a drink of his tea, he grimaced. 'I'll never get used to the taste of London water.'

Noticing a tremor in his hand as he put the mug down, something occurred to her. 'You're not back on the booze, are

174

you?' Callum had admitted that after getting out of prison he'd dived into the bottle, only getting clean before he came looking for her.

'No. Still going to AA meetings every week, I promise. Atoning for my sins.' The words could have sounded bitter, without the broad lopsided smile that always reminded her how handsome he'd once been.

Cassie recalled how her mum, on her sad days, would say, *Daddy will be home soon*, like a mantra, and when his big smile came through the door it would light up her face, like the surface of the moon illuminated by the sun.

'Anyway, I've got an interview tomorrow.' Looking mock-proud of himself. 'Warehouse stacker at a builders' merchants on the Holloway Road.'

'And your record is no problem?'

He shook his head. 'They're one of those employers who work with rehab charities to take on old lags like me.'

'It's so unfair. You're innocent!'

He chuckled. 'That'll be official soon enough.'

They fell silent, and Cassie knew they were both thinking about her mother.

'How are you doing, anyway?' he asked, scanning her face. 'You seem a bit . . . brighter in yourself?'

She nodded. 'Things are better at work.' She still felt a reluctance to share stuff she might tell Babcia – like about being on antidepressants.

'Ah, that's great.' He nodded towards her hands. 'The rash is looking better.'

It was true: in place of the angry-looking hives there was only pinkness, the grazes where she'd scratched herself almost

175

healed. Impossible to know whether that was down to the calamine and hypo-allergenic gloves or her improved mood.

He dropped his gaze to examine the contents of his mug. 'You know . . . your Auntie Siobhan is bringing one of your wee cousins over from Belfast soon.' He raised a hand. 'No pressure at all, but the offer's there whenever you feel ready to meet them.'

The thought of a whole new family descending on her filled her with panic. 'I'm really busy at work right now. Maybe later in the year?' Then, trying to ignore his disappointed look, she said, 'It's great about the interview! You'll ace it.'

When she stood to go, she noticed a pale patch of scalp shining through his dark curls. 'Look, Dad, I'm going to sort you out a GP appointment,' she said. 'Just to check you over.'

He looked down at his hands for a moment blinking rapidly, before smiling up at her.

'I love it when you call me Dad.'

FLYTE

'Dean, would you pop in?' After hanging up, Steadman said, 'I take this kind of thing very seriously, Phyllida.' His expression troubled. 'You're sure it was the same woman in the pub, a witness who Dean interviewed here?'

'I'm afraid so, boss.' Flyte's heart was jumping in her chest but having endured a sleepless night wondering what the hell to do she had woken with her mind made up.

'Consorting with witnesses in a pub is not a good look,' said Steadman, 'especially one of the opposite sex. We're under the microscope these days . . .'

And no wonder. It felt like barely a week passed without some new scandal involving cops behaving badly: having sex with vulnerable female witnesses, exchanging vile homophobic and racist comments on WhatsApp, strip-searching a black schoolgirl because she 'smelled of cannabis'. Overnight, Flyte had reached a decision: the only way she could live with herself as a Met police officer was by standing up to be counted.

A knock on the door.

Willets blinked to find Flyte there.

'Sit down, Dean.' Steadman laid out the charge: that he'd met a witness outside work for drinks.

'But, boss—'

'You know I won't tolerate that kind of behaviour, Dean. It's unprofessional and it opens you and the unit up to accusations of God knows what.'

Dean shot Flyte a look of pure venom. 'If I can just explain. That woman, she was a potential witness in the Hugger Mugger case, but simply by being in the same club as the victim. Her testimony wasn't much use to us – she only got a fleeting glimpse of him.'

'That's hardly the point.' Steadman sounded quietly livid. 'You took her phone number and met up with her for drinks?!'

'It's not what it looks like. She's a lettings agent!'

'Meaning?'

'We only swapped numbers because I was looking for a flat! She found me a good one. I just signed the contract, hence the drink.' He held his hands up. 'Look, I plead guilty to drinking on duty. But there is no sexual relationship of any kind with her, I swear.'

Flyte was listening to this with growing discomfort. A lettings agent? She had to admit his account had the ring of truth.

Steadman fell silent, eyeing Dean's face. 'You've . . . moved out?'

Dean folded his bottom lip under his teeth momentarily, a vulnerable gesture, and nodded. 'Yeah, me and Rosie, we're having a bit of a break.'

'None of my business,' said Steadman, raising both hands. He stood up and stared at the ceiling for a few seconds. 'OK, Dean, I am minded to accept your explanation. I'll let you know what I decide. But I won't be referring it to the DPS.'

'Thanks, guv.'

'Don't thank me yet,' Steadman growled, aiming a finger at him. 'And next time you need a lettings agent or hairdresser or any other darn thing in future, do me a favour and google it like everyone else.'

Dean left and Flyte met Steadman's eye. 'Boss, I'm so sorry, I had no idea . . .'

He waved away her apology. 'Phyllida, you saw something that looked dodgy and called it out. It takes guts to do that. Public trust in the police is in short supply, and it relies on the good cops doing the right thing.'

'Thank you.'

'I'd take bets that Dean won't be drinking Prosecco with witnesses again any time soon.'

Steadman's reaction made her feel better, at least for the sixty seconds it took to get back to the incident room. Gathered round Willets' desk was a little gaggle of his acolytes, who dispersed as they saw her, avoiding her eye.

So, that's how it was going to be.

Willets came over and planted both hands on her desk. She felt everyone's attention trained on them. 'I'd like you to look after the door-to-door enquiries as well as the CCTV.'

It was low-level work but after what just happened she was in no position to argue.

'Look, Dean, I realise I should have spoken to you first—'

'Oh, don't worry about it,' said Dean, a glassy grin on his face. 'It's good to have a stickler on the team.'

Flyte picked up the less-than-subtle emphasis on the word 'team'.

He turned to go before turning back, doing a little pantomime of remembering something. 'I almost forgot, when was it you visited our other witness, Cassie Raven, on her boat?'

Hell's bells. How on earth did he know about that? The implication was clear – that Flyte had done exactly what she'd just accused him of, paying an unofficial call on a witness before Kavanagh's death had even become a case.

'Umm, it was, er, a few days ago – to do with the identification of Sean Kavanagh.'

'Really? Why go to her private residence and not the mortuary?' Dean was enjoying himself and she could visualise every ear in the place angled towards them like an array of radar dishes.

She didn't even bother trying to defend it. 'She didn't complain, did she?'

'Uh, complain?' Dean frowned. 'No . . . I didn't actually know you'd been there, it was just a lucky guess.' And with a smug smile he walked off.

A sick feeling settled on Flyte. She'd given Willets a hold over her which he'd no doubt use when it suited him. Reporting him to the boss for what turned out to be a fairly minor infraction might just have effectively ended her career in Major Crimes before it had properly started.

Thirty seconds later, her phone pinged with a message from Seb. He was on the other side of the room but must have heard everything.

It read: *Ouch! Fancy dinner later?*

They went for a pizza in a tiny Italian place in the backstreets, or at least Seb had pizza while Flyte pushed a Caesar salad aimlessly around the bowl.

Seb was sympathetic, but it was clear that he would never have done what she had, grassing up Willets.

'So where is the line, for you?' she asked. 'If you knew for sure that Willets had dated a witness would you report him?'

He lifted one awkward shoulder. 'Look, I'd never do anything like that myself, obviously. And if Dean was taking backhanders or something that would be totally different. But when it comes to dating someone.' He made a face. 'I know a couple of people who went out with girls they met as witnesses and who went on to marry them. It's a grey area, don't you think?'

She resisted the urge to correct that irritating 'girls', telling herself he wasn't using it to be dismissive or derogatory. 'But imagine you've been mugged – or sexually assaulted – and then the officer who takes your statement starts chatting you up?'

Seb's expression acknowledged the point.

Flyte went on, 'So Willets – Dean – has split up with his wife?'

'Yeah, so I hear. She threw him out apparently. Bit of a shocker, they've been together for ever – like, ten years? Dean's good at putting on a front but underneath I think he's taking it quite hard.'

As he topped up her wine glass, she scanned his face, thinking that his comment displayed emotional intelligence.

'So did you get anything from your contacts at Finsbury Park on Sean Kavanagh?' she asked.

'Not much. I could only find one old lag, name of Bevan, still there from eight years ago. He said Sean was a lovely guy, popular, not the type to make enemies, but didn't have close friends, not in the Job anyway.' He glanced at her. 'He also said he was a "pussy hound".'

'Charming.'

'Apparently the lads used to call him Heinz.'

'Really? Did he have a German connection?'

'No, but he had fifty-seven varieties of girlfriends?' Seb grinned. 'They took the piss out of him because he spent every spare minute working out and splashed his pay cheque on designer gear, the latest trainers, etcetera.' He hesitated. 'He did sort of hint that Sean blotted his copybook once, a year before he resigned, but apparently there was no official censure.'

'Blotted it how? Inappropriate behaviour with witnesses?'

'Nah, Bevan said it was just like a drunk and disorderly, or a minor driving infringement, something like that.'

'You've told Willets?'

'Yeah, Dean said it was all just canteen gossip. There was nothing in his personnel file.'

'What did the desk sergeant say about him leaving the Job?'

'It came out of the blue, apparently. He just didn't turn up for work one day, sent his resignation by email a couple of days later. Asked for his DNA and fingerprint records to be destroyed.'

'More likely his murderer did. Nice touch.'

Having removed his prints and DNA from the system, the killer must have been feeling pretty confident, eight years on, that his body might never now be identified. A gamble that had come close to paying off. It also suggested that Sean hadn't been killed by a random stranger: whoever killed him must have known he was in the police and that a fake 'resignation' was needed to head off any investigation into his disappearance.

Flyte pushed her barely eaten salad aside. A uniformed cop's take-home was modest, and yet Sean had a pricey clothes habit and presumably wined and dined his string of girlfriends. Had he supplemented his pay by taking backhanders from villains? And shared the cash with Bethany?

Whatever his transgression had been, it seemed like it had been hushed up – as police officers had done for each other since time immemorial. She found herself watching Seb while he ate, telling herself that he at least was different. One of the good guys.

Chapter Twenty-Three

Cassie and Archie had met at the nearest pub but wasted little time before getting back to the boat and into her not-quite-big-enough bed.

But in the early hours she was jolted out of a deep sleep by a shout next to her ear, followed by the boat violently rocking.

What the . . . ?

Finding Archie no longer at her side she got up and wrapped the sheet around herself toga-style. Blinking in the cockpit, she was met by a sight that made her laugh: Archie, naked, walking back along the towpath with one hand over his groin.

'Archie, what happened?'

'It's not funny. There was somebody looking in through the window.'

'Porthole,' she said automatically. 'Are you sure?'

'Yes! It freaked me out.'

'I can imagine,' she said. 'What did he look like?' Despite her casual tone her heart was beating too fast and the hairs on her forearms prickled.

'No idea. I'm not even sure whether it was a man or a woman. Whoever it was legged it when I shouted and by the time I jumped off they were gone.'

Back in the cabin, Archie stood effortlessly on one long leg to pull on his boxers, the quadriceps in his thighs tensing beneath the skin. He was muscled but still slender, a natural-looking physique she found far more attractive than the over-pumped body of workout addicts like Sean Kavanagh. Clearly there must be some women who went for that overblown look but it wasn't for her.

'Hey, you've cut yourself,' she said, seeing a smear of blood on the pad of his foot. 'Sit down.'

After she'd TCP-ed the cut and put a plaster on it, he looked at her, all serious. 'It's not safe here, Cassie.'

'Look, it was probably just one of the homeless guys who hang around the towpath. They're perfectly harmless.'

Archie seemed about to say more, to join the litany she got from people like her dad telling her what to do, but thought better of it. Instead, he got up to run a glass of water from the tap, his back to her. 'So . . . was this a one-off or does this mean we're back together?' His tone studiedly casual.

Oh crikey.

'The thing is, Archie, I'm just not very good at relationships. I probably never will be. You'd be better off finding yourself a regular gal.'

'I don't want a regular gal.' He turned to look at her through those ginger-fringed eyes, slate-grey and serious.

Oh my.

'Well, don't say I didn't warn you.' Dropping the sheet she'd wrapped herself in, she reached up to him. 'Come back to bed, boyfriend.'

In for a penny.

FLYTE

As ever, Flyte's first waking thought was of Poppy, turning to greet the serene little face in the photo on the bedside table.

Her second was the memory of ending up in bed with Seb last night. Rolling over she sniffed at his pillow, inhaling the faintly iron filings smell of male sweat mixed with his fresh-smelling cologne. She'd been half asleep when he had kissed her goodbye in the early hours, saying he had to go, a dental appointment or something.

The memory stirred differing emotions: anxiety at having made herself vulnerable at work by sleeping with a colleague, but satisfaction too; the sense that after her long period of grief-stricken celibacy she had rejoined the human race. She had forgotten how gratifying it felt to be desired, although for her the sex had been, as ever, more about intimacy than passion: she could still feel the imprint of his arms around her as they'd fallen asleep. For the first time in years she had allowed herself to fantasise about the possibility of having another baby.

'What do you think, Poppy?' she murmured to her picture. 'Is he a keeper?'

But Poppy wasn't offering any relationship advice.

Flyte was making coffee in her wildly expensive machine, frothing her oat milk, looking forward to a lazy Saturday when her phone chimed. It was a text from Cassie Raven: *I need to see you! It's about Sean Kavanagh.*

She paced the kitchen for a few minutes, on the verge of saying no, paranoid about Willets finding out and dropping her in it. In the end, she texted back: *Somewhere quiet – I can't be seen with you at the moment.*

Half an hour later, Flyte was pretending to peruse the bookshelves on the first floor of the Pancras Square library in King's Cross when Cassie sauntered in.

Coming alongside her she grinned. 'Good choice. This is the last place we'd run into any cops.'

Ignoring the jibe, Flyte nodded over to an alcove with a table where they could chat; although happily the library was more or less empty.

'So, what is it?' she asked, scanning Cassie's face, noting how much healthier – and prettier – she was looking. Lately, her skin had appeared sallow but now not even the pale goth-style make-up she favoured could hide the pink in her cheeks, and her black-kohled eyes were bright.

'I remembered something about Sean's body which didn't strike me as significant before. I think it's worth checking out.'

'Go on.'

'He was pretty pumped, remember? Big biceps and quadriceps, highly developed trapezius muscle' – setting both hands either side of her neck where it met the shoulders – 'which is what gives bodybuilding addicts that humped look.'

'So what? We know he was a gym enthusiast,' said Flyte, struggling to keep the exasperation out of her voice.

Cassie went on, 'Do you remember when he first came in, he had quite bad acne across both cheeks?'

Flyte shrugged. 'Yes, but acne in adults isn't unheard of.'

'Maybe.' Cassie picked up her phone. 'But then I pulled up the prof's PM report and had another look at the photos of the body.' She swiped through the images before finding one and zooming it up. Turning the screen towards Flyte, 'OK, see here? More acne on his chest. And look at this on his upper back.'

She peered at the images. In the patches where decomposition hadn't discoloured his skin she could make out silvery spider trails. 'All I can see is stretch marks.'

'Exactly.' Cassie shifted around in her seat as if this was exciting. 'He had them across his shoulders as well.'

'What's the big deal?' asked Flyte, squinting at the marks. 'Maybe he just put on a lot of muscle fast . . .' Her head shot up and she looked at Cassie. 'Ohh . . .'

She nodded. 'Yep. I'd bet serious money that Sean Kavanagh was abusing steroids.'

Chapter Twenty-Four

First thing that morning, when Archie had left to play rugby, it had still been dark beyond the curtained portholes but Cassie hadn't been able to get back to sleep, images of Sean's over-pumped legs, arms and trapezius playing on a mental loop. So in the end she'd given up and, opening her email, pulled up the images from the PM report.

'I'm annoyed with myself that I didn't clock it earlier,' she told Flyte now. 'Acne and stretch marks are classic side effects of anabolic steroid abuse.'

'If you're right, could it have been a factor in his death?'

'No.' Cassie shook her head. 'The PM found no evidence of any of the serious side effects like heart disease, atherosclerosis, or hepatitis steatosis.'

Flyte fixed her with a steel-blue gaze. 'In English, please?'

'Uh, sorry, arterial plaque build-up or fatty liver. But Sean was young and it can take years of abuse before any damage becomes detectable.'

'Doesn't it alter mood?' said Flyte.

Cassie tapped at her phone. 'I did a bit of research into that. No one's run a large-scale study but some steroid abusers do report having bursts of irrational anger. It's called "'roid rage".'

'OK,' said Flyte, rubbing her brow with long fingers. 'Maybe he got into a fight with a jealous boyfriend or husband, which could explain the blow that fractured his sternum.'

'If Sean had been caught with steroids, I'm guessing as a cop he'd be in big trouble?' asked Cassie.

'Absolutely. You can't be prosecuted for taking them, but selling them is a crime. Simply by buying them Sean would have been guilty of knowingly engaging in an illegal transaction. He'd have been sacked, no question.'

'Which could explain why he called himself Shane at the gym, to hide the fact that he was a cop,' said Cassie. 'Maybe his dealer found out who he was and started blackmailing him?'

Flyte made a non-committal gesture but Cassie could read her better these days. 'You've got an idea who was flogging him the gear, haven't you?'

She was saved from answering by her phone going off – a cascade of chiming bells – but after checking the screen she killed it.

Her gaze returned to Cassie. 'Please tell me the tox screen will automatically pick up steroids?'

Cassie shook her head. 'You'll need to request specific tests on Sean's urine and hair samples for half a dozen different steroids. And they're not cheap.' Seeing Flyte's face fall she asked, 'I'm guessing the authorisation has to come from that twat Willets, right?'

Flyte made a grimace of agreement. 'He'll probably say I'm flying a kite. And it won't help that the idea came from you. He already thinks we're in cahoots.'

Cassie tried not to smile at the old-school phrase.

Chapter Twenty-Five

The next evening Cassie and Callum went for Sunday dinner at her grandmother's.

Afterwards, they agreed to Cassie's suggestion of Monopoly. She was guiltily aware of the two of them deliberately avoiding the subject of her mum, knowing she found it difficult, but she was grateful for the simple interaction that playing a daft game allowed them.

'*Brawo!*' said Babcia, clapping her hands as Cassie's throw landed her little dog on Mayfair, which her grandmother owned. Peering over her glasses at her card she said, 'Let me see, with one house . . . you owe me £200 rent.'

Cassie counted her few remaining notes – she'd had an unlucky run of throws. 'Um, can I owe it to you till I pass Go?'

'Sorry, *tygrysek*, rules are rules.' Her grandmother's eyes glittered with acquisitive glee. 'You could give me one of your properties instead?'

'Babcia! You're ruthless! Dad – lend me some cash?'

Callum shook his head, pulling a rueful grin. 'Sorry, Catkin, you won't catch me getting between you and Nana Rachman there.'

Cassie had to mortgage two properties to pay her debt, grumbling, 'This is the closest I'll ever get to having an actual mortgage.'

Callum's go landed him on King's Cross station. Cassie whooped – as the closest property on the board to Camden Town she had snapped it up – but Callum had gone very quiet.

'Come on, Dad, it's only £25 and you're loaded.'

Callum half rose from his chair before his legs folded and he half sank, half collapsed to the floor.

'Dad!!'

The next few minutes were a flurry of panicked activity. Cassie kept it together enough to check he was still breathing and had a decent pulse – *Thank God!* – while Babcia called 999. The sight of his pale and sweaty face made her chest hurt. 'Come on, Dad, wake up,' she murmured.

Eventually, he opened his eyes and managed a smile. 'Hello, Catkin. What's occurring?'

At A & E, the nurse, who recognised her, sent them straight to resus – which dealt with potentially life-threatening emergencies. Callum had recovered some during the ten-minute ambulance ride and by the time a junior doctor arrived in their curtained alcove to take a history he was almost back to normal although still candlewax pale.

'I just had a funny turn is all,' he told the doctor. 'I don't want to waste your time.'

'We'll see,' she said dismissively, looking at her clipboard rather than him. 'Is this the only time that you have lost consciousness recently?' Her accent was the kind that took years of private schooling to acquire.

'Yeah, unless you count a bender I went on in 1995.' Grinning, he sought the doctor's eyes but she ignored him.

Cassie wanted to slap her. She could only be in her twenties but she was already the type of medic who saw herself as superior

191

to the grubby masses, no doubt on a fast track to private practice at the first opportunity.

'Any nausea or vomiting?' she asked.

'No.' Callum shook his head.

'Dad, you threw up at Babcia's a couple of days ago!'

He was sat in a chair with Cassie standing behind him, giving her a view of the top of his head. She noticed that he'd lost more hair in just the last couple of weeks – and the bald patches were randomly spaced, which wasn't typical of male pattern hair loss. Running a hand through his hair in what looked like a simple gesture of affection, she found it came away holding a couple of dozen dark curly strands.

Nausea, hair loss, fainting . . .

Jesus! She broke into the doctor's next question. 'Dad, remember you complained that your tea tasted funny? What about other drinks?'

The doctor huffed. 'I'm sorry—'

Cassie cut her off with a chopping gesture.

'Now you mention it, drinks do taste a bit off. Food sometimes too.'

'Metallic tasting?'

His eyes widened. 'Yeah, how do you know?'

The doctor had turned a furious red. 'Now, look here—'

'Look, I'm pretty sure my dad has overdosed on zinc supplements. How many of those tabs do you take in a day, Dad?'

'Oh, maybe five, six? The more the better right?'

'You're only meant to take one.' She turned to the officious medic. 'If he's been taking five or six of the tabs I gave him every day that's 150 grams a day.'

'A zinc overdose?' She sent Cassie a death-ray stare. 'That is highly unlikely. I'm going to run checks for myocardial infarction. A heart attack, in layman's terms.'

Cassie opened her hand under the snooty medic's nose to show her the dark hairs still clutched there. 'Does a heart attack make your hair fall out?'

FLYTE

'I can't get away from work today.'

It was eight o'clock on Monday morning and Zeke, the security guard who had come forward to ID Sean as 'Shane' – a supposedly casual acquaintance at the gym – didn't sound enthusiastic at the prospect of another audience with 'the Feds'. But when Flyte said sweetly that it was no problem, she could come to his workplace, he managed to find some space in his schedule.

She had a hunch that Ezekiel Drew hadn't told her the whole truth about his dealings with Sean Kavanagh – 'dealings' being the appropriate word. Of course she ought to inform Willets of her suspicions and have Zeke attend the station for a more formal interview, but her gut told her that the combination of Dean Willets and the inside of a nick would make him clam up for good.

She and Zeke met in the same cafe up in Kentish Town, the air thick with the sweet-savoury smell of bacon. But this was a very different Zeke: jumpy and defensive. 'I already told you everything I know,' he shot at her before she'd even sat down.

'There's just a few things I wanted to clear up,' she said reasonably. 'We now know the guy whose image you recognised in the paper was Sean Kavanagh, a Met police officer.'

No reaction.

'Sean's death is now the subject of a murder investigation,' she said. Seeing Zeke unconsciously clenching his jaw muscles, she felt a little flare of excitement: this was a man under stress. 'We need to find out who killed him and bring them to justice. Remind me, why did you call him Shane when his name was Sean?'

Zeke shrugged and looked away. 'I dunno. It's what people called him. Maybe I heard it wrong.'

'You also said he didn't advertise the fact that he was a police officer. Why do you think he wanted to keep it quiet?'

'I don't know!' Anger fraying his voice. 'The Feds aren't exactly flavour of the month round here, y'know.'

She smiled. 'You see, I've been wondering if there's another reason. That he was perhaps engaged in some activity which as a police officer could land him in serious trouble.'

Zeke blinked.

Leaning across the table, she hardened her tone. 'We believe that Sean Kavanagh may have been using anabolic steroids. A restricted Class C substance that it is illegal to produce or supply.'

'I don't know nothing about that.' But the look he threw at the door, instinctively checking for an escape route, suggested otherwise.

Flyte saw the sheen of sweat under his eyes. 'I think that you were selling him those steroids and when you found out he was a police officer, you used it to blackmail him.'

For a moment Zeke looked bewildered – before pulling a grin so wide it revealed a gold pre-molar. 'You've got it all wrong, lady.' He shook his head. 'It was *Shane* who was selling the 'roids.' His smile faded. 'But it's no surprise that you go: "the black guy must be the dealer".'

Flyte stared at him, experiencing the vertiginous feeling of being utterly wrongfooted. Going by the sudden relaxation in his demeanour he appeared to be telling the truth.

She kicked herself for her schoolgirl naivety: it had never occurred to her that Sean – a police officer – would be the one selling the steroids, committing a criminal offence.

'Do you have any evidence of that accusation?' she asked stiffly.

'How could I? It was eight years ago. I only bought them off him a few times and they made me depressed, so I went natural.' He slapped his little pot belly. 'My days of getting shredded are ancient history.'

Of course, even if Sean had been the dealer and Zeke just one of his customers, he could still have been blackmailing him – and for even higher stakes.

'Did you ever threaten to report his activities to the police?'

Zeke looked her straight in the eye. 'I'm no grass. I'm only telling you now cos he's dead.'

Flyte felt deflated: his body language had changed to one of somebody with nothing to hide. 'If what you're saying is true, who else was he selling to?'

'Loads of guys,' said Zeke. 'Whenever Shane come in the gym the word went round' – he adopted a conspiratorial whisper – "Candy Man's here!"'

'So you had the impression he was selling a lot of product?'

'Uh-huh. He was minted, you know, always wearing designer threads and talking about fancy restaurants he'd been to.'

'Did you ever see him with a girlfriend? Or his fiancée Bethany?'

'Nah.' Zeke examined his fingernails, closing down again.

'Can you think of anyone who might have been trying to blackmail him?'

'I never heard nothing like that,' said Zeke, checking his phone screen. 'Look, I need to get back to work.'

Flyte finished her tea to give Zeke a five-minute head start. The last thing she needed was anyone from work spotting her with a witness before she'd worked out how to share the steroids lead with Willets.

FLYTE

On reaching the nick Flyte's mood was anxious but determined.

Seeing Dean Willets already at his desk on the other side of the incident room, she was steeling herself to brief him on her discovery that Sean Kavanagh had been selling steroids, when he got up and made a beeline for her. His demeanour seemed less cocksure than usual, probably due to something Seb had intimated: it was nearly a week since the Kavanagh case had become a murder investigation, and without a single lead, IO Willets was feeling the pressure.

'I've got Bethany Locke coming in for another interview at ten,' he told her, checking the time.

'Oh, right.' Eyeing him warily.

He perched on the edge of her desk. 'I think you should sit in.'

'Really?'

'You've met her and, you know, fellow female and all that. You might pick up the non-verbal stuff?'

Maybe since his wife had thrown him out, Willets was questioning his abilities as a reader of women.

'Sure, I'd be happy to. Are you treating her as a suspect?'

He screwed up his face. 'Not really. I still can't see her hauling a body in and out of a car and into the canal?' He paused. 'What do you think?'

Holy moly. Dean Willets asking her for advice?

Since Luke the reporter had bearded her in the street about Sean's former fiancée, Flyte had been replaying their encounter at her flat in the Barbican. She had suspected then that Bethany was withholding information about Sean – significant information – and now she had a good idea what it was.

Sean's pricey lifestyle – clearly beyond that of your average uniform – had evidently been funded by a lucrative sideline dealing in steroids. Was it plausible that Bethany had known nothing about it? Or had she been a partner in the enterprise herself?

'I don't think she's being upfront with us,' she told Willets. 'How could she carry on with buying a flat in the Barbican after Sean jilted her?' She knew that 'jilted' sounded old-fashioned these days, but disliked the brutality of the more modern term 'dumped'. It seemed to her that the world had become an unkinder place.

Willets shrugged. 'No way of knowing without looking at her bank account history, and we've got no grounds to apply for a warrant for that.'

In order to investigate her account they would need to convince a judge that Bethany had benefitted from the proceeds of crime. Time to share what Zeke had told her.

'Remember the security guard who recognised Sean from the photo in the paper? I was about to come and tell you I saw him this morning, to see if he'd remembered anything about Sean's contacts at this gym they used to go to.'

Dean eyed her face curiously. Would his hunger for a lead outweigh his instinct to slap her down for not running it past him first?

'Go on,' he said.

'He told me how Sean was able to throw money around.'

Bethany had changed her look for the interview, her hair up in a demure chignon, wearing a sober navy dress and ecru jacket, only natural-coloured polish today on her acrylic nails. If she were auditioning for a movie role it would be 'betrayed yet sorrowful ex-fiancée'.

Willets led Bethany through the routine stuff before homing in on the split with Sean. 'I appreciate that it's a long time ago but could you walk us through what happened again?' he asked, pouring her a glass of mineral water. It was the first time Flyte had seen him in charming mode.

'Thanks.' Bethany sent him a dazzling smile. 'Well, I knew when I met him he had a reputation – I was the latest in a massive list of girlfriends. But when he asked me to marry him I thought he was putting all that behind him.' It sounded as if she'd rehearsed what to say in front of a mirror.

'Then, I . . . saw a message come in on his phone. I can't recall what it said but it was obvious it was someone he was seeing. Sleeping with.' A tremor of genuine disgust briefly ruffled her expression.

'What was her name?' Willets asked.

'Who?' The question was unremarkable but she looked startled. 'Oh . . . Zara, I think.'

'Like the shop?' asked Flyte with an edge of sarcasm. It felt like she'd pulled the name out of the air.

'Did you know a Zara?' asked Willets.

Bethany shook her head. 'He didn't even try to deny it. Said that the engagement was a mistake. He was sorry, blah, blah, but he'd realised he was too young to settle down. I called him a lot of names and he left the same night.' Her expression hardening.

'You must have been furious,' said Willets. 'It would be understandable if you lashed out? Hit him?'

'No! I wouldn't give him the satisfaction. Next thing I hear, he's upped and gone to Canada.'

'Who told you that?' asked Flyte.

She shrugged. 'I think I saw a post on Facebook.'

Or you put up his posts yourself, thought Flyte.

'Did you know his Facebook password?' she asked.

'No. He was cagey about stuff like that – for obvious reasons.'

'But sloppy enough to allow incriminating messages to show up on his phone screen?' Flyte was smiling but going by Bethany's expression she'd caught the insinuation.

'We all slip up I suppose.' She tapped a glossy fingernail softly on the tabletop, apparently unaware of the gesture.

'You and Sean can't have earned that much back then – I'm guessing what, fifty, maybe sixty grand between you?' asked Willets, still working the charm. 'How were you able to afford the flat in the Barbican?'

Bethany shrugged defensively. 'The proceeds from my flat, plus savings from modelling, and an aunt left me some money in her will.'

'Enough to go ahead even after you and Sean broke up?' asked Willets.

'Yes.'

Flyte jumped in, 'Sean had some expensive tastes – designer brands, fancy restaurants and so on, didn't he? How did he manage to fund all that on a police officer's salary?'

Bethany's eyes flicked from Flyte to Willets and back again. 'I don't know. I wasn't his keeper.'

'You never asked?' Flyte lent her voice a sarcastic edge. 'As in: "Darling, you've just spent five hundred quid on clothes – how can you afford it?"'

'I never really thought about it,' said Bethany, sending her a flame-thrower look.

'Just to be clear, you're saying you were completely unaware of any other income source Sean might have had?' It was a classic tactic: trying to catch someone out in a provable lie.

Bethany shook her head, that fingernail going tappity-tap on the table.

Flyte looked at her notes. 'What about the anabolic steroids he was selling down the gym?'

Blinking rapidly, Bethany made as if to say something before apparently thinking better of it.

'You told me that the flat you shared at the time was tiny,' Flyte went on. 'Boxes of pharmaceuticals in the quantities needed for dealing aren't easy to hide.' She paused as if something had just occurred to her. 'Unless you two had a little lab somewhere to manufacture them?'

'No way.' Bethany shook her head vehemently. 'If he was doing what you say then he must've kept them in a locker at the gym.'

'Sean sounds like a generous guy. But you're telling us he never sent any of the cash he was making your way? Seriously?' Folding her arms, Flyte sat back, impassive, enjoying her bad cop role.

Dean leaned forward, wearing a sympathetic expression, his hands steepled like a priest in the confessional. 'Is that how you could afford to buy a flat in the Barbican, Bethany? It'd be better if you came clean – after all, it wasn't you who was selling the gear.'

Would she bite?

Bethany let out a breath before saying, 'OK, I knew what he was doing but I swear I had nothing to do with it. I was always on at him to stop selling that filthy stuff before he got caught and lost his job.'

Chapter Twenty-Six

After her dad's ECG had come back normal the stuck-up doctor had finally – if huffily – agreed to Cassie's demand to run blood tests for zinc overdose.

It was midday the following day and Cassie was back at his bedside when a different doctor – *thank Christ* – came to tell them the results. It confirmed her hunch: Callum had more than three times the safe level of zinc in his system.

They hooked him up to an intravenous infusion of drugs to 'chelate' the excess zinc from his system. Having looked up the word on her Classics app, Cassie discovered that it came from the Greek *chele* meaning claw. The chelating drug molecules would storm through Callum's bloodstream to seek out the molecules of zinc, locking them in a claw-like embrace and carrying them out through the urine.

After the doctor left, Callum took her hand and sought her gaze. 'You should get back to work. Listen, Catkin, it was my own stupid fault. You warned me to be careful how much I took but your old dad isn't very bright. I stupidly thought zinc was like vitamins. Promise me you won't go stressing about it.'

Cassie pasted on a smile but every look at his grey complexion and patchy hair was an agonising reminder that in her misguided efforts to get her dad healthy she had poisoned him. If his collapse hadn't landed him in A & E he might have suffered organ damage. Were all her relationships doomed to end the same way – hurting the people she loved?

Outside the hospital she saw a bloke in an NHS-issue dressing gown hooked up to an intravenous drip stand smoking a fag and bummed one off him, which she smoked fierce and fast on the short walk across the hospital car park to the mortuary. Why the fuck hadn't she spotted the symptoms of zinc overdose earlier? She needed to be more on the ball monitoring Callum's diet and supplements, making sure he took his emphysema meds, getting him to exercise more, eat healthily . . . Although truthfully the idea of having to play nursemaid filled her with gloom.

Seeing DS Flyte walking up and down outside the mortuary entrance, Cassie took a last draw on her fag before chucking it. Despite her mood, the sight of that ramrod spine, the pent-up impatience in her pacing, brought a smile to her lips.

'What can I do for you?' she asked, swiping her entry card.

'I was passing so I thought it would be quicker than calling. I've got approval for the extra steroid testing on Sean Kavanagh's samples.' She unleashed one of the rare smiles that revealed her dazzling prettiness.

'Well done,' said Cassie. She'd clearly invented an excuse to be here, probably wanting to share her achievement. 'So, I'm guessing you found the guy who was selling him the gear?'

Flyte's mouth pruned and she seemed about to invoke confidentiality or some such bullshit, before relenting. 'Strictly between you and me? It turns out it was Sean who was doing the dealing.'

'Wow. Says who?'

'A guy who used to go to the same gym as him up in Kentish Town.'

'Which explains how he could afford the flash gear he was wearing when he came in' – picturing his sodden Nike Airs.

In the body store, Cassie opened a workstation to access her email.

'So, I already spoke to the toxicology lab,' she said, 'and they sent over a list of anabolic-androgenic steroids they would advise running tests for.'

Leaning towards the screen Flyte read out, 'Testosterone, nandrolone, clenbuterol, stanozolol ... there's more than a dozen here! Are they injected or taken as pills?'

Cassie could smell lavender soap mixed with the warm scent of her skin.

'Um, both apparently. Guys looking to bulk up will inject one kind over several weeks and then supplement it with different drugs orally. It's called stacking.'

'It sounds dangerous.'

'Oh, it is, if you do it for any length of time. How your body responds to having its hormonal profile pharmaceutically hacked is a genetic lottery.'

Their shared look lamented the stupidity of it all.

'If I'm honest, I feel sorry for men,' said Cassie. 'This obsession with washboard abs and getting stupidly pumped and shredded, they're just falling for the same old shit women have put up with for years.'

She filled in the official request for steroid tests and mailed it over to the toxicology lab, but Flyte didn't seem inclined to dash off.

'How would you describe Bethany Locke's reaction when she viewed Sean's body?' she asked.

Cassie screwed up her face, remembering Bethany's vehement whisper: *You bastard.*

'She was furious with him.' She lifted a shoulder. 'But that's not especially unusual in the bereaved. Probably an irrational response to being abandoned.' Thinking of her dad disappearing when she was four. Remaining irrationally convinced for years that he'd turn up to read her a bedtime story.

'Well, he had been unfaithful to her, and broken off their engagement,' said Flyte. 'It sounds as though he never really stopped chasing the ladies: he had quite the reputation at his nick in Finsbury Park. His fellow officers described him as a "pussy hound". . .' Flyte made a face like an Edwardian great-aunt sucking a lemon.

Something Bethany had said came back to Cassie.

The worst thing is, he never really wanted me.

Her eye fell on drawer number six, marked up 'Sean Kavanagh', with the alias he'd used in brackets. Feeling an idea starting to take shape – like egg white dropped into simmering water. 'You told me that he called himself Shane at the gym?'

'Yes?' Flyte frowned. 'For a police officer who was illegally dealing drugs, that would make sense.'

'Maybe that wasn't the only thing he was trying to keep under wraps.'

Flyte looked blank. 'Meaning?'

Cassie recalled her phone conversation with Sean's mother about his funeral. The only emotion she'd expressed: relief that his father wasn't around to hear that his son had *gone and got himself murdered.* Like he had asked for it.

'Tell me more about the guy who told you Sean was dealing.'

'He's called Ezekiel – Zeke – black guy, works as a security guard.'

'And how did he take the news that Sean was dead?'

Flyte flexed her brow, remembering. 'He seemed genuinely upset.'

Cassie raised an eyebrow. 'Over some guy he barely knew, who he hadn't seen for eight years?'

'What are you suggesting?'

'Come on, isn't it obvious? This Zeke and Sean were lovers.'

Seeing Flyte's sceptical expression, Cassie went on, 'If Sean-stroke-Shane was just this guy's dealer why would he stick his neck out by talking to a cop?'

'It's an interesting theory,' said Flyte, handing her a patronising smile, 'but Zeke is married with two kids.'

'Do you live under a rock?' Cassie shot back angrily. 'Have you seriously never heard of a gay guy marrying a woman?' She widened her eyes meaningfully. 'Or a gay woman marrying a man?'

Seeing a blush flood Flyte's cheeks, Cassie regretted the jibe immediately. What business was it of hers if Flyte chose to live her life in the closet?

'If Sean was gay, how do you explain his string of girlfriends, the Casanova reputation?' asked Flyte coldly.

'A smokescreen? Is it easy, do you think, coming out as gay in the Met?' Cassie went on, 'I'm sick of hearing, "Oh, it's no big deal being gay these days." There are loads of people who still have a problem with it.' People like Sean's mother, estranged from her son, probably because she'd found out he was into men. But it was clear from Flyte's expression that she'd closed down.

Flyte picked up her bag, the blush only just starting to fade from her cheeks. 'Thank you for getting the test request in so promptly,' she said in her 'official' voice. 'Let me know when you receive the results, would you?'

FLYTE

Seb was off work that day but towards the evening he messaged her to see if she wanted to meet up, an offer she declined nicely. It felt . . . too soon after their first tryst. And in truth since sleeping with him she'd been feeling somewhat conflicted about the relationship, for no good reason she could think of. He was attractive, single and solvent – a solid long-term prospect as a husband and a potential parent. She just didn't feel any magnetic pull towards him.

Magnetic pull? Stuff and nonsense, Phyllida! she scolded herself, channelling her mother. *You're far too old for schoolgirl crushes.*

Her thoughts kept returning to her fractious encounter with Cassie. Could Sean's string of girlfriends, his ladies' man reputation really all have been a diversionary tactic? Pops would have called it 'chaff'; a wartime term used to describe the practice whereby planes flying over enemy territory would disperse a shower of tiny metal fragments in order to confuse radar systems.

But seriously? For him to go to the effort and expense of wining and dining a stable of girlfriends for years just to maintain his reputation as the Casanova of Finsbury Park nick? She just didn't buy it, or his supposed affair with Zeke.

She'd seen Cassie in combative mode before but for her to try and shore up her theory by implying that Flyte was a closet lesbian, well, that was beyond the pale.

Recently, Flyte had come to terms with occasionally finding herself attracted to women – had even felt attracted to Cassie, once she'd got to know the real woman beneath the challenging veneer. But that didn't make her gay. She still considered herself heterosexual and her vision of a successful relationship was unchanged: a nice normal marriage to a nice normal man like Seb and, God willing, another baby. Anything else struck her as too . . . messy to contemplate.

She promised herself a night in with an M&S ready meal – salmon in a low-calorie lemon sauce with mange tout and a mini-bottle of Sauvignon – followed by an old episode of *Midsomer Murders*. She found its countryside setting soothing – a comforting antidote to the sordid day-to-day reality of policing Camden.

It was just as well she had opted for an early night because the next morning she was jerked from sleep before dawn by her work phone's ringtone. It was the Camden nick patrol sarge, telling her that a body had been found on Hampstead Heath. By some historical quirk the Heath fell under the jurisdiction of the City of London Police, but since they were two detectives down they'd asked for Camden to send someone to attend the scene.

It was six thirty with the sky only just starting to lighten when she arrived on the eastern fringe of the Heath. The branches of the trees hung low, heavy with rain after a sharp shower which had left the wooded slopes misty and out of focus. She paused under an oak tree, squinting at the coordinates she'd been sent, then cursed as it offloaded a stream of rainwater down her neck. By the side of the path, she saw a shiny scatter of silver bulbs – used canisters of nitrous oxide – laughing gas. Hippy crack, they called it; not as dangerous as crack cocaine but still a high that killed several idiots a year.

Middle-class Hampsteadites saw the heath as a pastoral haven, a slice of natural wilderness amid the brick and concrete, but to Flyte it was about as 'natural' as the population of scabrous city foxes who scavenged bins to survive.

A flutter of blue and white police tape loomed out of the mist, encircling a wooded dip, and she recognised the uniform standing there.

'What have we got, Jethro?' she asked, taking nitrile gloves from her pocket.

Amid a circle of trees, their rain-bent heads like mourners at a funeral, she saw the outline of a man wearing a beige coat, half seated against an oak, his head bent, almost touching his knees.

Flyte felt her heart start to hammer, but her conscious brain lagged a second or two behind.

Bending down, she put her gloved hand under his chin and lifted his head to see his face – but she already knew who it was.

Luke Lawless, crime reporter for the *Camden Gazette*.

'His flies are open,' she noted.

'Yep.' Jethro nodded at a wrinkled condom a few feet away and raised an eyebrow. 'It's a popular spot with the gay fraternity. I'm giving evens on a chemsex overdose.'

Remembering Sean Kavanagh's open flies – a deliberate misdirection by his killer – Flyte gave him a sharp look. 'Let's not leap to conclusions. And get that condom bagged, would you?' Jethro sighed windily but took a glove from his pocket.

She would never admit this publicly, but she had never understood the appeal of outdoor sex or why it was so popular with gay men – even those who, in the parlance, were 'out'. They were bound to get their clothes dirty, there was nowhere to shower afterwards, and in the UK it would be uncomfortably cold most of the year.

She set the back of her hand against Luke's cheek. From the chill damp of his skin, he'd clearly been dead for hours. His eyes were half closed, as if dropping off to sleep, and his face was blotchy, but she couldn't see any obvious signs of violence. Dipping a gloved hand into one coat pocket then the other she felt the touch of glass and pulled out a small vial containing some kind of liquid. Jethro's guess of a fatal OD during a drug-fuelled sexual encounter looked likely to be accurate.

Flyte would never have guessed Luke was gay but then maybe her gaydar wasn't that finely tuned. Scanning his face, she tried to understand why an ambitious young man, so focused on his journalistic career, would risk it all for a moment of pleasure? The way some people – usually men – allowed their sexual needs to lead them by the nose had always mystified her.

She continued to check all his pockets. 'No phone or wallet,' she said, looking up at Jethro. 'So he's having sex with someone, he ODs, and then they rifle through his pockets?'

Jethro shrugged, evidently bored with the whole thing.

Looking around, she spotted a man, up on the crest of a hill looking down at them, rubbernecking. She raised her hand, indicating he should wait. He wore running gear and seemed for a moment to be considering whether to ignore her and resume his run, before seeing her purposeful stride and deciding against.

By the time Flyte reached him, she was a little out of breath. Flashing her warrant card, she asked if he'd ever seen Luke in the area, describing him and what he was wearing, but the guy, who said his name was Max, shook his head, seeming defensive. She took in his spotless Gymshark joggers and coordinated hoodie, the box-fresh trainers – all a bit chic for the average straight guy and suspiciously clean for anyone on a proper run.

'Listen, Max,' she said, locking eyes with him. 'I'm well aware that people have . . . liaisons on the heath, and I'm not remotely interested. I just want to know whether Luke might have been cruising, whether he was a regular here. If somebody else is implicated in his death then we need to track them down, for everyone's protection.'

Max visibly relaxed before shrugging. 'Sorry, but I honestly don't know the guy.' He nodded down the slope. 'But I can tell you that's a popular pick-up spot.'

'Did you see anyone hanging around here last night – or any night? Perhaps someone you didn't recognise?'

He shook his head.

'OK, let me know if anyone else did, would you?' She gave him her card.

After Max resumed his run, she headed back down towards the wooded dip where Luke's body lay. And between the low-hanging branches she glimpsed Jethro lifting his phone. From his stance it was clear he was using it as a camera, and from the direction in which it was pointed he could only be photographing Luke's body.

She took the last few metres at a near-run.

'Give me that phone.'

'But, Sarge . . .' Jethro's expression said 'caught red-handed'.

214

'Now!'

He handed it over reluctantly.

In his photos, she found half a dozen images of Luke's body.

'You were going to share these, weren't you?'

Jethro appeared to be taking a sudden interest in his shoes, but he didn't try to deny it.

She thrust the phone into his face. 'Do you know how much it damages us when this kind of behaviour comes out? We're the police for fuck's sake. The good guys! It's our job to protect the public, not to share degrading images of them with our . . . twisted friends!' Flyte paused for breath, aware that she was ranting but finding that she just didn't care. 'You're a disgrace.' Clicking the phone's lock button she said, 'I'm confiscating this as evidence and I'll be taking it up with DCI Steadman.'

Jethro had the nerve to look aggrieved. 'Come on, Sarge, the WhatsApp group I'm in, they're all Job.'

'Keep going, Jethro, it's all going in my report.' She pocketed the phone.

Jethro blinked, disbelieving. 'But seriously, Sarge, you can't take my phone!'

She pulled a sweet smile and enjoyed the glimmer of hope on his face. 'Don't worry, Jethro, I'll write you a receipt.'

Chapter Twenty-Seven

Cassie said no to meeting up with Archie that evening, telling him she was still feeling a bit drained after her dad's zinc-overdose drama a couple of nights back – which was true, if not the whole story. Now and again, she just craved her own space, something that some of her previous lovers had found hard to handle. Her live-in girlfriend Rachel had said that when Cassie was in that mood it was 'like trying to communicate with someone through perspex'.

And the bad-tempered spat with Flyte hadn't helped. It was none of her business, of course, but the woman's self-delusion about her sexuality, her all-consuming need to stay on the 'right side' of some unbreachable sexual preference line – it was exasperating. And yes, OK, Cassie couldn't help but take it as a negative comment on her own love life.

A breeze was ruffling the water of the canal, which the setting sun had turned quicksilver-blue shot with lemon. She could feel the air temperature dropping a bit further as dusk fell earlier every evening. This time of year had always made her melancholic: the long months of winter yawning ahead like an endless tunnel.

When Gaz popped his head out of his cabin and asked if she wanted to come over she decided a bit of no-pressure company would be good for her.

They sat on Gaz's deck drinking whiskey.

'Gaz, can I ask you something?' Cassie asked. 'Would you ever live on land again?'

'Like, in a flat?'

She'd been going over Archie's idea of them getting a place together, and wondering whether she could ever hack being part of a conventional couple: arguing over how to load the dishwasher, going to B&Q on a Sunday, all that domestic crap ... Shivering, she zipped up her leather jacket. On the other hand, with winter coming, central heating held an undeniable appeal.

'Nah, I'm a free-range chicken.' Gaz gave a wheezy chuckle. 'I haven't lived indoors since the early nineties. Walls freak me out.'

Remembering Archie's report of someone peering in through the porthole – and the weird feeling she'd had the previous week that someone had been in her cabin, she asked, 'You haven't seen anyone hanging about around my boat lately?' Both events had left her feeling more rattled than she cared to let on.

Gaz's eyes disappeared into the rugged terrain of his face. 'Nah. I mean there's Copernicus but he's harmless. Not a junkie tea leaf.'

Copernicus?

Seeing her expression, Gaz clarified, 'He was a professor of cosmology.'

Cassie remembered the homeless tweedy guy sat on the edge of the towpath, waiting for Jupiter to rise, telescope clamped to one eye.

'Seriously? Yeah, I've seen him around. How did he end up here?'

'The word is he was a don at Cambridge, or Oxford, I forget. Won all kinds of awards till he went crackers.' Spinning a finger at the side of his head.

High-flyers and geniuses who'd crashed and burned weren't uncommon among the homeless.

Gaz topped up Cassie's glass. 'How's your water holding up?' he asked, tipping his head in the direction of *Dreamcatcher*.

'About forty litres left.' She was lucky that she could shower at work.

'No problem, next week we can take her upstream to fill the tanks.' He squinted at the sky. 'If we don't get some proper rain soon I'll be running low myself.'

Gaz was like an unofficial outpost of the Met Office, keeping a daily weather diary recording rainfall, temperature and hours of sunshine.

He squinted over her shoulder, his eyes tiny bright spots in a sun-darkened face that reminded her of a vintage leather satchel. 'They're getting ready to blow that place up.'

She followed his gaze: forty metres upstream on the opposite bank the bright neon-yellow of two men in hazard jackets glowed through the gathering dusk like fireflies. They were stood on the blocked-off section of towpath that ran alongside the abandoned housing estate, next to the big 'Hazard' board warning off trespassers. As she watched, they appeared to tinker around with the mesh security fence. It was hard to tell but it looked like they might be making it more secure.

'We'll have a front row seat when it happens,' she said, taking a swig of whiskey. 'We should sell tickets.'

FLYTE

Back in the office after attending Luke Lawless's body on the heath, Flyte had kept an eye out for Seb leaving his desk to make coffee.

Since her early morning rant at Jethro she'd been having misgivings about the wisdom of making an official complaint against him. The fact that she had known Luke, albeit only slightly, had probably contributed to her furious outburst at seeing him disrespected in death.

Finally, what seemed like an age later, she saw Seb get up, and after a decent pause she followed him out and into the tiny staff kitchen.

As she told him the story, sotto voce, his expression grew increasingly sombre, his eyes widening when she reached the confiscation of Jethro's phone.

'What else could I do?' she pleaded. 'He'd just have deleted the images and left me without a leg to stand on.'

'But you say he hadn't even shared the photos? So, what has he done exactly?'

'He admitted he was going to share them, no doubt to make tasteless jokes about the dead gay guy.'

'Do you take milk?' Seb's tone changed and she realised that Terry, one of the office workers, had come in behind her. But after retrieving his lunch from the fridge he left again.

'Look, it's up to you,' said Seb under his breath. 'But grassing Willets up for having a drink with an estate agent didn't exactly make you Ms Popular, and everybody likes Jethro. Do you really think the boss is going to pin a medal on you for bringing him more grief?'

Flyte bit her lip. She remembered Pops using the military slang 'Bravo Foxtrot' to describe someone with a reputation for snitching on his brothers-in-arms to the higher ranks. Years later, she had googled it and found it stood for 'Buddy Fucker'.

She chewed the side of her nail. 'So what would you do?'

'Delete the photos, give Jethro all the really shit jobs for a month and tell him that if he ever does it again you'll drop him in it from a great height.'

By the time Steadman called her and Willets in for an update on the Sean Kavanagh case that afternoon, Flyte had decided reluctantly to take Seb's advice. It was rank cowardice but she couldn't afford to get a rep as the Bravo Foxtrot of Major Crimes. Ironic that having done nothing wrong, it should be she who was worrying about blotting her copybook.

At least her relations with Willets had moved from sub-zero to tolerable since she'd delivered the steroid dealing lead.

'Good work uncovering this new line of enquiry, Phyllida,' said Steadman, sending her an approving look.

'Thank you, boss,' said Flyte, feeling warmth rise in her cheeks.

'If it stands up, the press will have a field day, especially in the current climate,' he sighed. '"Dead cop was drug dealer." But, regardless, we must pursue this without fear or favour.'

'Absolutely,' said Flyte. 'We'd like to apply for a court order to access Bethany Locke's bank account from eight years ago, on the grounds that she must have benefitted from the proceeds of Sean's dealing.'

Steadman frowned. 'Even if she did, how would that make her a suspect in his death?'

'I see the two things as interconnected,' said Flyte. 'She could have killed him in a jealous rage when she found out about his infidelity, but then later transferred the remaining drug-dealing proceeds from his bank account so that she could still buy the Barbican flat. Chances are she knew his passwords.'

Steadman leafed through the document on the desk in front of him. 'According to the interview transcript she admitted to knowing about the dealing but denied benefitting from it financially. Right?'

'Well, yes. She claims it was a "legacy from an aunt" that allowed her to go ahead with the flat purchase, but we don't buy it,' said Flyte. She shot a sideways glance at Willets, expecting backup, but he was examining his fingernails.

Steadman blew out a breath. 'It's all circumstantial, I'm afraid. We need more substantive evidence. If we took this to a Crown Court judge as things stand it would be dismissed as a fishing expedition.'

Willets turned to her, his smile edged with spite and adopted a patronising tone. 'The onus is on us to prove that the money was the proceeds of crime, not on Bethany to prove that it came from an inheritance.'

Flyte felt her cheeks flame, with fury this time. Just ten minutes ago, Willets had agreed that Bethany was their prime suspect and that they should ask Steadman to apply for the court order, but now he had hung her out to dry.

'I'm afraid the court would take the same view of Sean's old bank account. Even the dead have rights to privacy.' Steadman stood up from behind his desk. He took a boiled sweet from a bowl, his gesture inviting them to take one. 'I took up these to help me give up smoking. That was four years ago . . .'

After unwrapping the sweet and popping it into his mouth, he started to pace up and down, as was his habit when he was thinking. 'In any case, I'm having trouble with the idea of Bethany as our suspect. I can see how she might have snapped and killed him for being unfaithful, but how did she shift the body and where did she keep it frozen for eight years? We know Kavanagh was a muscular guy, while she probably weighs . . . what?'

'About nine, nine and half stone,' admitted Flyte.

'Right. She'd have to get him out of their flat, into a vehicle, and then into a freezer somewhere. Then eight years later she would've had to drag his body out of the cold store and into another vehicle to dump him in the canal – all without being spotted in one of the busiest parts of London.'

Put like that, it did sound pretty unfeasible. 'I was thinking she might have had an accomplice,' said Flyte.

Steadman made a non-committal sound before sitting down and tipping back his swivel chair. 'Any other thoughts on an alternative motive, suspects? . . . Dean?'

'For me it has to be the steroids dealing, guv. It's a multi-million-dollar business – but to make the serious money you've got to be smuggling it in from overseas on a big scale. Hundreds of tonnes of the stuff is brought in from India.'

Willets was talking as though he was the world's expert on steroid smuggling when Flyte knew that the entirety of his knowledge had been gleaned from a cursory Google search.

'I think Kavanagh got greedy,' he went on, warming to his theme. 'Maybe he started thinking why buy his supply from a gang and pay their huge mark-up when he could scale up and ship it in himself at a fraction of the cost?'

Steadman moved his sweet from one cheek to the other. 'The hypothesis being that his existing suppliers found out he was setting up his own operation, and took him out.'

'Exactly, guv.'

'That sounds like a more promising theory. A drug gang would have the resources to put a body in long-term cold storage and then get rid of it when they think it's safe.' Steadman turned to his computer screen, signalling the end to the meeting. 'OK, Dean, set up a call with the NCA, see if they have any intel about steroid smugglers' activity around the time Kavanagh went missing.'

The National Crime Agency – the big boys who handled organised crime. Willets would get off on that.

Chapter Twenty-Eight

There were only two bodies on the PM list the following morning – a woman in her fifties who had died of a cardiac arrest during an appendectomy and a man found dead on Hampstead Heath of a likely chemsex overdose. Cassie tried to deal with the female guests when possible – knowing that some women might feel uncomfortable at the idea of their naked body being handled by a man.

But as she and Jason retrieved the bodies from the body store, she said to him, 'Could you look after Mrs Maddox? I'm taking the heath guy.'

Jason just gave a bored shrug. 'They're all the same to me, sweetheart.'

Refusing to rise to the wind-up she wheeled thirty-year-old Luke Lawless to her autopsy table, while Jason set the radio to her least favourite station, which played back-to-back Ibiza house and dance music. At least the wall of noise would mean she could talk to Luke without being overheard.

Flyte had messaged her just after six that morning to tell her that he was coming in and to ask her to 'keep her eyes peeled' for anything odd. Cassie was half tempted to tell her to sod off – with no suspicious circs Luke was only getting a routine PM – but instead she just sent back a curt 'OK'.

Removing Luke's clothes was a struggle: with his major muscles in peak rigor mortis, it was like undressing an unco-operative child. She folded them all carefully into a plastic bag and sealed it. If the case did end up going forensic they might hold fibres or hairs left there by someone else.

Scanning the front of his naked body, she could see no obvious injury. The skin below the neck was the colour and texture of uncooked dough, but his face was a dark red. According to the notes he'd been slumped forward, so it was possible the blood had pooled there post-mortem. The only visible blemish was a cold sore on the corner of his mouth.

'What's the story, Luke?' she asked him under her breath. 'Were you high? Did you meet someone on the heath?' She didn't get anything back. 'The police are going to inform your dad as soon as possible.' The notes said that Luke's father was a widower who'd lost his wife only a year earlier. 'Meanwhile it's our job to find out what happened to you.'

The front of Luke's body showed no sign of any injury. Gently lifting a half-closed eyelid with gloved fingers, she saw a curved red-brown band of discoloration across the eye and the iris, repeated on the other eye. Known as *tache noire*, it happened when the eyes didn't close at death. After several hours, the area of eye surface open to the air dried out, leaving this darker slash, like an exposed film.

If only Kühne had been right. A nineteenth-century German scientist, Kühne came up with the theory that the last image a dead person saw would be recorded on their retina. After experimenting, he did manage to photograph the rudimentary outline of a barred window captured on the retina of a dead rabbit, and early pathologists attempted to repeat the trick on murder victims, but the images recovered were nowhere near clear enough for identification purposes.

She heard the door to the clean side open and Archie's cheerful tones saying, 'Morning, Jason . . . Cassie.'

As he began his external exam of Luke's body, they shared a complicit look.

'This is Luke. Thirty years old, found on Hampstead Heath yesterday morning,' she said. 'The police report no suspicious circs, and found a vial of liquid in his pocket, so they're thinking it's a probable chemsex OD during a gay hook-up.'

'They've sent the liquid to the lab?'

She nodded. 'It'll almost certainly be GHB.' A party drug popular among gay men, GHB caused euphoric feelings and intensified sexual sensation. It was relatively easy to OD on, especially if mixed with alcohol or other drugs, and was also highly corrosive. Cassie had done her fair share of pharmaceuticals but she drew the line at a liquid that could burn through plastic if insufficiently diluted.

Archie flipped Luke's eyelid open with less delicacy than she'd used. 'The *tache noire* suggests at least a seven-hour interval since death. Rigor of the limbs consistent with a TOD of between seven and ten hours. Face congested.'

Eyeing Luke's face, she became aware of a tingling in her mouth which quickly became a burning sensation, like lemon juice on a mouth ulcer. Her hand shot to her cheek.

'Cassie?' Archie looked worried. 'What's up?'

'It's OK,' she said. The burning had disappeared in an instant but it had left a thought buzzing round her brain.

She bent over Luke and pulled his lower jaw to open his mouth. 'Shine your torch inside,' she told Archie, who complied with a puzzled half-smile. 'See anything?'

226

'Umm . . . oh, hang on. Yes, there appears to be a lesion inside the right-hand cheek . . .'

Bingo.

'Don't touch him – I'll be right back,' she said, stripping off her gloves.

'Where are you going?'

Cassie was already heading to the quiet of the body store to call Flyte. *Come on, come on*, she mouthed, until she heard her clipped tones with their edge of impatience. 'DS Flyte.'

'Hi there. Did your Heath guy, Luke Lawless, have a water bottle or anything else to drink on him?' asked Cassie, being extra polite after their falling-out the last time they'd met.

'Um . . . no, there wasn't anything like that recovered at the scene. Why do you ask?'

'If the liquid he was carrying is GHB it's highly corrosive and Luke has an area of what looks like burned tissue inside his mouth.'

'I don't understand.'

'Anyone who takes GHB knows it causes burns if you drink it neat. You have to heavily dilute it first.'

Cassie could hear Flyte working it out.

'So while he might have misjudged the dilution, you would still expect to find a bottle of water close to hand. Are you suggesting that somebody forced him to drink it neat?'

'Or planted some in his mouth after killing him.' She saw Archie push open the door from the autopsy suite, his expression telling her there was more. 'I'll call you back.'

Back at her workstation, Archie lifted Luke's chin and played the beam of his torch along the jawline. 'Can you see that? It's not easy to make out because of the congestion.'

'Yeah! There's like . . . a double line?'

227

'Yup, it's a patterned contusion. Possibly the seam of a sleeve.'
They looked at one another.

'You think somebody had him in a chokehold?' she asked.

Archie gave a shrug. 'Above my pay grade,' he said. 'But it means one less job for me today. I'll let the coroner know this chap is going to need the full bells and whistles PM.'

FLYTE

Flyte couldn't tell Willets what Cassie had shared; she just had to endure the suspense until an email arrived from the coroner's office just before lunchtime. It summarised Dr Cuff's preliminary findings and said that a Home Office pathologist had been instructed to conduct a forensic PM on the body of Lucas Lawless the following day.

Minutes after she'd forwarded it to Dean Willets, he ambled over.

'So your heath guy just got promoted to a category one,' he said. 'Sounds like my Hugger Mugger case is back in business.'

In light of the discovery that Luke had likely been killed in a chokehold, a possible linkage between the two cases had occurred to Flyte. But she'd decided it didn't bear much examination. 'If someone did plant the GHB on him, then they were almost certainly trying to put us off the scent by painting this as an OD,' she told Willets. 'The MO is totally different. Whatever the motive, this isn't a straightforward mugging gone wrong.'

'Well, his wallet and phone were gone.' Willets raised his eyebrows sarcastically.

She raised hers right back. 'Maybe his assailant was removing evidence that might implicate them.'

'Or perhaps this reporter was out cruising, was new to GHB so didn't know how to take it, and fell foul of our Hugger Mugger.'

Willets pulled a patronising smile. 'Let's wait and see what the forensic PM says, shall we? A uniform can do the death knock and Seb can check out Lawless's flat when he gets in later.'

The death knock: visiting his next of kin. 'Wouldn't it be better if I did both? Seeing as I met him, and attended the scene?' Keeping her tone light, unchallenging.

'I'd rather keep your talents focused on the Kavanagh case. The NCA is sending over mugshots for members of drug gangs with a history of steroid smuggling. I'd like you to show them to Bethany Locke in case she recognises any of them as Sean Kavanagh's associates.'

As Willets sauntered off, she mouthed a rude word at his back.

Could it really be coincidence that just days after Luke Lawless had told her he was probing the murder of Sean Kavanagh, he should turn up dead in highly suspicious circumstances? But arguing the point with Willets without a scrap of proof was pointless. Ordinarily, she might have considered taking it to Steadman, but he was away at a national conference for the brass in Birmingham for a few days.

After logging into Luke's case, she found his home address, provided by his boss at the *Gazette*, as well as the name of the lettings agent who held a spare key. Seeing it was nearly 1 p.m. she left a Post-it note on her computer screen saying 'Back by 14.30' and sauntered out. If she picked up the key en route to his flat and had a quick sniff round nobody would be any the wiser.

Within half an hour, she was unlocking a grimy front door next to a Korean fast-food joint off the Camden Road. She climbed the narrow stairway with its stained and threadbare carpet to

Luke's first-floor flat, the whole place smelling like it had been marinated in Korean spices.

Pulling on a glove, she knocked at the front door – no answer – before unlocking it, aware of her heart beating faster, although not in an unpleasant way. Pushing the door open, she held her breath and listened for a long moment, but could detect no movement within.

The place was tiny, the kitchen area and living–dining space only about three by four metres, an unmade bed visible through an open door. Up here the smell of spiced chicken and kimchi was even stronger.

She started to scope the place, knowing what she was looking for: the tan-coloured Moleskine notebook Luke had used during their first meeting.

The living room was surprisingly tidy for a young guy living alone, making her task easier, but there was no sign of the notebook. On the coffee table lay a copy of the latest *Gazette*, open at Luke's feature on the Kavanagh case, and on investigating the sideboard, on which a modest-sized telly stood, she found only old fast-food receipts, and bits and bobs. Nothing in any of the kitchen units either.

Moving into the bedroom, she saw two framed photographs beside the bed, reminding her of her precious image of Poppy. One held a selfie of Luke making a silly face alongside an attractive young woman, her eyes intelligent behind glasses: clearly a lover, although no doubt Willets would dismiss this as the window dressing of a closeted gay man. The other showed a couple, presumably Luke's parents, on a hot-looking beach sitting either side of a two- or three-year-old in a sun hat. Toddler Luke was intent on prodding a hole in the sand with his spade, but his mum and dad only had eyes for him. The dad who'd recently lost his wife and who was now having to deal with the fact that his only son had been murdered.

A swift but thorough search of the bedside table and chest of drawers was fruitless. Returning to the front room she was starting to think that maybe Luke's assailant had taken his notebook along with his phone and wallet when she heard something.

The traffic noise from the street below increased as if the volume had been turned up, before subsiding again: the only clue that somebody had opened and closed the door downstairs to the street.

Flaming focaccia!

She moved swiftly to the front door, quietly snibbed the lock, and waited, trying to quiet her breathing.

Stupid! Since no keys had been found on Luke's body, it was a good bet they were in the hands of his attacker. Straining her ears, she couldn't hear any footsteps from the stairs but ten seconds later she could sense someone on the other side of the door.

A scraping noise as a key was put in the lock. Flyte held her breath, her pulse thudding double-time in her throat. Now the key rattled uselessly in the lock, the snib holding firm. What would the visitor do now? It would only take a couple of well-aimed kicks to knock the lock off the door frame. Then a silence that seemed to last an eternity, before she heard steps retreating down the stairs.

Back in the front room she opened a gap between the dusty wooden blinds, but could see only innocent-looking passers-by in the street below.

Holy moly.

Her pulse was still hammering. When Luke's assailant took his key had he planned to burgle his flat? That was possible, but there was a more compelling motive: that they were both there for the same reason – to recover any evidence that might point the police towards Luke's murderer. Like a notebook.

It gave her the impetus to renew the search with more urgency. Who knew when the unknown visitor might return, determined to gain entry? Luke was practically welded to that notebook; it had to be here somewhere. What would his idea of a clever hiding place be? After pulling all the cushions off the sofa and checking the linings, she returned to the bedroom to look under the mattress, inside the duvet cover and pillowcases, under the bed and bedroom furniture.

Zilch.

In the kitchenette, she clambered on a chair to check out the top of the kitchen units, which were clear except for a quarter-inch of fatty grime. In the cupboards she opened a biscuit tin and peered inside open packets of rice and cornflakes. Maybe this was a hiding to nothing.

The fridge was empty but for a pint of milk and some half-eaten noodles. The freezer compartment held a single bag of oven chips and she was about to close the door when she stopped. Behind the chips: the blue edge of a ziplock bag. Inside it, wrapped in a second plastic bag, was Luke's Moleskine notebook.

She smiled. Of course it would fit with Luke's sense of drama to hide it in the deep freeze, just as Sean Kavanagh's body had been.

Flipping through the book with gloved hands, she saw a mix of shorthand notes and scribbled words. The last page contained just a couple of lines that might as well be hieroglyphs.

A bunch of scrawled numerals and initials, hard to decipher. What looked like '5K' – five thousand? – followed by '0PD!! AO=NDW' and then two words she was able to make out.

Abney. Caution?

Clearly scribbled in haste, perhaps even on his way out to meet his assailant on the heath? But at the last minute something had made Luke leave his notebook in its safe place. Was that why he'd written and underlined 'Caution'?

It was nearly 2 p.m., and aware that Willets might come looking for her at the nick after lunch she took photos of as many pages as she could before returning the double-bagged notebook to the freezer compartment. Since Luke's death had been declared suspicious a search warrant had been issued for his flat, but if the notebook were to be used in evidence against his killer it ought to come to light during an officially recorded search.

Letting herself out onto the street, Flyte spotted a cafe across the street that offered a clear view of the flat should the intruder return. She didn't even know whether it had been a man or woman. Presumably only a man would have had the requisite strength to kill someone in a chokehold, although that didn't rule out a female accomplice. She took a window seat, feeling a little stunned at how far off-piste she had gone, but also feeling more alive than she had for a long time.

Making a call, she said, 'Hey, Seb . . . Listen, Willets wants you to check out Luke Lawless's flat in Kentish Town right away . . . I was up this way so saved you some time by picking up the key.' Feeling her cheeks redden at the egregious dishonesty she went on to tell him where she was.

Seeing Seb push open the door of the cafe, Flyte closed the image of Luke's final note, suddenly unsure how much she wanted to share with him.

'So Dean tells me we've got another victim of the Hugger Mugger.'

'Hmm, maybe,' said Flyte.

'You don't buy it?' asked Seb with a half-smile.

Flyte was in a quandary: still not sure how much to tell him. Maybe it was because he had seemed to put himself on the side of Dean Willets and Jethro when they had misbehaved. She eyed his face. If push came to shove would he be more loyal to her, or to his buddies? But then without trust there could be no future for them.

She shared her hunch that Sean and Luke's deaths might be connected and told him what had happened in the flat, watching his eyes get wider and wider. 'Wow! And I always had you down as Ms Rulebook!'

She shrugged awkwardly. 'We're entitled to search his flat for evidence relating to his death, so my only misdemeanour is following up a lead Willets seems determined to ignore. Anyway, now we know that somebody else was keen to check out Luke's place.'

'It could have been his cleaner, or some workman sent by the landlord,' said Seb. He tipped his head towards the flat. 'Have you seen anybody going in since?'

A headshake.

'So are you going to show me this mysterious code?' Seb asked.

She could hardly say no. She opened the image and turned her phone to face him.

He made a face. 'I get a bunch of meaningless numbers and initials. "Five K – zero PD" two exclamation marks, then "AO 'equals' NDW" followed by "Abney" and "Caution?"

She pointed to the 5K. 'I thought that was a "five" too at first. But I think it's an S. As in SK.' Seeing if he would get it.

'You think it stands for Sean Kavanagh.' His shrug was non-committal. 'What about the rest?'

She bit her lip. 'That's what I'm struggling with. Could it be some reference to steroids? The A in AO could be anabolic? Is Abney a person?' She took her phone back. 'I'd like us to put this in front of Bethany Locke, see how she reacts.'

Seb frowned. 'You haven't heard?'

'No, what?'

'When Dean tried to call Bethany Locke he got a voicemail saying she was going "out of town" for a while.'

Chapter Twenty-Nine

There was nothing quite as unnervingly silent as the silence of a therapy room, thought Cassie, trying not to fidget under the kind but unrelenting gaze of Pauline Martinez.

She had considered quietly cancelling her second session with the shrink, blaming workload, but Doug had asked her how it was going only the previous day so she'd decided better to grin and bear it.

After some small talk about work, followed by one of Pauline's trademark yawning silences, Cassie found herself offloading about how she'd poisoned her father with zinc, and how bad it had left her feeling.

'Killing him with kindness,' said Pauline with a rueful look.

'Almost literally. I mean how stupid was I?! I *know* how crap Callum is at reading instructions, and how dangerous mineral supplements can be in excess.' She shook her head. 'I've got to be more on the ball with him. He's not a healthy man.'

'Do you always call him Callum?'

Only when I'm feeling conflicted about him.

'I guess I'm still getting used to having a father,' she said instead. 'And I've been stressing about my boyfriend. He wants us to live together and I'm not sure it would work out. It never has before.'

'Why do you think that is?'

'Oh, I don't know,' said Cassie impatiently, having turned it over in her mind a thousand times. 'I like my own space, I guess. Maybe I just don't need other people? I'll probably end up one of those old ladies who picks up other people's rubbish in the street.'

She didn't mention the dead magpie she'd rescued from the towpath after her first Pauline session. Unable to leave him there amid the discarded fried-chicken boxes and fag ends, she'd taken him home and stowed him in the freezer compartment of her fridge for now.

'What are you worried will happen if you move in with your boyfriend?'

'That he'll end up leaving.' She spoke without thinking, but it was the truth.

'That you'll lose him.'

'. . . I suppose so, yes. I mean why can't we just keep things as they are?'

She remembered something her grandmother had said to her when she was a teenager: 'Better to have loved and lost than never to have loved at all.' It had made her quietly furious: it was patently obvious that you'd be better off never exposing yourself to loss in the first place.

'The risk is too great?' Pauline asked.

'Yes! I mean I see it every day in my job, what people go through losing the ones they love.'

Pauline nodded, considering this. 'And do you think they would be better off never having loved the person who died?'

Cassie blew out a breath. If you put it like that . . . Would Acantha and Seffy have been better off if their mother had died when they were babies? Would Becka Bennett's grieving husband Dan be wishing right now that he'd never met her?

'You've known a lot of loss in your life,' said Pauline. 'It's only natural you should respond by trying to protect yourself from any more – by not letting your father, your boyfriend, get too close. All relationships involve risk but perhaps you need to consider what you stand to lose by closing off what they offer.'

For some reason, what came into Cassie's mind wasn't Archie or her dad, but the severely beautiful geometry of Phyllida Flyte's face.

Cassie made her way back to the mortuary, taking the longer route along the canal. The sun was making an effort to break through and the occasional peep and squawk of the waterbirds, the *shhh* of the water lapping against the canal-side soothed her.

Then her phone rang. No name, but the number didn't look like spam so she answered, warily.

'It's Bethany Locke. You said I could call you.'

Interesting.

'Absolutely. How are you doing?'

'I don't know why I'm calling,' Bethany said. 'I barely know you but it feels like apart from me you're . . . closer to Sean than anyone? Probably sounds daft.'

'Not daft at all,' said Cassie. The bereaved did sometimes felt an instant intimacy with the person who'd last handled the person they'd loved. 'Sometimes a stranger is the best kind of sounding board.'

'I think I'm in trouble.' A hoarse sigh. 'The cops, they think I was involved in Sean's death.'

'Really?' Sensing something performative in Bethany's emotion, Cassie repressed the urge to say, *And were you?*

'Yes. You don't have any idea why they would think that?' she went on.

So that was it. Bethany had called to pick her brain about what the cops knew.

'I'm sorry but I have no idea,' said Cassie. 'They're hardly gonna tell me something like that.'

'They must have questioned you though, since you were the one who found Sean?'

A detail that hadn't been made public. Probably Bethany had played grieving fiancée and batted her falsies at one of the cops – probably that tool Willets – and he'd let slip about Cassie having found the body. Was Bethany the figure she'd glimpsed on the bridge that time? Might she even have been the intruder who'd left a citrusy scent in the cabin?

'Yep, they did,' said Cassie, keeping her voice unconcerned. 'They wanted to know if I'd seen or heard anything.'

'And you hadn't?'

'Uh-uh . . . So what is it that makes you think they suspect you?'

'I knew he was selling steroids at his gym but I told the cops I had nothing to do with it.' Sounding vehement. A pause before she added, 'I think he got in too deep, pissed off some drug gang and got himself killed. But I suppose I'm an easier target. You hear of innocent people going down for stuff all the time, don't you?'

Thinking of the seventeen years Callum spent inside for something he didn't do, Cassie couldn't disagree. But at the same time she wasn't convinced that Bethany was an entirely innocent person.

FLYTE

When Flyte got back to the office, she asked Willets about Bethany Locke's disappearing act but he was dismissive. 'She's probably gone to Southend on some hen do,' he said.

But then he'd never been able to accept the idea that a woman could have killed Sean and hidden his body. Flyte wasn't so sure: Bethany could be lying about her involvement in the steroids dealing, and she had motive as the betrayed fiancée. From their first encounter, Flyte had her down as a hard case, someone who might count among her social circle the sort of person who could disappear an inconvenient corpse.

Back at her desk, she kept reopening the image of Luke's note, puzzling over his gnomic scribble, which resembled a thorny equation from a school chemistry lesson.

When Seb returned from Luke's flat, he went straight to Willets' desk and she saw him handing over an evidence bag containing the Moleskine notebook from the freezer. He was trying to look nonchalant, which made her feel guilty for putting him in a position where he had to fib to Willets.

She was too far away to hear what they were saying but it was obvious Willets was questioning Seb, seeming taken aback at how thoroughly he'd searched the place. But after a brief exchange, Willets set the bag aside and carried on tapping at his

241

keyboard. Catching Seb's eye as he walked back to his desk, she mouthed, 'Sorry!' Getting an awkward grin in return.

A few minutes later, Willets shook the notebook out of the bag and used a pen to turn the pages. When he reached what she would bet was the final note with its cryptic abbreviations he seemed to become very still, before casting a would-be casual glance around the office. Luckily, she was half hidden behind her screen. Maybe it was just her paranoia but something about his body language set her nerves jangling.

Where had Bethany Locke got to? Her disappearance might not necessarily be sinister but Flyte remained convinced that she was withholding information about Sean's death.

She pulled up the transcript of her interview and started to read through it, pausing at the point where Bethany mentioned the incriminating message she'd seen on Sean's phone, and Willets' supplementary question.

What was her name? he'd asked.

And Bethany's reply: *Who?*

It had been the obvious follow-up but Flyte remembered Bethany looking totally blank for a moment before saying: *Oh . . . Zara, I think.* As if she'd said the first name that came into her head.

Why would she do that?

She reread Willets' question. *What was her name?*

Her name. Was that what had thrown Bethany? Because the question should have been *his* name? *Zara* pulled out of the air because the real name had been *Zeke*.

Had Cassie Raven's hunch about Sean and Zeke been right after all?

242

Going over to Willets' desk, she said, 'Bethany's still not answering so I'm going to drop in on Ezekiel Drew, the security guard who went to Sean Kavanagh's gym?'

Willets squinted up at her, looking preoccupied. 'I thought you said that was a dead end, the guy didn't even know Kavanagh's first name?'

'True. But he did buy steroids off him a couple of times so I want to push him on who else was buying, whether the staff knew, etcetera.' Which was true – if they really had been lovers Zeke would likely know more about Sean's business than he'd been letting on.

Willets turned back to his screen with a shrug. 'Knock yourself out. I've got a Zoom with the NCA about steroid gangs.'

Zeke's phone kept going to voicemail and he wasn't replying to texts, but she remembered Luke Lawless mentioning that he worked at a wine and spirit warehouse, and after a bit of googling she found the only place that seemed to fit the bill. It was called Drinkzone, and it was five minutes' walk from the cafe where they'd met previously.

It was nearly 5 p.m. by the time she'd found the place. Praying he was on duty today she texted him: *I'm outside your warehouse. Shall I come in or would you rather meet me out here?*

That got his attention. Less than ten minutes later, she saw him crossing the car park towards her.

As he drew near, she said, 'Sorry to turn up unannounced but I have left you a ton of messages.' Trying not to sound accusatory.

'Yeah, sorry, I've had a lot going on.'

She had to stop herself staring at his face.

Around his eye socket and reaching halfway down his cheek the skin was purple. Bruising that looked to be a couple of days old.

It was two days since Luke Lawless had been murdered.

He took her around the corner where there was a tiny park with a few benches.

'I've come across something on the Sean Kavanagh investigation that I wanted to run past you, see if it rings any bells?'

'OK,' he said, sounding guarded.

She showed him a screenshot of Luke's final note, with its jumble of abbreviations.

'Anything?' she asked, eyeing his face. 'Abney could be the guy who imported the steroids? Do you recall anyone of that name down the gym? Staff member?'

Gazing down at the image Zeke touched his bruised eye, seemingly unconsciously. He shook his head, but she could see the note meant something to him.

'Zeke, it could help us find out who killed Sean.'

He met her gaze properly for the first time – his eyes troubled. 'Are you saying that this has something to do with his murder?'

'It's possible.'

After giving her back the phone, he stared down at his hands for a long moment. 'Abney isn't a person, it's a place. Abney Park Cemetery in Stoke Newington. It's a cruising spot, or at least it used to be.'

Flyte kept her expression neutral. 'Go on.'

'Shane – I mean Sean – told me he used to hang out there, said there was a lot of guaranteed action in and around a loo block.'

She left a pause. 'I have to ask, how long had you two been lovers?'

He blew out a long breath. 'Six months or so? I thought we might get serious, you know. But then one day he just didn't

244

turn up to the gym. His phone was turned off. I knew by then that he was a Fed but he never said where he worked. Anyway, it's not like I'm gonna stroll into the cop shop and start asking for him, am I?' Having taken the biggest step – of admitting to the relationship – he seemed keen to talk.

'Did his fiancée, Bethany, know . . . about you two?'

'Yeah, he told me she saw a text message I sent. They had a big row and he called off the wedding. This happened just before he went missing so when he did his vanishing act I thought maybe he'd got back with her and couldn't handle telling me.' He opened his hands. 'Not that I could complain, being as I was married . . . Then eight years later I see his pic staring at me online.'

'That must've been awful for you.' She paused. 'Can I ask what happened to your face?'

He touched his eye as though he'd forgotten about it. 'My wife thumped me.'

'She found out that you're gay?'

He tipped his head. She had no doubt he was telling the truth.

'Oh, Zeke, I am sorry. How did she—?'

'I told her.' A steely note entering his voice. 'Discovering that Sean was dead, it set me thinking. Nobody really knew who he was. You know he never even told me his real name?' He shook his head slowly. 'But then I was the same – living a big fat lie. Anyway I couldn't go on cheating on my wife. It ain't right.'

It had often struck Flyte, when some long-married male public figure came out and everybody cheered his bravery, that barely anybody acknowledged how devastating such news must be for his wife and family.

'Do you think Sean ever considered coming out at work?'

Zeke looked at her as if she'd said something ridiculous. 'He said if the other cops knew he fucked guys his life wouldn't be worth living.'

Flyte recalled the homophobic 'banter' she'd heard over the years, the way male cops used 'gay' as an insult meaning laughable or weak, the conflation of paedophilia with homosexuality . . .

Zeke shook his head. 'He said that the day someone found out was the day he'd have to pack it in. Not even because of the grief he'd get, but because it would make him an outsider on his own team.'

Having felt like an outsider all her life, Flyte experienced a surge of fellow feeling for Sean, the double life he'd led, the string of girlfriends – the reputation he'd spent so much effort cultivating.

She made a sympathetic noise, stuck for something to say that wouldn't sound over-personal or patronising. In the end she just said, 'Thank you for your help, Zeke, I truly hope everything works out for you.'

So Cassie Raven's intuition about Sean and Zeke had been spot on – *damn and blast her* – thought Flyte as she headed back to the nick.

But Zeke's revelation raised more questions than it answered. So Abney Park and Hampstead Heath, where Luke's body had been found, were both gay cruising spots. Were Luke and Sean murdered by the same person? Could the motive be entangled with Sean's secret life as a gay man? But then she didn't believe Luke had been gay, even if his killer wanted the police to think he was. The condom found at the scene had been unused – a piece of set dressing. So was it all a smokescreen? Was a steroid-smuggling operation still the real reason behind both killings?

Then there was Bethany, who had lied to them about the nature of Sean's infidelity. Why would she do that? Thinking of Zeke's black eye, she pictured Bethany's likely reaction to Sean revealing he'd been unfaithful to her with men. Had she inflicted the blow that killed him? Or bided her time and hired someone else to do her dirty work?

Chapter Thirty

Cassie had gone to bed early, before 11 p.m. She wasn't even working the next day but the session at the shrink had left her feeling wrung out.

As she dropped off she started dreaming that Sean's body was washing up against the hull, his skull once again gently rapping the boards.

Knock. Knock-knock.

Then suddenly the volume increased. Realising it came from the towpath side, she sat up, reaching for the boat hook she'd started keeping next to her bed.

Blinking, she saw a face at the porthole through the gap in the drapes.

Bethany Locke.

As she stepped into the cabin along with a gust of cold night air, words poured out of her. 'I'm really sorry. I didn't know where else to come. I don't have anyone else to talk to.'

'Hey, don't worry. Here, sit down. Vodka?' Knowing that Bethany must have followed her from work at some point to find out where she lived, Cassie propped the boat hook within easy reach. Sometimes women were the ones to fear; she had the scars to prove it.

After pouring them each a large shot, Cassie sat down opposite her guest on the bench seat and waited, an encouraging but neutral look on her face.

Bethany downed her iced vodka in one – not her first drink of the evening going by her unfocused look and bloodshot eyes. 'I don't know what to do. I think I'm in really big trouble.'

'About Sean?'

A nod. 'I really did love him, you know. He was so sweet. My previous boyfriends had all been so . . . full of themselves, you know?' She pulled her hair back off her forehead to show Cassie a silvery scar. 'The previous one gave me this, banged my head against a kitchen cupboard for "talking back". . . Sean wasn't like anyone I'd been with. Right from the start I thought, this one's a keeper.'

She looked at Cassie, her eyes intelligent through the alcohol haze. 'He left me, but it wasn't for some other woman. He was . . . having sex with men.'

'Oh. Did you ever suspect?' asked Cassie gently.

'No. Yes.' She shook her head. 'I think deep down, maybe I did? All the chummy chats with waiters and barmen, the lingering look when we passed a hot guy in the street. I always closed my eyes to it cos I loved him so much. When he told me he was . . . gay, I was beyond furious. I could've killed him right there and then. Other women would be bad enough, but men?' She tugged at her hair. 'Can you think of anything more humiliating?'

Cassie made a sympathetic face, but she was thinking that in Bethany's place she'd probably find it *less* humiliating – Sean wasn't choosing a 'better version' of her by having sex with men. *Apples and oranges.*

'Why come to me?' she asked gently, topping up their glasses. 'Why not talk to the cops?' Was she about to hear a murder confession? Albeit hearsay and inadmissible in court, as Bethany probably knew.

'I don't like that Flyte woman.' Bethany's lips pruned, her face hardening. 'I could tell from the off she was looking down her nose at me. Thinking, *how could someone like* you *afford a flat in the Barbican?*'

'And could you? Afford it?' The lack of class divide between them allowing her to ask.

Bethany put both hands flat on the table. 'Look, I'll tell you cos I trust you and right now I need some advice.' Cassie noticed that the polish on two of her perfect nails was chipped. 'When Sean left we'd already exchanged on the flat and put down ten per cent but we hadn't completed. I had the proceeds from my previous place plus some money an aunt left me, but he was supposed to put in the rest. Without it, I faced losing the flat. Anyway, after we split I kept trying to call him but his phone was turned off. Then I saw on Facebook that he'd emigrated to Canada, so I messaged him to say I needed that money . . .' Lifting her chin, she sent Cassie a defiant look. 'I told him straight: if he didn't help me out I'd tell the cops that the money in his bank account came from dealing steroids.'

Cassie hoped she never had cause to upset Bethany Locke.

'What did he say?'

'He wrote straight back, saying it was a lifelong dream moving to Canada blah, blah – although he'd never mentioned it to me. He said he felt bad about leaving me in the shit over the flat purchase and that he was transferring some money to me. It would be his way of saying sorry.'

'How much did he send?' asked Cassie.

'A hundred and fifty grand.'

'Wow. That's a lot of sorry.'

'I know. He said it would come from a Canadian account that wasn't in his name but not to worry about it.' Looking at Cassie for her reaction. 'The money came the next day.'

'And you guessed it wasn't from him?'

'I knew it wasn't from him.'

'How come?'

'Because when I checked in the hiding place where we kept important documents, his passport was still there.'

Chapter Thirty-One

Bethany said that barely a week had elapsed between Sean leaving and the Facebook message, supposedly from Canada, promising to send cash. Not enough time to get a new passport.

'Anyway, I messaged back to thank him for the cash and said I'd pay him back some day.'

'But by now you knew it wasn't really Sean you were talking to,' said Cassie.

'The message didn't sound like him: the spelling was far too good.' Bethany pulled an awkward shrug. 'I'm not stupid. Even if he was making big money off dealing steroids, who hands over £150k just like that?'

'True. What did you think had happened to him?'

'I thought that he was dead.' She picked a fragment of chipped polish off a nail.

'So who did you think sent the cash?'

'It's obvious, isn't it? The people who killed him. My guess would be whoever he was buying the steroids from. They didn't want me going to the cops and £150k probably wasn't a big deal to them if it meant me keeping my mouth shut.'

Cassie thought that sounded feasible. 'And you never told anyone this, until now? His passport sitting there, the cash arriving from Canada . . . ?'

Bethany folded her arms. 'Look, I've had a difficult life. My mother put me into care when I was six and I was brought up in a string of foster homes. I won't give you the whole sob story but I've had to make my own luck in life and I've done pretty well for myself. Why should I lose that flat just because he got himself in trouble? It wouldn't have made no difference if I did tell the cops – they'd have taken the money and probably still not found his killers.'

Bethany's self-absolution sounded like something she'd honed and polished over the years.

'Do you remember the name of the account the cash came from?' asked Cassie.

She nodded. 'It was N. Toussaint. Ms N. Toussaint.'

Cassie's eyebrows shot up. 'A woman?'

'Yeah, but the account was probably opened with a stolen ID.'

Despite her steady vodka intake, Bethany appeared to have sobered up during their exchange. Or maybe it was the act of confession that had steadied her. Did she have a conscience after all?

'You said you wanted my advice,' Cassie reminded her.

Bethany met her gaze. 'If it was you . . . would you tell them? The cops, I mean?'

Cassie pulled an awkward affirmative shrug. 'Yes, I would. Sooner or later, they're going to access your bank statements and work it out for themselves. If you take the lead it might persuade them that you had nothing to do with Sean's death.'

Finding it hard to decipher the expression on Bethany's face a thought popped into Cassie's head.

Whether that's true or not is another matter.

FLYTE

The following morning, Flyte got in early, as did Dean Willets, but after an hour he still hadn't said a word about Luke's notebook – not to her anyway. Seeing Seb head for the kitchen she left it a few moments before following him out.

'Want one?' he asked, dropping a tea bag into his mug, which bore the legend '*I'd rather be playing golf*'.

An impatient headshake. 'Did Willets say anything to you about the notebook hidden in Luke's freezer?'

'No, nothing. Why? It wasn't exactly a smoking gun, was it?' He looked at her admiringly. 'You're looking particularly beautiful today, you know.' He put his hand on her waist but she shook it off.

'Don't,' she hissed, nodding at the door. 'Do you remember the final note in Luke's notebook?'

Seb shrugged and reached into the cupboard for the biscuit tin. 'It was gibberish, wasn't it?'

Flyte had read and reread Luke's hieroglyphic note a hundred times since yesterday but it was only on waking up that morning that something had occurred to her.

Sitting on the edge of her bed in her satin pyjamas, she had read the note again, and felt a smile tugging at her lips like it did when she completed *The Times* Sudoku – 'Fiendish' version.

SK – 'zero' PD!! AO=NDW. Abney. Caution?

It wasn't a 'zero' in front of PD: it was a capital O. OPD.

Now, moving to the kitchen door she pushed it closed with a soft click. Lowering her voice to a murmur, she said, 'I've worked out part of it. I think Luke discovered that Sean Kavanagh had been caught cottaging in a place called Abney Park, a big Victorian cemetery in Stoke Newington. This was about a year before he was murdered. He was querying whether he'd got a caution for OPD.'

OPD was the acronym for 'Outraging Public Decency' – the splendidly Edwardian-sounding offence of participating in a public sex act where passers-by might see you. Flyte was annoyed with herself for not deciphering it earlier but until Zeke had come clean about he and Sean being lovers she'd been totally focused on the steroids dealing. The only consolation was that Seb hadn't spotted it either.

'Seriously?' Seb's face grew a frown. 'Even if he was let off with a caution it's an indictable offence.'

'Which for a police officer would have meant instant dismissal. I know.'

'So what, you're saying that Kavanagh mounted a cover-up? How? You can't alter the computer record.' Seb pulled a face. 'Sounds to me like this reporter was a conspiracy theorist. Hiding his notebook in the freezer isn't exactly normal, is it?' He stirred milk into his tea. 'Show me the note again?'

Pulling up the image, she handed him her phone.

'What is it?' she asked, seeing a flicker cross his face.

'Nothing. Still looks like gibberish to me.' He picked up his mug. 'Anyway, some of us have work to do. You want to grab a drink later?'

'Sure.' Feeling deflated by his response, she didn't press the theory that Sean and Luke's murders could be linked. Given that it was the last note Luke had taken, it seemed likely that whoever he had arranged to meet on Hampstead Heath the night of his murder was somebody he believed could tell him more. Which surely pointed to Luke being killed because he was investigating Sean's murder.

She had just retrieved her Tupperware box of lemon segments from the fridge to make her own tea (she didn't trust anybody – not even Seb – to make it to her specifications) when she got a call from Cassie Raven.

'I got a surprise visitor last night,' she said, before relaying what Bethany Locke had told her. When she reached the part about the £150,000 that Locke had admitted receiving from a mysterious Canadian bank account after Sean's disappearance, Flyte had to stifle a gasp.

'Do you think she's telling the truth? That she really has no idea who sent the cash?'

Cassie hesitated. 'I honestly couldn't tell you.'

After a pause, Cassie added in a casual tone 'In case it's relevant, she also said that Sean was being unfaithful to her with other men. I think she found that aspect of his infidelity really hard to take.'

'Yes, I know. You were right about that,' said Flyte stiffly. 'Anyway, thanks for this – leave it with me.'

Her cooled tea left undrunk, Flyte marched over to Willets' desk. He was on the phone but she ignored his dismissing headshake and stood there until he hung up. 'I hope this is good,' he said.

'Oh, it's pretty good,' she said with sarcastic false modesty before bringing him up to speed. 'Locke agreed to let Cassie pass the info onto us,' Flyte told him. 'She claims it's to "show that she's innocent and willing to help". It could all be smoke and mirrors, of course.'

'Didn't I say all along this was about the steroids?' said Willets, lounging back in his chair. 'That kind of money? It's got to point to a smuggling operation.'

Flyte made a non-committal sound. Having been stung by Seb's 'so what?' response to her interpretation of Luke's note she wasn't going to risk a slap-down from Willets. He sent her a suspicious look. 'Why didn't Locke come to you directly? Why use the mortuary girl as intermediary?'

Flyte shrugged. 'She lied to us, and now she's scared.' She wasn't about to pass on what Cassie had said, that Locke supposedly thought she was snooty or some such nonsense.

She handed him the note she'd taken. 'This is where the money came from. The payment reference was in Sean Kavanagh's name but the account wasn't. Probably opened using a fake ID.'

The note said 'First Vancouver Bank; Ms N. Toussaint', followed by the account number and sort code.

As Willets frowned down at it, he seemed to become very still.

'Dean? Does it mean anything to you?'

'Not a thing.' He shook his head. 'Leave it with me,' he said, turning back to his screen. 'I'll get onto the Vancouver bank when they wake up over there.'

Chapter Thirty-Two

It was Cassie's day off and that afternoon she sat in the cabin drinking tea and stroking Macavity who was stretched out beside her on the bench seat like a discarded black fur stole. She couldn't stop thinking about her recent exchanges with Flyte, which had been at best businesslike; at worst, chilly since Cassie had tried to persuade her that Sean and Zeke had been lovers. Regardless of the fact she'd been right, she knew that she'd overstepped the mark. Remembering her insinuation that Flyte, like Sean, was a cop in the closet made her cringe. She should have apologised right there and then, and now it felt too late, too *loaded*.

Feeling the boat rock, she turned to see her grandmother climbing on board.

'Babcia. This is a nice surprise.'

'Since you couldn't come to dinner tonight I thought I'd drop by on my way home from Sainsbury's.'

Guiltily aware that she'd been ducking dinner with her dad, she made some fresh tea – with lemon, the Polish way – while Weronika took something out of a carrier bag. 'I got you some twaróg ice creams from the Polish shop – you used to love these when you were little.'

'Aww, Babcia, that's so kind.' She remembered adoring these bars of chocolate-covered ice creams. They looked like a small version of the standard choc ice but being made from sweetened curd cheese they were far less sickly.

Before Cassie could stop her, Babcia had opened the door to the freezer compartment.

To her credit, Babcia didn't flinch at the sight of a deep-frozen magpie, simply picking up the stiffened corpse in its clear plastic shroud and putting it on the side before stowing the ice creams. Closing the fridge door, she regarded it with a sad smile. 'It is beautiful. Just like that one you brought home the first time. You must have been four, just after your mama passed. God rest her soul,' crossing herself.

Without thinking, Cassie found herself repeating the words in a murmur.

Her grandmother met her eyes. 'Why don't we give this little birdie a burial at sea? Hmm? Like we did with your very first one.'

During the 'animal undertaker' phase of Cassie's childhood it had been the only way she could be persuaded to part with her decomposing charges; she and her grandmother would launch them with some ceremony in the canal, sometimes in a shoebox that passed for a Viking-style boat, the bodies surrounded by fresh or dried flowers rather than pyrotechnics.

'OK,' said Cassie, finding the idea oddly appealing. 'No coffin though. The last thing the canal needs is more junk.'

A few minutes later, they stood twenty yards upstream where the towpath dipped briefly closer to the surface of the water. Cassie opened the ziplock bag and coaxed the magpie head first into the water, its blue plumage turning briefly green then purple as it caught the final rays of the sun breaking through strands of pink cloud. Behind her, she heard Babcia start to sing, in a surprisingly strong voice.

'*Speed bonny boat, like a bird on the wing . . .*'

It was a song Cassie had learned to play on her Dziadek's piano during a brief early teenage enthusiasm – before she'd discovered boys and girls, weed, and goth bands.

They stood watching as he floated out, beak up, one wing still pointing up at the sky like an Old Testament prophet in a painting. He travelled lazily across the gilded water drifting only slightly downstream with the current. Near the middle of the canal, he finally rolled over and sank, his cocked wing the last thing to disappear from view.

Her grandmother said, '*Pożegnanie, ptaszku,*' – farewell, little bird – and they both crossed themselves.

Walking back to the boat, Cassie felt lighter than she had for a long time.

Her grandmother took her hand and said, 'Come to dinner with your father soon? He's looking much better now. Good as new.'

Picturing his crooked smile made her chest hurt, and she realised she'd been missing him.

'Yes, all right.'

She glanced back at the spot where the magpie had sunk, and a dimly remembered religious phrase popped into her head from nowhere.

Let the dead bury the dead.

FLYTE

Willets had spent the rest of the day popping in and out of the office, and since he always took his phone with him, he evidently didn't want his calls to be overheard. Bang on the dot of five he had put on his jacket and slipped out, without the usual banter-strewn farewells to his acolytes. Whatever was bugging him, Flyte was convinced it had something to do with the Canadian account that Bethany Locke's hush money had been sent from. It was only just 9 a.m. in Vancouver when the bank offices opened so if he was calling them he wanted that conversation kept private, too.

Half an hour later, she and Seb met up in a trendy bar overlooking a piazza behind King's Cross station, an area that had been transformed from one of the worst parts of London – awash with down-and-outs, prostitutes – male and female – and junkies – into a buzzy leisure hub. Cassie Raven would no doubt bemoan its loss of 'character' but Flyte found the spotlessly clean piazza soothing after the ingrained grime and edginess of Camden Town.

She went straight in for the kill. 'Look, Seb, why did Dean seem to freak out when he read the note in Luke's book?'

'Did he?' Seb frowned into his craft ale. 'No idea.'

'Don't give me that. Once I told you that the note was to do with a public sex offence you spotted something, I could tell.' Her gaze scoping his face like a laser scanner.

261

'Look, it's probably nothing.' He looked uncomfortable.

'Go on.'

'Show me the note again.' He pushed his pint aside, and taking her phone, angled it so they could both view the image.

'AO=NDW,' he said, looking at her.

A headshake. 'I don't get it.'

'AO could stand for Arresting Officer.'

'Really? It's not an abbreviation anyone in the Job would use.'

'No, but it could've been the reporter's own shorthand.'

'And the NDW?'

Seb bit his lip. 'The N could stand for Nigel.'

'Meaning?'

He blew out a breath. 'Dean's first name is actually Nigel. He prefers to use his middle name, not surprisingly. Nigel Dean Willets. NDW.'

'For fu—' She managed to stop the rest of the profanity slipping out. 'Are you saying it was Willets who arrested Sean Kavanagh in Abney Park?'

'I don't know! I shouldn't have said anything. Who's to say this reporter was right? He sounds like a bit of a nutter.'

'Does Hackney nick cover Abney Park, i.e. Stoke Newington?' she asked.

Seeing Seb nod, she cursed her ignorance. Any London-raised Met officer would have known that.

'You told me that when Willets was a uniform at Hackney he ran a sweepstake to see who could nick the most gay men!' She felt excitement warming her cheeks. 'Luke must have found out it was Willets who collared Sean and contacted him. If it was Willets whom he went to meet on the heath . . .'

'Whoa, Phyllida. Hold on a sec.' Seb made a shushing motion with his hand, scanning the nearby tables. 'You're not seriously accusing a fellow officer of murder.'

She replayed Willets' handling of the Sean Kavanagh case: how he'd initially dismissed it as just another drunk who'd fallen in the canal, the way he'd focused on the steroids angle to the exclusion of everything else, and how keen he seemed to pin Luke's death on the Hugger Mugger.

'If he has nothing to hide then why wouldn't he mention knowing Sean? He saw his picture enough times.'

'If he did arrest him – *if* – it was nine years ago!' said Seb. 'He must've nicked hundreds of people since then. I'm sure there's some other explanation.' But he was looking uncomfortable. Picking up the menu, he said, 'Shall we order some food?'

Flyte needed to be alone, to process things. Reaching for her bag she said, 'I've got to go.'

'Aren't we having dinner?'

She kissed him on the top of the head. 'Sorry. Maybe tomorrow?'

As she left she heard him say, 'Phyllida! Don't do anything stupid.'

Chapter Thirty-Three

When Cassie set down Macavity's evening meal, he seemed more interested in her hand than the food, and she realised he must still be able to smell *eau de dead magpie*.

Giving her hands a proper wash at the sink, she looked out across the canal. With no boat traffic it was as calm as an infinity pool and the alchemy of a London dusk had turned the surface silver. She pictured the way the magpie had floated out, drifting only slightly downstream, barely troubled by the current.

She jumped down onto the towpath and went next door to Gaz's boat. He was swabbing the aft-deck – aka mopping the bit to the rear of the cockpit.

'Silly question, but I assume rainfall affects the current, right?'

Gaz sent her the pitying look of a boating veteran to a newbie. 'Yeah. It's not strong at the best of times but when it's been dry for this long it's almost non-existent.'

'And when did you say it rained last?'

He squinted up at the darkening sky, his satchel face creasing further. 'Don't recall off the top of my head. I'll go and get the log.'

He went below deck, his gait bow-legged to accommodate any sudden movement of the boat, and returned with a pink and purple diary.

'Is that, um . . . My Little Pony?' asked Cassie, trying not to smile.

'Yeah,' said Gaz with a chuckle. 'I got the brightest colour I could, makes it easy to find.' He sent her a look. 'You wait till you get old, you'll find out.' He leafed back through the pages, murmuring to himself. 'Ah, here you go. Second of September – storm. Three and a half inches of rain. Sorry, I'm still on the old money.'

'And you're sure that was the last time it rained?'

Gaz sent her a steely look. 'I might be an old git but I never miss a day recording the weather.' He turned the diary around so she could see it and turned the pages: 'See? *sunny & dry . . . overcast & dry . . . drizzle overnight . . . broken sun & dry . . . a light shower two days ago . . .*'

Counting backwards, Cassie calculated that when Sean had washed up against her boat it hadn't rained for ten days. She strained to remember what Willets had said when she'd asked where the body went in. 'Way upstream,' he'd said, much closer to the lock.

'So if a body washed up at my boat after ten days of dry weather, how far would you say it would've travelled to fetch up here?'

'Ahh, we're talking about your floater.' He looked upstream. 'With the current this sluggish? No distance at all really. Maybe thirty, forty metres?'

She pointed diagonally across the canal towards the hulking profile of the derelict estate. 'Like round about there?'

Following her gaze, he nodded. 'Yeah, possibly. I'm no expert but the lock-keeper's a mate. I'll give him a call.'

As he went below deck, Cassie looked out over the water, picturing herself pulling Sean's body through the water, and how still it had been.

At this hour – gone seven – office workers had gone home but it was too early for clubbers, making it as silent as the inner city could ever get. Which meant that the scoot of a stone underfoot followed by a man's muttered curse travelled clearly across the water. Squinting across the canal towards its source, she saw something odd: a man in a suit making his way down the unused section of towpath between the canal and the abandoned estate. That side of the canal was already in deep shadow, but from his halting progress it looked like he was having to pick his way through undergrowth. Her gaze swivelled to where the path dead-ended in a high mesh barrier.

Where the fuck was he going?

Reaching the dead end he turned to face the fence, his back to her. He appeared to fiddle with something at waist height and then he was through, pulling a section of fence closed behind him. As he turned, a sliver of his face was lit by the orange security lights just for a moment. It was enough, together with his silhouette and his walk, for her to recognise him.

FLYTE

On the way back to Camden, Flyte passed Old St Pancras, the medieval church where Poppy's naming ceremony would be held in two days' time. Seeing that the lights were on, she tried the ancient oak door and found it unlocked. As she went in, a couple of young women came out, one of them carrying a cello case. Presumably an early evening rehearsal.

Taking the steps down into the cool and hush was like lowering herself into well water. Sitting in one of the empty pews she imagined the thousand-year-old stone walls enclosing and embracing her, unwinding her shoulders and spine muscles. Already she felt as though she could sense Poppy's presence here.

Flyte had only once visited the hospital memorial garden where her daughter's ashes had been scattered to the winds, mixed willy-nilly with those other babies. *Never again*. It had felt like a municipal space: anonymous and unloved, planted with the sort of low-maintenance shrubs you saw in supermarket car parks.

Her mind circled back to what she was going to do about Willets. Her every instinct rebelled against the idea of a police officer being capable of murder – two murders, if Sean and Luke really had been killed eight years apart by the same person. But if it was true that Willets had on another occasion caught

Sean Kavanagh committing a public decency offence and never mentioned it, he had some serious questions to answer.

Maybe Luke Lawless had got the wrong end of the stick and the whole thing really was about steroid dealing – with Bethany in it up to her neck. Perhaps Willets had caught Sean dealing and started taking backhanders to keep quiet? A year ago she would never have believed it, but given the recent deluge of police misconduct scandals – like the outflow from a broken sewer pipe – she no longer ruled anything out.

Those stories made her sick to her stomach, even more so because she knew the scumbags represented a minority among hard-working officers committed to making people's lives better, even if in somewhere like Camden that could seem like a Sisyphean task.

What to do, though? Confront Willets? He was hardly likely to confess, and if she was wrong it would make their current relationship look like a warm rapport. It was an unenviable position to be in, and one that could end with her having to leave Major Crimes for a new job. Traffic duties in deepest Essex, probably. The only person senior enough to discuss it with was DCI Steadman. He was still away at his conference, but she could get him on the phone and just lay it out to him in a matter-of-fact way? Then it was off her plate and onto his – or more likely the Directorate of Professional Standards.

And what if she was wrong? She'd already informed on Willets once, for something that had turned out to be no more than a minor transgression.

She had never felt so torn: if she did the right thing, she risked everything blowing up in her face. But if she let it slide, she could be covering up police involvement in a serious crime.

Hearing her phone chiming, she silenced the ring tone and stepped outside.

'What can I do for you?'

Feeling that familiar muddle of warmth and irritation at hearing Cassie's voice, saying, 'You might want to get down here.'

Chapter Thirty-Four

'Where's the fire?'

Cassie turned to see the tall and impossibly straight-backed figure of Flyte climbing on board, one elegant ankle briefly exposed as the hem of her trousers lifted. It was the first time she'd taken her eyes off the point diagonally opposite where the man had disappeared through the fence. She pointed across the canal. 'A guy just went into that derelict estate – there, where the towpath ends.'

Flyte squinted through the thickening darkness. 'I've been over there; the estate is all fenced off.' Her tone making it crystal clear that if she'd been called out on a wild goose chase she'd be pissed off.

'Well, my eyesight's pretty good and I'm telling you he went inside,' Cassie retorted. 'The only people I've seen over there are workers, and that was in the daytime. This guy was wearing a suit for Christ's sake.'

'You're not telling me you've dragged me out here to report a trespasser?' huffed Flyte, folding her arms.

Struggling to keeping her temper in check, Cassie realised she'd need to do more to convince her. 'Listen, that estate has been uninhabited for months. I think it could be where Sean's killer dumped him in the canal.'

Flyte perched herself cautiously on deck next to Cassie, looking every inch the landlubber in her office-girl suit, and peered across the canal. 'It's only what, thirty, forty metres upstream of here? Apparently the current would have carried the body one or two *hundred* metres or more.'

'Only when there's been heavy rainfall!' said Cassie, shaking her head. Reaching for Gaz's notebook, she ignored Flyte's raised eyebrow at its lurid My Little Pony cover. 'Look, the last rainfall worth talking about was at the start of September.' Flipping through the pages, she pointed out the entries with a black-painted nail. 'Dry . . . drizzle . . . dry . . . dry . . . dry. See? Ten days without rain right up to when I found the body. When there's no serious rainfall the canal has barely any current beyond what's caused by lock gates opening and boats going to and fro.'

'Says who?'

Cassie sent her a hard stare. 'The lock-keeper.'

'Really?'

'Really. My neighbour knows him. He said that after a long dry spell a body would only drift a short distance.'

'How short?'

'"A stone's throw",' he said.' Bending her head towards Flyte's, she extended her arm upstream and sketched a line from the estate opposite, a little way upstream, across the canal, ending at the bows of her boat. The scent of warm skin and some cologne with the undernote of something bracing like rosemary rose from Flyte's neck. Feeling suddenly awkward, Cassie straightened.

Two pink spots had appeared in Flyte's creamy cheeks. She cleared her throat before saying, 'Describe this man you saw over there.'

271

'I can do better than that,' said Cassie.

'What do you mean?' Her tone suddenly steely.

'I think it was that tosser who came to interview me about finding Sean.'

Flyte stared at her. 'Dean Willets?! Are you sure?' she asked in a harsh whisper.

Her reaction took Cassie aback. 'Pretty sure, yeah. So what's the big deal? I assumed he was just checking out the estate. I wanted to let you know in case he was keeping you in the dark – which he obviously was.'

Flyte ignored her question, asking, 'What's the quickest way to get across the canal?'

'Front crawl?' said Cassie, but Flyte didn't crack a smile. 'You have to go up to the road bridge and back down again the other side. Maybe fifteen minutes if you go at a lick?'

Flyte jumped down onto the towpath with surprising athleticism, leaving Cassie to shout foolishly at her departing back, 'Are you going to tell me what the fuck is going on?'

FLYTE

The sky was dark and the night air cooling fast but within five minutes Flyte's shirt clung wetly to her chest and back as she half jogged, half ran west towards the road bridge.

Her mind tracked back to the first case conference on Sean's murder, replaying the discussion about why, having stored the body for eight years, the killer had suddenly decided to dump it. She'd suggested then that perhaps he or she had been moving house. If the body had been hidden in a flat on the estate then the upcoming demolition would have had the same effect.

After crossing the road bridge, she had to pause, bending to rest her hands on her thighs, to get her breath back.

Of course, Willets might just be over there having worked out it was a possible dumping spot, but she wasn't so sure. If Luke Lawless had been on the right track, Willets had encountered Sean Kavanagh in Abney Park a year before his disappearance. Then there was his reaction to seeing his own initials – NDW – in Luke's notebook and his shifty behaviour ever since she'd handed him the details of the Vancouver bank account.

Above all, Willets was an unapologetic homophobe. If he really had arrested Sean in a gay cruising ground a year before his disappearance, he could have encountered him there again. Her train of thought always stopped at that point. Homophobia was one thing; a fellow detective committing murder was beyond the boundaries of her belief system.

After taking the stairs back down to the canal two at a time, she jogged along until she could see the orange haze over the estate shed by the security lights. On reaching the steel safety barrier that blocked the towpath, she found it was only secured to the fence on the right. Lifting it inwards, she was able to squeeze past it on the canal side, aware that any slip would send her into the dark water to her left.

The undergrowth beyond the barrier appeared to have been trampled, and recently. She rolled up the legs of her Jaeger trousers so they wouldn't get snagged and high-stepped carefully over the tangled brambles and stunted buddleias, squinting through the gloom.

Her left ankle sent up a flare of pain as it folded sideways beneath her.

Hell's bells! Bending to rub it, she saw the culprit: an old length of scaffold pole hidden in the undergrowth.

On reaching the dead end where the steel mesh fence turned to block the path, she aimed the torch on her phone to her right through the fence bordering the estate – and saw a passageway beyond. Cassie had been right: the estate did have direct access to the canal. Seeing that the section of fence hung loose, she played her torchlight down the join, and found a black plastic zip tie on the ground, its plastic edges cleanly severed. The demolition workers had done a slipshod job of securing it, leaving anyone armed with no more than a penknife easy access.

Pulling open the loose section like a door, she shone her phone torch down the passageway. It was narrow, hemmed in by eight-feet-high brick walls and her beam didn't reach the other

274

end. The sensible thing to do would be to call for assistance. But it just wasn't possible. She was off duty, with no plausible excuse to be hanging round a mothballed estate and if Willets was here it would be obvious she had been tailing him.

She wondered whether she should call Seb.

To say what exactly? 'If my body ends up floating in the canal tell them it was Willets . . .'?!

Chapter Thirty-Five

Cassie stayed on deck after Flyte left, so she could keep an eye on the estate opposite. Shivering, she zipped up her leather jacket and sparked up a Camel, prompting Macavity to throw her a look of outrage before jumping down to land on the catwalk with unnecessary force.

'Look, once this pack's gone, I'm giving up. OK?' she told him. As he walked away, the tip of his tail twitched once as if in sceptical disgust.

The nicotine helped her to think. She had called Flyte that evening to tell her Sean's body might only have travelled the short distance from the estate opposite to her boat, and to alert her to the movements of that shiny-suited creep Willets. Flyte had been the only person to show any interest when Sean had been just another anonymous floater rather than a murdered cop, and Cassie had always hated the idea that Willets might hoover up the praise for solving the case.

But Flyte's reaction had startled her. It was much more than the weary annoyance of a woman who'd been sidelined by a male colleague. Which set Cassie thinking. That time she'd detected a citrusy smell in the cabin of the boat and wondered if an intruder had been on board; and lately she'd thought it was Bethany, if anyone.

But it had only happened a couple of days before Willets paid her an official visit with that uniform in tow, to ask her what made her think that Sean's body had been frozen. Could he have been the intruder? He'd been sceptical about how she'd reached her conclusion. Had he been sniffing around to see if she was hiding any evidence? But if so, why go about it in such a high-risk way?

Making a decision, she hopped down to the towpath and went to Gaz's boat where the cabin lights glimmered around the edges of the drapes covering the portholes. When he came out into the cockpit, she said, 'You know the rough-sleeper guy who hangs around here, the cosmologist?'

'Copernicus?' Gaz scratched his stubbled chin. 'Yeah? I saw him today actually.'

'Whereabouts? Does he kip down round here?'

Gaz leaned over the side and pointed upstream along the towpath. 'He has a little den in the bushes by the scaffold yard, up there next to the bridge.'

Cassie was off up the towpath, throwing thanks over her shoulder at a bemused Gaz.

FLYTE

On the other side of the canal, Flyte was making her way down the darkened brick passageway from the canal into the estate. Her ankle was sending up a thump-thump of pain, and there was more rubbish underfoot which slowed her progress. Emerging from the passage, after her eyes had adjusted to the sinister tangerine glow of the security lights, she peered up at the estate. A sprawling seventies monstrosity about ten stories high, it stood on concrete stilts with one central stairway and lift shaft. Facing it, across a narrow roadway, was a row of lock-up garages stretching for some hundred metres, which would have been let to residents, for parking or to use as overflow storage.

She felt a rising sense of excitement. A chest freezer in a lock-up garage would be the perfect place to store a body for eight years without fear of discovery. Only when the estate had emptied of tenants and demolition loomed would its disposal have become urgent. She swung her beam back up the passageway; armed with a proper torch it would take less than two minutes from here to the waterfront, even dragging a body.

But which of the garages? There must be a couple of dozen and she couldn't see any light leaking from any of the doors up ahead.

Double-checking that her phone was on silent, Flyte started out cautiously down the line of garages, hugging the half-metre that was in shade and careful to minimise the tap of her heels on the concrete underfoot. The only sound here was the distant background hum of the city that never disappeared, even in the small hours. She realised with a pang that she missed the silence of the countryside, above all, missed being able to see the stars, hidden by the ever-present corona of light that hung over the city.

In between the concrete stanchions in the gloomy undercroft to her right, she made out a jagged silhouette of domestic waste left by the previous tenants. Then her eye snagged on something even deeper in the shadows. Something white and angular. Leaving the lee of the garages for a moment, she went closer to investigate.

It looked a lot like a chest freezer.

Chapter Thirty-Six

Cassie couldn't find Copernicus at the spot in the undergrowth Gaz had described, but then she heard a raised voice nearby that sounded familiar. She headed for its source and found him sat on a bench, one leg neatly crossed over the other.

'No, you listen,' he was saying in an accent unmistakably forged in the crucible of public school and Oxbridge. 'Dark matter is assuredly not a WIMP or an axion, or indeed any other kind of particle.' He jabbed a finger at his imagined opponent. 'It isn't even matter!' Leaning back, he nodded to himself triumphantly.

Then, lowering his voice, he replied to himself in an elaborately courteous tone, 'I'm afraid I must disagree – and I'm hardly alone in this – lightest supersymmetric particles are by far the most compelling candidate—'

Seeing Cassie, he fell suddenly silent, a wary look closing his face.

'Sorry to bother you,' she said, sitting down at the other end of the bench and offering him the open pack of fags. After a moment's hesitation, he reached out and took three, putting two in the breast pocket of his suit jacket, and accepted her proffered lighter to light the one between his lips. 'I live on a narrowboat five minutes' walk down there.'

'*Dreamcatcher*,' he said with a smile, as if remembering an old joke.

'Mmm. That's right,' she said, hoping Gaz was right about him being harmless. 'I know you sometimes hang out round that bit of the towpath and I was just wondering, have you ever seen anyone going onto my boat when I'm not home?'

'No, no, no, no,' he said, shaking his head, his eyes widening in alarm.

'You're not in any trouble,' she said, breaking eye contact and leaning back on the bench. 'It's just between you and me, I promise.' Telling herself that it wasn't really lying since no way would this guy ever make a witness in a court of law. She held out the pack of Camels. 'Here, would you like the rest of these?'

A look of calculation, so childlike it made her want to smile, came over his face. 'He gave me a ten-pound note,' he said pointedly, taking the pack anyway and disappearing it conjuror-style into the folds of his tweed greatcoat.

'Did he?' She fished in the inside pocket of her leather jacket, pulled out the folded twenty she kept there for emergencies and smoothed it out on her lap. 'Who was this then?'

'It was all perfectly above board,' he said in a haughty tone.

'Is that what he told you, when he realised you'd seen him?' Keeping her voice matter-of-fact, unexcited.

'I had good reason to believe he wasn't a common thief or vagabond,' he said, eyeing the twenty.

'Oh, yes? Why was that?'

'He was an officer of the law,' said Copernicus, plucking the twenty from her hand.

Squinting through the gloom at the white outline of the freezer in the recesses of the undercroft, Flyte navigated her way through piles of trash and old furniture. Wrinkling her nose at the smell of old urine – and worse – she pushed an old foam mattress out of the way with her foot. A lithe furry shape shot across her path. *Flaming focaccia!* Realising she'd gasped out loud in shock, she ducked behind an old wardrobe, listening out for any sign that somebody had heard her. Nothing.

What was she scared of? Did she seriously think Dean Willets murdered Sean Kavanagh? And Luke Lawless, too? *Of course not*, she told herself. But if Sean's body had been kept in one of the lock-ups then the real murderer could be close by.

Having kept vigil for a few moments without seeing or hearing any movement, she carried on towards her goal, scanning the floor with her phone torch to head off any further encounters with Camden wildlife.

The freezer was an old-school monster of the kind she recalled from the family garage when she was little: six feet long and more than three feet deep – large enough to hold three bodies, let alone one. Pointing her beam down on the litter-strewn floor and back towards the roadway outside, she thought she could make out an indistinct pathway through the detritus – as if someone had pushed the freezer here to hide it deeper in the undercroft and then attempted to cover their tracks.

Feeling breathless with excitement, she scrabbled in her pocket for a nitrile glove and wrapped it round the freezer handle. The lid wouldn't open but finally the rubber seals parted with a sticky *tock!* and a bad smell wafted out. She played her phone torch into the interior and leaned in as far as she could, one foot off the ground. It looked grubby but empty – except for some scraps of plastic packaging. She was struck by an illogical feeling of disappointment. What had she expected to find? Another body?

She heard a noise behind her. Before she could react, strong hands had gripped her by the knees and upended her into the freezer. Her nose and forehead crashed into the plastic side of the freezer, a hand pushing her legs in behind her. *Good job I'm not wearing a skirt*, she thought, absurdly. Before she had time to cry out the lid slammed shut, leaving her in the foul-smelling darkness.

Cassie jogged across the bridge towards the derelict estate, wishing she was wearing her Doc Martens instead of plimsolls. Having had her own run-ins with the police during her squatting days, she hadn't been surprised by the recent press stories about the behaviour of some male cops, but to find out that a cop had broken into her boat properly spooked her. It suggested someone with something serious to hide. Something that had to be tied up with Sean Kavanagh's murder.

Whatever it was, Flyte needed to know sharpish that one of her colleagues was not to be trusted.

Flyte had been left in a heap, face down on the floor of the freezer.

Scrabbling to get onto her knees, she tried to turn her body in order to reach the lid. There was barely any room to manoeuvre and her hands and feet couldn't get any purchase on the slippery plastic walls. Then she heard a metallic clunk echoing through the cabinet like the crack of doom. Somebody had put something good and heavy on the lid.

Twisting herself onto her back she bent her knees to set both feet on the underside of the lid and pushed. Nothing, not even a smidge of movement. Cocking an ear, she heard the sounds

283

of someone retreating through the rubbish-filled undercroft. Whoever had tipped her in here had gone – for now.

Fuck, fuck, fuck.

In some situations, only full-fat swearing would do.

She started shouting, hammering her fist on the inside of the lid. *Stupid.* As if her assailant would change his – or her – mind and let her out.

More likely, whoever it was would come back and finish her off. Immediately followed by another thought.

What if he never came back?

A musty, faintly meaty smell invaded her nostrils sending a chill slithering up her spine as she remembered that Sean's body had lain here for eight years. *Don't panic.* She'd had her phone in her hand when her attacker tipped her inside. Scrabbling on the floor, her fingers found its reassuring outline and she drew it towards her.

The sight of the lit screen and a single bar of signal lifted her spirits.

Huzzah!

Then the single bar disappeared.

Her forehead and right cheekbone had started to throb where they'd struck the side of the freezer. She had tried to manoeuvre herself into a sitting position but her head hit the underside of the lid, so she had to stay half bent, her neck muscles complaining at the stress position.

She concentrated on breathing in through her nose and out through her mouth to calm herself and viewed her situation logically. Her attacker might not come back and she remembered something else that lifted her spirits: Cassie had said she'd seen workmen on-site prepping the place for demolition. When they arrived, probably first thing the next day, she would shout her lungs out and they'd rescue her.

A memory elbowed its way to the surface of her thoughts. When she was little, no more than six or seven, her mother had caught her standing on a chair leaning over the open chest freezer, spooning ice cream straight into her mouth. The sting of a slap on the leg. 'You must never do that again, Phyllida! If you fell in and the lid closed you would suffocate.'

Freezers were airtight.

Chapter Thirty-Seven

Reaching the estate, Cassie used her phone torch to navigate the dead-end section of towpath, finding the rough track that recent feet had trodden through the undergrowth. Flyte would almost certainly be pissed off at Cassie tailing her while she was on police business, but fuck it. Since she wasn't answering her phone there was no other way to pass on Copernicus's revelation.

Emerging at the end of the passage, she stopped, checking out the row of garages, and the crumbling hulk of the abandoned estate looming over her. Feeling suddenly anxious, she realised it was the silence that was unnerving her. She was missing Camden's reassuring soundtrack of partygoers, music, the rumble of a bus, the shrill of a police siren.

She made her way down the line of garages, ear tuned to any sound. The place was pretty creepy, especially the shadowy area under the estate, piled high with dumped waste. It looked like rat city under there. Cassie shivered; she had a thing about rats. She squinted, half expecting to see Flyte's slender outline, picking her way fastidiously through the litter, the pale flash of her wheat-blonde hair.

Maybe she'd never even made it here, had gone home instead. Cassie pictured her eating an M&S ready meal and watching some cosy box set in her leisurewear. She smiled. *Freshly ironed leisurewear, obvs.*

Flyte's phone told her she'd already been trapped in here for around thirty minutes. As soon as the oxygen issue had occurred to her, she'd frantically calculated the dimensions of the freezer and how much air it held. Two metres long by a metre wide and maybe one and a half deep, at a guess. Minus whatever her own mass displaced. Flyte had routinely come top of her maths class at school but now she'd happily be innumerate. She had once read somewhere that an average human needed 150 cubic feet of oxygen-rich air a day, and by her calculation the freezer held less than 60.

That gave her ten, maybe eleven hours of oxygen. Her phone told her it was half past eight.

If she wasn't found by seven thirty tomorrow morning she would suffocate.

Poppy's face, radiating calm, came into her mind along with the hushed interior of the church where she would finally claim her name. *Poppy Flyte-Howard.* Matt's surname as well as hers, to give her a mum and a dad.

'Don't worry, darling,' Flyte murmured. 'Nothing is going to stop me getting out of here.'

There was no point wasting her oxygen shouting and banging. She just had to wait till she got a bar of signal back and use it – fast. If she wrote a text now wouldn't it send instantly when the signal returned? But whom to message? Seb? His flat was probably closest but something stopped her. Cassie? Probably drunk or stoned, or both, by now, and in any case only a civilian. She needed somebody senior, someone with the clout

287

to send manpower double-quick, to get her out of this plastic coffin and find the bastard who'd put her in it. She started to tap out a text to Steadman. Pressed 'send'. Got the little red exclamation mark and 'Message Undelivered'.

To save precious battery life she'd just have to wait and hope for signal.

Averting her eyes from the creepy-looking undercroft, Cassie carried cautiously on down the row of lock-ups, feeling a mixture of fear and excitement. With the canal so easily accessible she was convinced that Sean Kavanagh's body had been stored in a freezer that lay behind one of these doors . . . If it was still there, it would almost certainly hold traces of his DNA – and his killer's.

About a dozen garages down the row she halted, listening.

Yes! It was only a faint burble, but from the single voice and the pauses – it was somebody talking on the phone. *Flyte? Or Willets?*

It seemed to be coming from a lock-up just up ahead. On reaching the double doors, she saw a glimmer of light coming through the crack between them. Whoever had been speaking had fallen silent so she held her breath until the voice started up again. It was clearly male but he must be facing the other way because as much as she strained her ears she couldn't identify him.

So where the hell was Flyte?

She retraced her steps – grateful now for her rubber-soled plimsolls – and once she'd put some distance between herself and the lock-up, darted silently across the roadway. Then she stepped cautiously into the foul dumping ground amid the massive columns holding up the estate, trying to keeping her feet clear of anything that might be a rats' nest. Going behind one of the columns she tried Flyte's number again.

Flyte could have wept if she hadn't felt so furious and ... impotent.

A bar of signal had briefly appeared, allowing her to re-send her text to Steadman but it hadn't been read yet. He was probably still out of town at the conference, and was right now knocking back beers with his fellow officers in the hotel bar. A terrible thought occurred to her: what if he stumbled back to his room and went to bed without even checking his messages? She'd just started tapping out a text to Seb when her phone rang. It must have got flipped off silent mode when it fell into the freezer. Seeing Cassie's name she immediately hit the green button, only to hear the line go dead.

Fuck, fuck, fuck!

Moments after she tapped Flyte's number Cassie almost dropped the phone. The muffled but unmistakable sound of chiming bells – Flyte's ringtone – was coming from close by, apparently somewhere in the piles of rubbish. Hastily killing the call, she started picking her way through the rat minefield towards its source.

Flyte tried to ring Cassie back and was getting no reply, when she heard something. The sound of tentative footsteps coming closer. *Shit.* Her attacker was back. Maybe the original plan had been to leave her to suffocate, but it was less risky to finish the job for certain.

She bit her lip so hard the ferrous taste of blood welled on her tongue. Balled her hand round her phone – her only weapon. She would play dead and then smash it in his fucking face.

Then she heard a voice.

Cassie bent close to the top of the freezer and murmured, 'Phyllida ... Don't say a word, but if you're in there tap on the lid.'

Three rapid little taps.

Christ on a bike!

'OK. Give me a minute, there's a fridge on top, I need to work out how to get it off without making a noise.'

Ignoring the muffled yet vigorous response, Cassie planted both hands on the fridge on top of the freezer and gave it an experimental push. It wouldn't be that hard to shift off the freezer but if it fell into the old tellies, strollers and assorted crap on the ground the racket would be heard across the canal, never mind in the garages opposite. Squinting around in the gloom, her eye fell on something.

Dragging the mattress over to the freezer as soundlessly as possible took a couple of minutes – luckily it was light, filled with foam rather than metal springs. After positioning it to the rear of the freezer, she stood to one side, picturing the fridge's trajectory, before making adjustments. Then she went back to the front, and putting her shoulder to the fridge, started slowly scooting it across the freezer top, aware of every little scrape and squeak. Once it was poised at the edge, she took a breath and gave it a final shove. The fridge landed more or less squarely on the mattress with a not-too-loud *whump* but it didn't stop there: Cassie could only watch in horror as it continued to roll, a journey that would end with an ear-splitting crash as it met the litter-strewn concrete. The fridge hung on its leading edge for a split second of indecision before rocking back and forward again. Then it settled on the mattress.

Cassie was reaching for the handle when the lid flew open and Flyte's furious blood-streaked face emerged. She used her arms to lever herself out and scissored her long legs over the side, ignoring Cassie's proffered arm, before sending her a look of pure rage. 'What the *fuck* are you doing here?' in a hissed whisper.

'You're welcome,' said Cassie mildly.

But she had to admit this new incarnation of the uptight cop was a thrilling sight. Her wheat-blonde hair dishevelled, the bloodied face, and the fury in her ice-blue eyes put Cassie in mind of a Viking warrior. *A Valkyrie.*

Flyte dusted down her stained trouser suit – pointlessly, since the torn cuff and stains meant it would never see active service again. 'You haven't answered me,' she said.

Cassie gave her a tissue, nodding at her forehead. 'You need some TCP on that.'

'Fuck TCP,' she said crisply. 'I need to find who tipped me in *there*.' With a backward jab of her head.

Cassie blinked, trying to recall if she'd ever heard Flyte swear before. 'I think I can help you there.'

When she told her that she'd heard a man's voice in one of the lock-ups over the way, Flyte said, 'Show me.'

At the edge of the undercroft, Cassie pointed out the garage and Flyte said, 'You need to leave. I don't want you anywhere near this situation. It could be dangerous.'

'I'm not going anywhere,' said Cassie, shaking her head slowly. 'And there's something else you need to know.'

She repeated what Copernicus had told her – that he was using his telescope when he chanced upon a plainclothes cop coming out of her cabin the previous week. 'I *knew* someone had been inside the boat. There was a . . . *lemony* smell I couldn't trace.'

'How did this homeless guy know he was a cop if he was in plainclothes?' asked Flyte, back in sceptical mode.

Cassie gave her a look. 'You lot stand out a mile. Anyway the cop realised he'd been spotted so he went over and told Copernicus he was there on police business and showed his ID.'

'Which could have been fake.' Flyte folded her arms. 'So, what did this guy look like?'

Cassie remembered Copernicus saying, 'Like a policeman,' as if that were enough. 'Yeah, he was a bit vague on that front. All he could recall was that the guy was wearing a suit and had brown hair.'

'Oh, great. That really narrows it down.'

FLYTE

Flyte managed to persuade Cassie to stay in the undercroft: at least there were hiding places there if things should turn nasty. The homeless guy's description of the man on Cassie's boat could fit Willets, but it was so imprecise it could also fit half the men in the office.

Including Seb. A thought she pushed away.

Approaching the lock-up Cassie had pointed out, she marched up to the double doors, leaking a sliver of light, and rapped out an authoritative knock. It sounded more confident than she felt. Her heart was beating so fast she could hear the *swish-swish* of blood in her ears.

Silence from within.

'Police. Open up.'

A moment later the lock was turned and one of the doors opened a crack and the face of Dean Willets peered out. 'What the fu—?' he said.

'Let me in, Dean.' In a voice that brooked no opposition.

A brief hesitation before he opened the door just wide enough for her to step inside. The light here wasn't as bright as the orange glare outside and she blinked as her eyes adjusted. A large portable lamp of the kind workmen used stood on a shelf at the far end, but the light it emitted didn't reach into the corners of the empty garage.

'What's going on, Dean?' she asked, looking around.

'I believe that Sean Kavanagh's body was stored in a freezer for eight years in one of these lock-ups,' he said. 'In fact, this lock-up.'

Flyte was taken aback. That was her line.

'What were you doing on board Cassie Raven's boat around a week ago?'

He pulled a sarcastic face. 'Er, interviewing her?'

'Before that – when she wasn't at home?'

Willets took a step towards her. 'What are you saying exactly?' A threatening edge in his voice.

During her incarceration in the freezer, Flyte had tried to nail what had happened nine years ago after the homophobic Willets had caught fellow police officer Sean Kavanagh having sex in Abney Park – had finally faced the unthinkable. Their paths had surely crossed again around a year later, an encounter that had ended in Sean's death.

Before she could decide whether to confront him head-on, there came a brisk knock at the lock-up door and someone pushed it open. *DCI Steadman.*

'Evening, guv,' said Willets. 'You must have made good time.'

'The A406 was clear for once. Evening, Phyllida. I didn't know this was a group effort. Good to see you two working as a team.'

'Hello,' she said, blinking in confusion. 'I thought you were in Birmingham.'

'I got back this afternoon.' Turning to Willets, he said, 'This better be worth it – I passed up a nice bottle of Medoc and my wife's boeuf bourguignon to come here.' He looked around 'So where's this freezer . . . ?'

Willets shot her a triumphant look before taking the lamp off the shelf and angling it towards the floor.

Steadman bent down, hands on his thighs and Flyte dropped to a crouch beside him.

Willets pointed out a rectangular outline of cleaner concrete on the floor. 'Looks to me like something was stood here for a long time. A chest freezer, for instance.'

Flyte bent her head closer to the floor and sniffed. 'Bleach. Somebody's been trying to clean up.'

Steadman nodded. 'Dean, care to share your working hypothesis?'

'Sure thing.' Willets had regained some of his usual swagger. 'Somebody stored Sean's body here but was forced to move it when the demolition became imminent. I've asked the council for the list of people who rented these garages.'

Which Flyte knew would only reveal the names of 'official' tenants, when it was common practice to sublet lock-ups on the QT to all and sundry. But her mind was struggling to keep up with the way events were unfolding. If Willets really had hidden Sean's body here, why on earth would he call in the boss? Had he realised she was onto him, and decided his only hope of regaining control of the situation was to get ahead of the game?

'How did you know which lock-up to check out?' asked Flyte. 'And how did you get in?'

'I tried them all but it was the only one that wasn't locked,' he said, shrugging.

Or the only one you had the key to.

295

'This is great work, Dean,' said Steadman, straightening up. 'Let's get forensics down here to properly check this place out, and try to find that freezer – if it's still in the vicinity.'

Flyte sneaked a look at Willets. Of course, his presence here would immediately explain any of his DNA turning up in the lock-up. But there might still be recoverable traces on the freezer out in the undercroft where Sean had been stored. She heard Pops's voice saying 'Keep your powder dry, Philly.'

Pulling out his phone, Steadman tapped at the screen.

'Marcus? Steadman here . . .' He chuckled. 'I know, no peace for the wicked . . . Listen up. I need you to send a couple of uniforms to secure a scene, on the canal . . . Right . . . And a forensic team for 0600 hours.'

After giving the coordinates of the estate, he hung up. Turning to Flyte a look of concern came over his face. 'Phyllida, you look done in. Go home and get some sleep, you can take over tomorrow first thing.'

As Willets went to set the lamp back on its shelf the upper rim of light flitted across something on a higher shelf. In that split second an image imprinted itself on Flyte's retina. The shape of something long and slim at the back of the shelf, loosely covered with a tarpaulin. *Not quite fully covered.* The inch or two she'd glimpsed looked an awful lot like the business end of a gun barrel.

Fighting to maintain her outward calm, she was remembering Willets' rabbit-shooting trips to Essex farms. Whatever he was playing at, he clearly couldn't be left here alone, at liberty to ditch the firearm and give the freezer the deep clean that must now be his urgent priority.

Steadman was turning to go. Whatever the risk to her career she had to speak up now.

296

'Boss . . . Sorry, but I need to ask Dean some questions while you're here.'

A look of irritation crossed Steadman's face. 'Can't it wait till tomorrow?'

'No. I'm afraid not.'

Steadman made a weary gesture, as if giving her the floor.

She turned to meet Willets' disbelieving scowl. 'It's come to my attention that you ran a game at Hackney nick, back when you were a beat cop,' she said. 'A competition to see who could nick the greatest number of gay men having sex in public.' He gave her a death stare, but made no attempt to deny it. 'Nine years ago, a year before Sean Kavanagh disappeared, you caught him while he was off duty having sex in Abney Park. I suggest that you encountered him again the following year. An encounter that ended up with him in a freezer.'

'Phyllida . . . ?!' Steadman was looking at her like she'd lost her marbles.

'Total rubbish,' Dean scoffed, but she could see the sheen of sweat on his forehead.

'That first time, he said he was a cop and you let him off – not wanting a fellow officer, even a gay one, to lose his job. Which was a risky thing for you to do.' Now for a leap into guesswork. 'You must have been furious when you caught him doing it again. It would be understandable if you lost your rag and hit him.'

Dean broke in, jabbing his finger at her. 'It's not the first time you've thrown bullshit accusations—'

Steadman waved a hand to quell his outburst before turning to her with an admiring look. 'You're a smart cookie, Phyllida, so I'm not surprised you've unearthed some bits and bobs, even if you they have led you down a blind alley.'

297

She blinked, thrown by his comment.

'But now you're part of the team I'm going to level with you.' Steadman paused for a moment. 'You're right about the distasteful game Dean here used to play at Hackney all those years ago. I was patrol sergeant at the time and as soon as it came to my attention I put a stop to it.'

He looked over at Willets who had dropped his head, staring at the floor.

'And it's true that Dean did nick Sean Kavanagh in the Abney Park public toilets. I happened to run into them when Dean brought him back to the nick. Dean got a call on the radio and Sean asked me for a word. He told me he was Job – right next door at Finsbury Park nick, too.' He sighed. 'As you know, even giving him a caution would have meant automatic dismissal. The offence had taken place at two in the morning, with no members of the public around to see him misbehaving. And so I took the view that it was a victimless crime.'

He scanned her face. 'I told Sean to get lost and sin no more, and made sure the arrest didn't get entered on the computer.'

Sweet Jesus.

Flyte was aghast. Officers could use their discretion in making arrests under Outraging Public Decency legislation, depending on whether there might be members of the public nearby whose decency might be outraged. So Willets had arguably been over-zealous arresting Sean in the first place – probably keen to bag an arrest for his stupid game. Had it been her, she'd probably have sent Sean off with a flea in his ear and a clean record. But once he had actually been arrested? It stuck in her craw to learn that Steadman – the patrol sergeant, no less – had intervened to cover it up. Police officers couldn't and shouldn't bend the rules, especially not to protect one of their own.

Something occurred to her. Why would Willets carry on with his gay-hunting game after getting a dressing-down from Steadman – his patrol sergeant and his hero? Her scenario, in which Willets caught Sean reoffending a year later, felt suddenly shaky.

'So why do you think Sean was killed?' she asked Steadman.

He lifted his big shoulders in a shrug. 'Either he had a falling-out with his steroid suppliers, or one of his lovers. But finding this place is a bloody good step towards us finding the perpetrator.'

Maybe he was right. Then she remembered Willets' reaction on seeing the details of the Canadian bank account from which Bethany had received £150k in hush money after Sean's disappearance. It had clearly meant something to him, but how could he have lain hands on that kind of money?

'Can I get back to my dinner now?' said Steadman, before turning to go – evidently considering the matter closed.

Flyte turned to Willets. 'Who is Ms N. Toussaint?' she asked.

Dean's alarmed gaze swivelled to Steadman.

A cascade of clicks in Flyte's brain, as if some elaborate mechanism was coming to life. Seb describing the glut of rabbits produced by Dean's shooting trips out to Essex. Which would have needed freezing. Steadman's wife – who made a mean rabbit casserole and was French.

Not French-French. French-Canadian.

FLYTE

Steadman had taken a couple of steps into the shadows and returned holding the rifle, unsheathed from its tarpaulin. The way he held it – one-handed, with casual confidence, told Flyte she'd got it all wrong. The gun wasn't Willets' but Steadman's, as was the lock-up.

'Tell her, Dean,' he said, positioning himself behind Flyte's shoulder. Close enough for her to smell lemon sherbets on his breath. Recalling his boiled sweet habit and the citrus smell Cassie had mentioned in her cabin.

He hadn't got here in record time due to lack of traffic; he'd been here before both of them. It was Steadman who'd been visiting his lock-up garage to do final checks, and Steadman who'd tipped her into the freezer when he'd found her sniffing around.

Of course there were no uniforms on the way to secure the scene: the call to the nick had been a piece of play-acting.

Dean's eyes were wide open, fixed beyond her on the gun. 'Guv,' he said tentatively.

Her every cell and fibre was on high alert, aware of the gun barrel just inches from her spine.

'Come on, Dean,' said Steadman. 'You must surely have worked it out by now?'

Willets looked frozen, queasy. His voice dropped to a whisper. 'I think Natalie Toussaint is the guv's wife.'

Steadman's wife had kept her maiden name.

'You opened a Canadian bank account in your wife's name to pay off Bethany Locke,' said Flyte.

In her peripheral vision, she could sense Steadman nodding and felt the barrel of the gun brush the back of her jacket, making her skin crawl.

'Well done, Phyllida,' said Steadman. 'Although of course you broke a key rule of interrogation. Never ask a question to which you don't know the answer.'

Should she try to run? She scrabbled to recall the ballistics lectures from her criminology degree. Assuming the rifle was the one he'd used for shooting rabbits it could only be a .22, but a single bullet of that calibre would be more than enough to kill a human – even at long range.

'So what did happen that night, boss?' Keeping her voice level. So long as he was talking he wasn't shooting.

'It was all just a . . . terrible accident,' said Steadman. 'It was a busy night so I took a car out on my own and I caught him at it again in the Abney Park toilets. His playmate did a runner.' Disgust lacing his voice. 'I admit I was angry. I had risked my own job to save his bacon. Then he turned his back on me. All I did was give him a shove, but he hit the hand-dryer on the wall pretty hard . . .' His voice became hoarse. 'I tried CPR but he never regained consciousness.'

Flyte wasn't tempted to ask why he hadn't tried calling an ambulance. She had no wish to hasten her own death.

She tried to catch Willets' eye, but he looked away. Not a good sign. He had a dog-like loyalty to his master. And he was in far too deep now. She pictured him helping Steadman drag her body back to the freezer.

'You know, Phyllida, I thought you were going to become my best detective.' Steadman spoke with finality and what sounded like genuine regret. 'I'm just sorry you got caught up in this.'

Jesus fucking Christ.

The next second was a blur. From the tiniest movement of the air behind her she knew that Steadman had raised the gun. In the same moment Willets launched himself past Flyte. In that small space the detonation sounded like a bomb going off.

Flyte couldn't recall hitting the ground, her entire being focused on the pain in her ears. Calling the gunshot 'deafening' was wrong – the high-pitched ringing whine in her head was unbearably loud. Then she tasted blood in her mouth. Not good. She knew a shot to the gut or liver could do that.

Next moment, she was blinking the scene around her into focus. Cassie Raven stood above her, legs planted apart, the rifle in her hands aimed at a point on the ground behind her. Her mouth was moving but Flyte couldn't hear what she was saying.

'Get your hands in the air and face the wall.' Then, still keeping the gun on Willets, Cassie went over to Flyte. Kneeling down, she opened Flyte's jacket, looking for any blood. Meeting her dazed gaze, the pupils so dilated by adrenaline there was barely any cornea visible, she mouthed, 'You're OK.'

The same couldn't be said for the big guy in his fifties who lay in a gently expanding lagoon of his own blood a metre or so behind Flyte.

Dropping to her haunches, Cassie cast a clinical eye over him. From the neat entry wound under his chin it was clear he'd

302

shot himself, the rifle bullet scything through soft tissue before ricocheting off bone and exiting his body through the left eye, leaving the socket a bloody void.

Cassie had heard everything unfold from the other side of the garage doors. After the shock of the gun blast she'd gone into automatic mode, operating in a bubble of unreality. Now the protective layer left her and the cold reality returned.

She bent to put her fingers against the big man's carotid artery.

His hand reached out and grabbed her wrist.

Fuck!

His grip was surprisingly strong, his fingers sticky with blood. She heard the rattle of blood or saliva in his throat. He tried to speak but a wet reflexive cough stopped his words. He gripped her wrist tighter. 'Tell Nat and Em . . . that I'm sorry.'

Cassie met his surviving eye. 'I will,' she promised.

His pulse was erratic, a fading whisper. Seeing his eye lose its spark, the pupil gently expanding, she was overcome by a feeling of dread and awe. She'd dealt with thousands of dead bodies, but she had never watched anyone die before.

FLYTE

The orange glow cast by the security lighting combined with the blue flashing lights from the ambulance and squad cars gave the scene an other-worldly quality. It flickered across the white suits of the forensics officers going to and fro inside the lock-up garage, now lit by high-wattage lamps. They would soon be joined by ballistics experts and a Home Office pathologist to analyse the scene and examine Steadman's body in situ.

Flyte had refused point-blank to go to hospital to be checked over. She was fine, she kept telling them all – the paramedics, Seb, the senior officer from DPS who'd be overseeing the investigation . . . In truth, she felt pretty terrible. The inside of her cheek still throbbed from where she'd bitten it as she hit the ground, the incessant ringing in her ears had been replaced by a piercing headache, and the adrenaline rush of immediate danger had long faded to leave a bone-deep exhaustion.

It must be an hour or two she'd been sitting here on the kerb, on a pillow the paramedics had given her, her gaze stapled to the scene in the depths of the undercroft. The freezer lay on its back now, its lid open and gaping at her, lit by two more lamps on stands either side. Kneeling before it like white-clad acolytes at an altar were a crime scene examiner she didn't recognise – and Seb.

Her eyes ached with the effort of her surveillance. Logically, she didn't really think they would be conspiring to hide evidence but then until tonight she would've trusted Steadman with her life. And Seb had been slow to tell her that the 'NDW' in Luke's final note matched Willets' initials. She couldn't stop wondering what else he had known.

Cassie sloped over, looking irritatingly insouciant even draped in a thermal foil blanket.

'Who was that who took my statement?' Cassie asked, lifting her chin towards a woman in her early fifties with well-cut greying hair who was briefing a detective and two uniformed officers.

'Zoe Stopford. She's a DCI with the DPS.'

'And in English?'

'Sorry, top brass from the Directorate of Professional Standards, the department which investigates police misconduct. She'll be assigning detectives from outside Camden.'

'Cops investigating cops,' said Cassie drily. 'What could possibly go wrong?'

'I'm inclined to agree with you.' Discovering that DCI Steadman had not only killed Sean, and probably Luke Lawless too, had torn a hole in Flyte's universe. Until tonight she had sometimes indulged in a comforting vision. In it she stood shoulder to shoulder with her fellow officers on one side of a fence watching over members of the public on the other side, happily going about their business, unaware of the ever-present perils of random violence and death that surrounded them. Her band of brothers and sisters might have myriad failings but they were united in one goal: protecting those oblivious punters from the bad people bent on doing them harm. Now the fence was down and she could no longer distinguish between the guardians and the villains.

How could she hope to trust her colleagues – or her own judgement – ever again?

'How are you doing?' asked Cassie in a gentler voice. 'It must be tough, having your faith in your colleagues crushed like that.'

'Crushed' was an accurate description. Things that had been crushed couldn't be reassembled. After a pause Flyte said, 'Anyway, I told you to stay in the undercroft. You could have been killed.'

'Yeah, but you know I'm not very good at following orders.'

'Have you ever actually fired a gun?' asked Flyte, genuinely curious.

'Sure.' Cassie adopted a modest look. 'I won a cuddly giraffe once.'

Flyte managed a smile – grateful for the attempt, however doomed, to cheer her up.

'Well at least you didn't shoot Willets.'

'I was tempted.'

Cassie had returned to her boat and the coming dawn was beginning to silhouette the roofline eastwards across the canal when Flyte saw Seb, weaving a route carefully through the trash of the undercroft, which would be undergoing a fingertip search. Lifting the blue and white tape between the concrete columns, he ducked beneath it and headed towards her.

After sitting down next to her on the kerb, his white suit rustling, he passed her a clear plastic evidence bag. It held a brass-coloured stud fastening of the kind used on button-fly style jeans. Making out the word 'Diesel' embossed around the edge, she felt a muted jolt of excitement.

'Ring any bells?' Seb asked her.

'Yep. Sean Kavanagh was wearing Diesel jeans, missing a stud.'

Seb looked at the ground. 'I guess it must have come off when he was being wrapped in plastic.' Flyte noted his use of the passive tense – avoiding any mention of who had done the wrapping.

'More likely when Steadman was unwrapping him prior to dumping him in the canal,' she said, pointedly naming him. 'It probably came off when he unbuttoned the flies. To make it look as though he fell in while relieving himself.'

Seb dropped his eyes. 'You don't think there was any . . . sexual motive, do you?'

Flyte had been wondering about that herself. Why had Steadman, who said he'd only taken out a squad car as it was a particularly busy night, returned to the public loo where Willets had first arrested Sean Kavanagh? Was he checking up on him? Or had he been secretly attracted to him when Willets delivered him to the nick – if only subconsciously? It was a possibility.

Seb ran a hand through his hair. 'I still can't take all this on board,' he said. 'I mean Steadman?! He was straight as a die! Do you think Dean knew anything?'

'Well, he knew that N. Toussaint was the boss's wife and did nothing.'

'I think he only worked that out yesterday.' Seb grimaced. 'He cornered me in the kitchen and asked me if I knew what Steadman's wife was called.' He shrugged. 'I remembered him calling her Natalie once, and that she had some French surname she kept after they got married.'

'And you didn't think to mention this to me.' Sending him an icy smile.

'I didn't think anything of it,' he said, making a hands-up gesture. 'Why would I be suspicious of Dean? Or the boss?' After a pause, he said, 'That's why he delayed his retirement, wasn't it? Not because his daughter was going to uni, but because of the loan he'd had to take out to keep Bethany Locke quiet.'

She nodded, remembering Seb's repeated defence of Willets as 'a good detective', his silence while Willets and his acolytes made their off-colour jokes, his advice to her not to report Jethro for taking photos of a dead body. The kind of groupthink that meant you never questioned a fellow officer, and certainly never reported them. The fact that Seb wasn't one of the bad apples, that he was a good man at heart, almost made it worse. Hadn't somebody once said it only took good men to do nothing for evil to flourish?

She eyed his face for a long moment. 'Listen, Sebastian . . .'

He raised a hand. His lips wore a smile but his eyes weren't invited to the party.

'You don't need to say anything, Phyllida. I knew by the way you looked at me when I got here – it's over between us, isn't it?'

Chapter Thirty-Eight

'How are you? How's the case going?'

It was midday before Cassie finally got hold of Flyte on the phone. Seeing how badly she'd been hit by the events of last night she'd been worried about her.

'I'm off the case – I'm a witness now so I can't be involved.' Flyte sounded tired, beyond caring. 'I shouldn't even be talking to you.'

'But the investigation will continue, right? To find out what happened?'

'Oh, sure. Steadman will be named at Sean's inquest as his killer and the case file will be closed. Willets will get the sack. But so what? All this sorry business will produce is a few lurid headlines about murderous cops and a public even less inclined to trust us.'

It disturbed Cassie to hear the cynicism – worse, the *defeatism* – in her voice. Flyte had always struck her as indefatigable.

'What about Luke Lawless? Doesn't his poor dad deserve to understand why he died? That Steadman killed him to stop him digging?' Eavesdropping through the lock-up door last night had allowed her to piece together the likely sequence of events. 'Otherwise all he knows is that his son was murdered on the heath in a known pick-up spot.'

'How much effort do you think detectives will put in to try and add another murder to a dead cop's rap sheet?' said Flyte and Cassie could almost hear her weary shrug down the line. 'And so far there isn't a scintilla of proof that it was Steadman who killed him.'

'Come on, Phyllida,' Cassie protested. 'It's obvious Steadman agreed to meet Luke because he'd got wind of Sean's arrest.'

'There's no evidence they ever even spoke to each other, let alone met. And Steadman would know better than anyone how to cover his tracks.'

This exchange only left Cassie more troubled about Flyte. Her apparently unshakeable certainty that she was on the side of the angels had clearly deserted her, and no wonder. Would she ever get it back?

Cassie had a good idea how she must be feeling. One of the things that made her job worthwhile was being able to tell those left behind what had caused their loved one's death. The truth might be painful, but it was still preferable to being tortured by uncertainty for the rest of their lives.

That morning Archie had forwarded her an email from Dan Bennett, whose wife Becka had died from an air embolism accidentally introduced during the insertion of a line ahead of an MRI scan. A scan that hadn't even been necessary; Archie's post-mortem report had identified the likeliest cause of Becka's severe headache as a hemiplegic migraine rather than stroke. Rather than kicking off about the medical accident that had led to his wife's death, Dan had written to express his gratitude for the answers the report had given him.

He said that his daughters were booked in to undergo genetic testing for the condition, so that if they ever presented with their mum's symptoms they would receive an accurate diagnosis.

She read Archie's accompanying email again.

All down to you, Sherlock! it said, with typical generosity, before ending with *When are we going to meet? I'm starting to think you're ignoring me . . .* Signing off with a silly clown face emoji to lay off any accusatory vibe.

She sat there a long time, thinking about Phyllida Flyte, thinking about Archie . . . who she hadn't even called to relate last night's clusterfuck.

Was it fair to keep stringing him along when they were so different? Archie deserved a nice girlfriend keen to settle down, do the whole domestic thing, not some misfit loner who felt more at home with the dead than the living. She felt conflicted: tempted to give it a whirl, to give up the boat and go share a centrally heated flat with him, or to just call the whole thing off before it all went Pete Tong.

Either way, she couldn't let things between them just drift. She started to tap out an email to him suggesting they meet.

FLYTE

'Obviously it's highly irregular, given that you're a witness to last night's shenanigans,' DCI Zoe Stopford's tone was brisk. 'But I've approved it.'

Despite having been locked in a cell in King's Cross nick since the early hours, Dean Willets hadn't exercised his right to a phone call, his only request being a bacon and egg McMuffin and a latte. But at lunchtime he had announced that he was ready to be interviewed – on one condition. He would only talk to DS Flyte.

The two women were heading for interview room one. Although Flyte was a good half a head taller, she had to quicken her pace to keep up with the stocky Stopford. She imagined they must look like a small but speedy tugboat pulling a sailing ship in its wake.

'Do I have to?' said Flyte, which brought a puzzled look from the older woman.

'I can't make you, obviously. But I'd have thought you'd welcome the chance to put your questions about this whole sorry affair to him directly? Unless you've had second thoughts and need to speak to a trauma counsellor?'

'No, I'm fine.' Her mantra since last night. Just get through today; tomorrow it was Poppy's naming ceremony and then she could face the question hanging over her: whether she still had a future in policing.

'He's still declining his right to a lawyer.' Stopford raised her eyebrows at Willets' bizarre decision before opening the door to the interview room.

Willets was already seated at the table. After conducting the legal formalities required ahead of an interview under caution, DCI Stopford opened the batting.

'Why did you not inform DS Flyte that you and DCI Steadman knew Sean Kavanagh, after he'd been pulled from the canal?' Her voice not unfriendly but crisp and businesslike.

'Because I didn't recognise him,' said Willets, with a shrug.

DCI Stopford frowned. 'Really. You expect us to believe that?'

'Really.' Willets' expression soured. 'I never knew his real name, cos he gave me a false one when I collared him in Abney Park. Anyway, I agreed to talk to Phyllida, not someone who drives a desk.' Sending Stopford a pointed look.

Flyte remembered hearing Willets bad-mouthing DCI Stopford after her appointment to DPS. 'The Muffia rides again,' he'd sneered – a homophobic dig at what he considered to be a cabal of lesbian officers promoted solely for diversity window-dressing.

Stopford didn't react to his latest insult, simply inclining her head to Flyte in invitation.

'Even if you didn't know Sean by name, how could you fail to recognise the post-mortem images of the body?' asked Flyte.

'His hair was . . . different, and it all happened nine years ago for Christ's sake. I nicked dozens of guys in Abney Park.'

'To earn points in your competition to see who could arrest the most gay men.'

He shifted in his seat. 'I didn't do anything wrong. We were getting a lot of complaints from people who funnily enough weren't that keen on seeing gays having sex in public.'

'Fair enough. But turning it into a game?'

'That was just a bit of a laugh. Office banter.'

Banter. Bantz. The secret language used by people like Willets, which meant that they owned the discourse, and decided whether you were in or out. And if you didn't go along with it you were a prude or a killjoy, or, worse, an eternal outsider.

'It's exactly the kind of thing that brings the police into disrepute!' Flyte had spoken with more force than she'd intended, but she sensed Stopford's silent approval alongside her. 'So . . . when *did* you realise that Sean Kavanagh and the man you'd arrested were the same person?'

'Not until I saw that reporter's notebook.' Dean opened his palms. 'Look, I had no reason to connect him with the guy I'd nicked. The boss – I mean Steadman – never even let on that Kavanagh was Job. He said he'd let him off because he'd heard whispers about the game and he didn't want me to get into trouble with the PC brigade' – throwing a glance at Stopford.

'You're saying you never once discussed Sean's arrest and its subsequent cover-up with Steadman in the intervening nine years?'

'No! Why would we? It was ancient history.' He shook his head. 'I swear, the first time it came up was when you started throwing accusations around in the lock-up.'

Flyte changed tack. 'At what point did you realise that Steadman had been involved in Sean Kavanagh's death? Was it when you found out that Bethany's hundred and fifty grand had been sent from an account set up in his wife's name, N. Toussaint?'

'I didn't know that! Not for sure. All I knew was that his wife was French-Canadian and it was only yesterday I found out her first name was Natalie.'

Which fit with what Seb had said. 'So why didn't you confront Steadman?' she pressed. 'Put the bank account details in front of him? Or go straight to the DPS.'

'I would have done,' he said, 'once I'd got more evidence.'

His words were unconvincing. Flyte knew that he would never have grassed on the boss. The likes of Willets viewed this bond of loyalty to a fellow officer as a positive; she saw it as akin to the Mafia code of omertà. She pictured what would have happened if she'd left as instructed by Steadman last night. With her out of the way he'd have gone back and stood Dean down, so he could continue with his clean-up operation before calling in forensics. And no doubt Dean would've quietly shelved the inconvenient bank account lead.

'Did you know Steadman had a lock-up on the derelict estate?'

'No! I had no idea. It wasn't in his name.'

Of course it wasn't – a former tenant would have sublet the lock-up to him, and taken the rent in cash.

'I'm curious, Dean. What prompted you to go there last night?'

'I started to review everything we knew, including where Kavanagh's body went in the canal. I got hold of the lock-keeper who said that there's been no rainfall for weeks so the current has been almost non-existent. I realised the estate would be the perfect place to conceal and dump a body without being seen' – a shrug – 'so I called the council and they told me about the lock-ups over there.'

'Why hadn't you found out about the current before?'

Dean made a sarcastic face. 'I could ask you the same question.'

Flyte pursed her lips. He was right: both of them had swallowed the bogus information that Steadman had fed the team at the first case conference. He claimed to have spoken personally

315

to the lock-keeper who'd said that the current would carry a body at least one hundred metres downstream. Nobody would dream of questioning Steadman's intel and so his lie had focused them on a false search area which kept them as far as possible from the soon-to-be-demolished estate. Flyte remembered it was she who had suggested the road bridge as the likeliest dumping spot – a theory that Steadman had of course encouraged.

'Look, Dean, forensics have barely started work on that freezer, and they've already found some hair and scraps of plastic used to wrap the body which they're analysing for DNA,' said Flyte. Knowing that the site would be cleared after demolition, Steadman hadn't seen any need to give the freezer a deep clean after dumping Sean's body, and by the time he'd decided to go back, armed with bleach, Willets and Flyte had been on his tail. 'If there's any chance of the lab finding your profile, you'd be better off telling us now.'

'There is zero chance of that,' he said, a mulish look on his face. 'Because I had nothing to do with it.'

Sensing that he was probably telling the truth, Flyte changed tack. 'And what about Steadman's murder of Luke Lawless?'

Willets became animated, sitting up in his seat. 'Come on, no way was the boss involved in that. Like he said, Sean's death was an accident. But committing a cold-blooded murder?' He gave a scornful shake of his head.

With both parties dead, it would never be confirmed what had happened when Steadman had caught Sean in flagrante in Abney Park a second time. Home Office pathologist Professor Arculus had already confirmed that Sean's xiphoid fracture could have been caused by a violent collision with the handdryer which fatally interrupted his heart rhythm. Forensics had been dispatched to Abney Park to measure the height of the dryer to check against the position of Sean's fracture.

Flyte tapped at her phone. 'The forensic post-mortem report on Luke Lawless came back this morning. Swabs from inside his cheek tested positive for GHB but none was detected in his bloodstream. The cause of death was "Compression of the neck causing venous congestion that starved the brain of oxygenated blood" ... "Evidence of patterning transferred from clothing to the jaw suggests the victim could have been held in a chokehold."'

'There you go!' Willets pulled a complacent smile. 'Fatally choked during a mugging, the exact same MO that put that drunk kid Harry Poppleton into a coma. Luke Lawless was just unlucky not to survive.'

Flyte looked sideways at Zoe Stopford. They had agreed in advance that she should deliver the latest development.

Stopford opened the file on the table in front of her. 'There's been a development in the Poppleton case. Two days ago the suspect known as the Hugger Mugger was caught red-handed putting a drunken tourist in a chokehold. After being shown the CCTV imagery from Camden he confessed.'

DCI Stopford spun the file round so that Willets could see him: a big wide-shouldered guy with a beard and a Mediterranean complexion glowered out of the arrest mugshot.

'And?' Willets shrugged.

'This was in Amsterdam.' Flyte levelled a cool gaze at him. 'He flew there shortly after attacking Harry Poppleton. Ten days before Luke Lawless was killed.'

Willets attempted another shrug but the look of smug certitude was draining from his face. 'Luke Lawless could have been a copycat killing – someone using the same technique.'

317

'Our hypothesis exactly,' said Flyte with a thin smile. 'Dean, you must remember the case conference, when DCI Steadman showed us how the Hugger Mugger choked his victims?'

Willets glared at the tabletop, clearly remembering the boss's demonstration: Steadman standing behind him, one big arm hooked around his throat.

'You're five nine, Dean. The same height as Luke Lawless,' said Flyte. 'And Steadman was around six foot two, just like the Hugger Mugger.'

Dean was shaking his head. 'No, no, the boss would never . . .'

'Planting the GHB on Luke's body was just set-dressing but Steadman went too far putting some in his mouth – not knowing how corrosive it was. He was hoping that Luke's death would go down as a bad reaction to a chemsex drug. But even if there were a forensic post-mortem, he knew the cause of death would be strangulation by chokehold – the Hugger Mugger's trademark. Steadman wasn't to know the real Hugger Mugger had already left the country.'

Dean was still shaking his head, but from his expression he was starting to face the unthinkable about his hero and mentor.

Still consumed by her own sense of disillusionment, Flyte had an idea of what he was feeling. The difference was that while Dean Willets' primary allegiance was to his fellow officers, her loyalty had always been to the institution of the police itself.

Chapter Thirty-Nine

'Come for dinner tomorrow night with your father, *tygrysek*.' It was clear from Babcia's tone that this was more instruction than invite, and Cassie knew she was right. Since her dad's OD she'd been texting him regularly to check up on his health but she'd been avoiding seeing him in person.

'Do you mean tomorrow and not Sunday, Babcia?'

'I haven't lost my marbles yet, thank you. We have a special guest I'd like you to meet.' But she refused point-blank to say any more about the mystery visitor.

After agreeing to go over, Cassie found her mind returning to the missing link between Luke Lawless and Steadman. Although Steadman had shot himself, she hated the idea that he would probably never be found responsible for Luke's cold-blooded killing.

An hour later, she was stepping through a shop doorway on the Roman Road in east London. It was the first time she'd knowingly set foot inside a beauty parlour – or whatever they were called these days – and the air keened with the reek of solvent. She asked the girl doing a customer's nails if Bethany was around.

When she emerged from the rear, Bethany looked startled to see Cassie there. 'Let's go next door, grab a coffee,' she said, picking up her fake fur jacket and saying to the young woman, 'Holly, I won't be long.'

In the Costa next door they sat looking out on pavements thick with punters. 'Good spot for a beauty parlour, I imagine?' said Cassie, eyeing Bethany's face. She was as thoroughly made-up as ever, but her eyes were bloodshot and there were streaks where she hadn't blended her foundation. And from the smell of alcohol coming through her pores she was drinking more than her liver could metabolise.

'Salon. Yes, it's been a really good little business. Keeps the wolf from the door.' Bethany fiddled with her vape device, unable to use it indoors.

'You've heard the news about DCI Steadman topping himself?' asked Cassie.

'Yeah. The cops called. They said they're working on the assumption that it was him who killed Sean.' Flashing her a look. 'Didn't I say you can't trust the cops? They asked me a load of questions about the money sent from Canada. Sent by this Steadman as it turns out.' Dropping her eyes as she said his name.

'Were you able to tell them anything useful?'

'I've told them everything I know.'

Cassie noticed that Bethany wasn't keen on eye contact.

'Anyway,' she went on, 'I've put the flat on the market and given notice on the salon. I've just signed the lease on a little place in Gran Canaria. I want to be a long way away when the tabloids start crawling all over Sean's life.'

'Yeah, I don't blame you,' said Cassie. 'By the way, did the cops mention a reporter called Luke Lawless? Who was found murdered on the heath?' Flyte had told her that Luke had door-stepped Bethany at her flat.

Bethany gave a shrugging assent, gaze slithering away again. 'I already told them he turned up asking all kinds of personal questions about me and Sean.'

Cassie left a silence until Bethany lifted her gaze reluctantly to meet hers. 'But he came back a second time, didn't he?' said Cassie.

Bethany's face crumpled.

It turned out that the day before he was murdered Luke had come to the salon to tell her about the lead he was following. He said that a year before Sean's disappearance he'd been arrested by a cop called Nigel Willets for a gay sexual offence in Hackney. This Willets was now a detective in Camden and Luke believed that he was responsible for Sean's murder.

'What did you do?'

'I sent him packing,' said Bethany, her voice harsh. 'Poking around in Sean's life – both our lives – to smear him, just for a sleazy headline?' She fidgeted with her vape. 'But . . . I couldn't stop thinking about Sean. I took that money from Canada, knowing that it must have come from his killer.' She looked at Cassie, regret in her red-rimmed eyes.

'So you decided you owed it to Sean to tell someone?' said Cassie gently. 'That Willets might have been involved in Sean's death.'

'Yeah. I thought it was tied up with the steroid dealing – maybe Willets was on the take, you know, and things turned ugly.'

'So you found out who Willets' boss was and went straight to DCI Steadman.'

She nodded miserably. 'I called him on Monday morning and told him everything Luke had said. He seemed to take it very seriously, and promised to look into it. Said he'd make it a "personal priority".'

Oh, he'd made it a priority all right. Luke had been murdered on Monday night.

'I swear I didn't even know that Luke was dead till today, when the cops called to tell me about Steadman.' Bethany paused, blew out a breath. 'Basically, I killed him, didn't I?'

'I get why you'd feel that way,' said Cassie. 'But there was no way you could have known what Steadman would do, what he was capable of. I mean, he was a senior cop.'

Bethany nodded eagerly. 'Exactly – and he was crystal about one thing: not to breathe a word about Willets to anyone. He said it would "compromise any investigation".'

And once Luke had been eliminated, the story would go away – or so he had hoped.

'You haven't shared this with the cops? The fact that you told Steadman about Luke's investigation just before he was murdered?'

She shook her head.

Cassie leaned across the table. 'Listen, Bethany, I totally get why you would want to sod off to the Canaries and start over, put this whole ugly business behind you. But there's still no proof that Steadman killed Luke as well as Sean.'

'What difference does it make?' She shrugged. 'Anyway, why the fuck should I help the cops clear up this mess?'

'Forget the cops. This is about Luke's dad. All he knows is that his only son was choked to death in a gay cruising spot with GHB on him.' She let that sink in for a moment. 'If you tell the police what you've told me they can't ignore it – they'll have to pull out all the stops to look for evidence that Steadman murdered Luke. It'll all get aired during the inquest and his dad will find out the truth: that his son was killed while going after a scoop.'

Bethany bit her lip, not yet buying it.

'How was it for you the last eight years, not knowing what had happened to Sean?' asked Cassie. 'Knowing he was almost certainly dead but not knowing who did it or why?'

Bethany fell silent. Then she said, 'There hasn't been a single day since he left when I haven't wondered about that. I never really stopped loving him you know. And I think he did love me. Is that possible? Even with him being . . . gay?'

'Yes. Not many people are one hundred per cent gay or straight. What you and Sean had together was real. The time you had together, it meant something.'

'Thank you for saying that,' said Bethany in a quiet voice. She blew out a long breath. 'OK. I'll talk to the cops.'

'You're doing the right thing,' said Cassie. And she was telling the truth. Not just for the sake of Luke's dad. For Bethany's sake, too.

FLYTE

In the cool silence of St Pancras Old Church, Flyte was putting the final touches to the flowers she'd arranged in vases either side of the altar while the Reverend Whitehouse – 'call me Toby' – disappeared into the vestry to get gowned up.

Flyte had only had one proper night's sleep since the business in the lock-up and she was still feeling divorced from reality, but nothing would've stopped her going ahead with Poppy's naming ceremony. She'd considered asking Cassie along but with only her and Matt attending, having her as the only guest would have stirred up emotions she didn't want to deal with today.

Checking the time, she felt a spurt of irritation. Matt was late, but then Matt had always been late. When the Revd Toby returned she was glad to see he wasn't wearing some trendy secular get-up but a dog collar and a proper long white robe with a green stole round his neck that hung down the front.

Then her phone buzzed. A text from Matt. No doubt with some lame excuse for his lateness.

Sorry Philly, I just can't face it. You name her for both of us. Matt xxx

She read it again, this time shaking with suppressed fury, especially at that 'xxx' sign-off. He might as well have used a crying face emoji. 'Could I possibly use your office?' she asked the rev.

Matt wasn't picking up – the snivelling coward – so she had to content herself with leaving a short but expressive voicemail. As Flyte hung up, she realised that the f-word was becoming a regular feature of her language these days. Once upon a time she'd have called it a failure of vocabulary, but maybe Camden Town was rubbing off on her.

When she returned to the nave, she found the rev talking to some tall slim woman in a hat with her back to Flyte.

Not some woman. *Her mother.*

'Sylvia?! What the . . . ? You said you couldn't come.'

'Did I?' Sylvia regarded her daughter as if she had a screw loose. 'Oh, you mean the cruise? I nixed that in the end. The weather in the Cyclades can be so unreliable this time of year.' She thrust a hand-tied bouquet at her daughter. 'The taxi brought me via Harrods. I thought these would be appropriate.'

White roses interspersed with deep red poppies.

Without thinking, Flyte stepped forward and hugged her startled mother, something she hadn't done in years – make that decades. 'Thank you, Ma,' she said in her ear, breathing in the once-familiar smell of Tweed perfume.

After the ceremony, they were sitting quietly in the first row of chairs facing the altar. 'Such a shame they ripped out the pews,' said Sylvia. 'But I must say he did a good job, your little vicar. Are they all gay these days?'

Flyte wasn't going to let her mother rile her. Revd Toby had evidently given a lot of thought to the service and his beautiful words had left her bathed in a feeling of peace which made all her other concerns seem small – for now. 'It was lovely,' she said. 'I thought the bit where he said naming Poppy made her part of a community of souls was very moving—'

Hearing a sound, Flyte turned to find her indomitable mother trying not to cry. As she watched, astonished, the tears spilled over and coursed down her face.

'I'm sorry . . .' said Sylvia.

'Shhh.' Flyte took her mother's hand, feeling all at sea. This surely couldn't be just about Poppy. 'Is everything OK? You're not . . . unwell, are you?' Picturing inoperable cancers – or worse.

Sylvia took a big breath of air, and producing a lace handkerchief from her sleeve, pressed it to her eyes for a moment. 'I'm fine. It just . . . this brings it all back to me.'

'Brings what back?'

'Losing Petica.' Suddenly looking every inch of her seventy-two years.

'Petica . . . ?'

'I don't think I ever told you, darling. Petica came a year before you, but she arrived too early. Her lungs weren't properly developed and they couldn't save her. Perhaps these days . . .' She waved her hand.

'I had a sister? Why didn't you tell me?' Flyte felt a surge of fury.

'Oh, there was no point in dragging it all up. Upsetting everyone.'

The rage quickly dissolved in a surge of empathy for her mother.

'How long . . . did you have her?'

'Four days. Four beautiful days.' A smile lit Sylvia's tear-smudged face.

'Oh, Ma ... How long was it after you lost Petica that I arrived?'

'Less than a year.'

Oh, too soon, thought Flyte. Far too soon.

'For months I slept – well dozed, really – in the armchair in your room, next to your cot. I would wake up constantly and put the back of my hand to your mouth to make sure you were still breathing.' She put her hand out as if cot and baby were still standing there in front of her. 'It drove your father mad, under-standably, so I stopped – but I never stopped worrying about you, thinking that something terrible would happen.'

Drove Pops mad ... ? 'Why didn't you have my cot in the bedroom with you both?'

A laugh. 'Gerald would never have stood for that!' Flyte's surprise must have been obvious because Sylvia went on, 'Your father couldn't really see the point of babies. But he was marvel-lous with you, as soon as you could talk.' She paused. 'I some-times felt a bit envious of how close you two were. Silly really.'

Sylvia gently removed her hand from her daughter's and blew her nose delicately into her hanky before folding it away into her sleeve. The heart-to-heart was over.

Now she looked at her daughter with something more like her usual expression. 'Your new hairstyle suits you. When you wore it up in a chignon you looked like a librarian.'

Flyte suppressed a smile. A compliment wrapped in an insult: normal service had been restored.

Chapter Forty

Cassie arrived at Babcia's flat for dinner at six that evening. She'd forgotten all about the 'special guest' her gran had mentioned until she opened her front door and the sugar and spice smell of freshly fried pączki rushed out to embrace her. Home-made doughnuts were a very special treat.

After kissing her grandmother's sweet-smelling powdered cheek, she said accusingly, 'What's going on? You never make me pączki!'

'Because you always complain they make you fat!' she scoffed. 'When anyone can see you are skin and bone.'

Callum stood up from the sofa looking a bit sheepish, and she gave him a hug, glad to feel some meat on his bones at last. 'Who's this guest?' she whispered but he just smiled and threw a glance in the direction of her gran that said 'more than my job's worth'.

'Come, come,' said Babcia, beckoning her. 'I put our guest in your room, I hope you don't mind?'

Was it a puppy? There had been talk of getting a dog once, before her grandmother's mini-stroke.

Cassie pushed open the door of what had been her bedroom from the age of four to seventeen, and found a small child cross-legged on her bed playing with two plastic figurines.

What the . . . ?

'This is your youngest cousin, Orla,' said Weronika, a smile beaming all over her face. 'I'll leave you two to get acquainted.'

Cousin? This must be the daughter of one of Callum's sisters. Cassie perched on the edge of the bed, trying to suppress a childish feeling of outrage at this miniature usurper occupying her space.

'So, how old are you then, Orla?' she asked.

'Five and a third.' Her accent, straight out of Belfast, made her sound oddly adult.

'And who are these you're playing with?'

Orla looked at her like she was stupid. 'He's an astronaut and she's a zebra.'

'Oh, right. Silly me.'

There was an awkward silence, until Cassie noticed a temporary tattoo of a dinosaur on Orla's upper arm.

'Cool tatt,' she said. 'Do you wanna see mine?'

By the time Cassie had dragged Orla to the dinner table the ice had been broken.

'Cousin Cassie says we can evix-er-ate my Barbie to see what her insides look like,' Orla announced as Babcia piled pierogi onto her plate. 'Barbie *does my head in*,' she added, clearly copying a phrase she'd heard adults use.

Cassie sent Callum an apologetic grimace but he was laughing silently, his shoulders going up and down.

'And when I'm sixteen I'm getting a skull tattoo like Cassie's.' Orla nodded once to herself like it was a done deal. 'It's *class*.'

'I think we said eighteen, actually,' said Cassie. *Jesus*, this one was going to be a handful.

Callum explained that Orla's mum, his sister, Siobhan, had flown in from Northern Ireland for a varicose vein operation, which apparently cost less in London, and Orla was staying over at Weronika's for the night.

Babcia poured a little melted butter onto Orla's pierogi and looked at Cassie delightedly. 'Do you see how much she looks like you?'

Orla started telling Babcia a complicated story about her swimming lessons back home.

'So, Dad, you're looking good,' Cassie told Callum. It was true: his skin was clear, his eyes bright.

'Aye, I'm grand.'

'Are you keeping up your new regime? Eating your five a day?'

'Yes.'

'Still going to the AA meetings?'

'Yes.'

'What about—'

'Catkin. Stop,' he said, raising his hand. He was smiling but there was a steeliness in his voice she'd not heard before. 'Enough with the Nurse Ratched routine.'

He glanced over at Orla to check she wasn't earwigging. 'Listen,' he went on in lowered voice, 'all those years I was away' – meaning his time inside – 'I had no control over my life – who I saw, what I ate, the hours I slept, when I could exercise . . . After I got my freedom back the hardest thing of all was suddenly being responsible for looking after myself. It's taken me years to get to grips with that, y'know? But it has to be my responsibility. Do you understand?'

Cassie nodded: she hated anyone trying to tell her what to do. 'Have I been a monster?' she asked.

'Well . . .' He bugged his eyes.

'Enough said.' She pushed the last pierogi round the plate, remembering Pauline the shrink suggesting that the important relationships in her life were shaped by a fear of loss. *Her gran, her dad, Archie – maybe even Flyte too?* 'When you came back into my life all those years after losing you and Mum, I suppose I wanted a guarantee that you weren't going to disappear again.'

'Ah, sweetheart' – he set his big hand over hers – 'nothing's certain in this life. But I swear I'll do my best to make old bones. As long as you agree to visit me in the old folks' home, feed me soup, let me blather on about the old days – you know the drill.'

'All right,' she said. 'I'll get off your case. But that cuts both ways.'

He frowned in incomprehension.

'You've got to stop going on about how dangerous it is, me living on the boat, walking home in the dark, etcetera. I've survived twenty-six years in the inner city, you know.' No need to tell him what had gone down in the canal-side lock-up a couple of nights ago.

He grinned at her. 'It's a deal.'

Chapter Forty-One

Lounging on the comfy sofa, Cassie was finding the buzz of the tattoo gun soporific, but then she wasn't the one getting inked today and from the look on her face, Detective Sergeant Flyte was finding the experience anything but restful.

It had come as a shock when Flyte, of all people, had called to ask her advice about getting a tattoo, and sensing her nervousness, Cassie had offered herself as chaperone for the ordeal. It had been nearly a week since the business in the lock-up and Flyte's mood seemed to have lifted, probably because she'd properly given her daughter a name at last.

'Owww!' said Flyte, glaring at Boo, the thoroughly inked and pierced tattoo artist, who grimaced in sympathy.

'Sorry!' she said. 'I know it hurts when I go over and over one area. Just a few more minutes and we're done. You OK to go on?'

'I'll survive,' said Flyte grimly.

'I'm really liking the image you chose. Very cool.' Boo winked at Flyte. 'Is it an opium poppy?'

'Hardly,' said Flyte stiffly. 'I'm a police officer.'

Cassie turned away to stifle her laughter.

Boo completed the rest of her task in silence, while Flyte rocked her impression of a medieval martyr getting burned at the stake. Finally, it was over and Boo cleaned the tattoo with antiseptic gel. 'You're done! I'll just go get a dressing.'

'So, are you happy with it?' asked Cassie.

Flyte frowned down at the design inked on her inner forearm – a delicate line drawing of a poppy in black, three or four centimetres long.

'I like it,' she said. 'Now I can just pull up my sleeve any time and find her there.' She sent Cassie one of her rare 100-watt smiles, which transformed her resting cop face into one of startling beauty.

Flustered, Cassie dropped her eyes and asked, 'So, what are you thinking about going back to work?'

Flyte's face darkened. 'I can't imagine going back to Major Crimes – if the Camden unit even survives. DCI Stopford wants me to apply for a job at the DPS.'

'*Quis custodiet ipsos custodes?*' said Cassie.

'Indeed. Guarding the guardians ... Apparently, I have acquired some useful experience of dodgy police officers.' A dry look. 'The other option is to just bail out, go and retrain as something else.'

'Listen, Phyllida, it's none of my business but I would say, take your time before deciding. A couple of weeks ago I was dead set on packing it in at the mortuary and going to work in a bar.'

'You? Working behind a bar?' Flyte's raised eyebrows were the exact shape of a seagull's wings. 'That could put a dent in their profits,' she said drily.

They shared a smile.

Cassie found it hard now to truly remember how grim she'd been feeling until just recently. Her lost connection with the dead, followed by her first ever major screw-up when she'd returned organs to the wrong body, had plunged her into a depression. The heavy feeling of bleakness had lifted now – maybe with a bit of help from the antidepressants. Plus she was feeling less conflicted about her dad, and now she had an amusing little cousin in Orla and a whole new family in Belfast to get to know.

But she also owed a debt of gratitude to Sean Kavanagh for restoring her bond with the dead. Picturing his body drifting across the darkened canal she was convinced that he had come knocking on her hull for a reason, even if she'd remained oblivious for too long to what he was trying to tell her. But then if it hadn't been for Flyte's persistence, she might have stayed that way.

'The cops need people like you, Phyllida. Without you asking questions about Sean Kavanagh's death he'd still be a John Doe, lined up for a pauper's funeral and an unmarked grave.' Hearing herself putting up an impassioned defence of the police was a weird experience.

'I hear that Bethany Locke came forward with information that directly links Steadman to Luke's murder.' Her laser-like gaze scanning Cassie's face.

'Oh yes?'

'Which means that line of enquiry is now getting the attention and resources it deserves. Between you and me, I hear they've already got CCTV of Steadman's Range Rover near the heath at the right time and they're doing house-to-house enquiries with his image.'

They fell silent as Boo returned to put a dressing on Flyte's tattoo and give her the aftercare instructions. Cassie recalled the conversation she'd had with Steadman's wife Natalie, passing on his last words as she had promised. It was clear she'd been completely in the dark about the bank account and the secret loan, but her husband's crimes would haunt her – and their daughter – for the rest of their lives.

After she'd gone, Flyte eased herself off the tattooing chair, careful to hold her inner forearm away from her body, and came and sat next to Cassie on the sofa.

'If I did stay in the police I'd have to go through the ordeal of joining a new team again. You've probably heard the classic question that gets asked of any new female officer . . . ?'

Cassie shook her head.

'"Bike or dyke?"'

Their eyes met for an awkward moment before each looked away, Flyte's alabaster cheeks tinged with pink.

Recalling the time she'd more or less accused Flyte of being in the closet, Cassie braced herself: saying sorry had never come easy to her. 'Listen, Phyllida, I want to apologise for having a dig at you, you know, when I was trying to persuade you about Sean and Zeke. It was mean and unnecessary.'

'You were right though,' said Flyte with a shrug. 'Two people are dead because a policeman didn't feel he could be upfront about his sexual preferences with his colleagues. I've thought about it a lot these last few weeks. The police still view themselves – and the institution – as white, straight and male. I've always argued that nothing will change until we start to look and sound like the people we're supposed to protect.' She hesitated. 'Now I see that an important part of that is about people on the inside being prepared to step up and admit to being . . . different.'

Was Phyllida Flyte coming out to her?

'You know, I've always admired your honesty.' Flyte's ice-blue eyes rested on hers and she spoke with a warmth – a humanity – that Cassie had glimpsed in the past. 'You've never let other people's attitudes prevent you from being true to yourself. So . . . whether I stay in the Job or not, it's high time I started being more honest with myself. About myself.'

In her discreet and restrained way, Flyte was acknowledging that she was attracted to women and – unless Cassie had lost her gift for reading people – she was also putting it out there that she was attracted to Cassie.

It threw her into turmoil. She'd been aware of her feelings towards Flyte for ages, but she'd always been able to file them under 'never going to happen'. Until now.

She felt a powerful temptation to lean over and kiss her. A temptation she had to resist.

Because last night she'd taken a different kind of leap. She had met up with Archie, and asked him something – half expecting him to say no.

How would you feel about coming to live with me on the boat? As a proof of concept.

And he had said yes.

Acknowledgements

First and foremost I'd like to thank you – the reader. Without an enthusiastic UK audience who have taken Cassie Raven to their hearts I wouldn't be able to continue her story and to discover where life will take her next. And without you, the series wouldn't have found an even wider audience in eleven different countries as diverse as Estonia and China, where a tattooed Camden Town mortuary tech seems to have caught the imagination of readers.

I am only sorry that you have a bit of a wait between books – that's partly a function of publishing slots but also down to the need for a ton of research into forensics and post-mortem processes. (Not many authors have a well-thumbed copy of *Knight's Forensic Pathology* on their bedside table . . .) If you'd like to be kept up to date with my news and be entered in the odd prize draw, you can sign up for my occasional newsletter here: www.anyalipska.com

I also owe huge thanks to an ever-lengthening 'panel' of experts from the world of sudden unexpected death.

The key person on the research front for *Case Sensitive* has been super-smart pathologist Nic Chaston – a patient sounding board for my half-baked ideas, a diligent checker of facts, and a new friend with whom to discuss gruesome CODs over Aperol spritzes . . .

337

Award winning APT and friend Barbara Peters has been on the Cassie journey from the start, and continues to be a huge help with mortuary practice, HTA rules, and the like, as well as a great source of insights into the toughest part of the job – dealing with the newly bereaved.

Former murder DI Paula James has once again been there to patiently put me right on police practices and procedures and now that she's left the Job for exciting pastures new I hope to spend more time with her picking her brains – and putting the world to rights over a bottle.

Former coroner turned North Wales sheep farmer Alison Thompson is a patient and thoughtful resource for my many questions re coronial practice – and also enlivens my writing day with photos of her favourite ram . . .

Psychologist – and dear friend of thirty-five years – Kate Gauci continues helping me to navigate the highways and byways of the human psyche and the long-term effects of bereavement.

My most recently recruited expert is Cheryl Kynaston, a Crime Scene Manager for the Met for thirty-eight years, who I met at my local gym. I have much enjoyed chatting to her about forensic crime scene practice, the intricacies of DNA and tox testing, and look forward to many more of our post-workout coffees.

And a very special thank you to the charity Tommy's, which advised me on stillbirths and which does such a wonderful job supporting bereaved parents. Anyone wishing to donate or needing their support can find them at: www.tommys.org

It's a pretty cool job that allows me to hang out with such an impressive list of women. Any mistakes that have snuck into the text (or occasional bits of artistic licence) are of course entirely down to me.

Much gratitude is also due to a bunch of people on the writing and publishing front: the fabulous community of crime writers in what can be a tough and lonely job, but especially to these uber-talented and supportive women: Domenica de Rosa aka Elly Griffiths, Jane Casey, Susi Holliday, and the legend that is Val McDermid. Special thanks go to my dear friend Isabelle Grey, AKA the superb author V B Grey, who did me the great favour of wading through an early draft and assuring me that no, it wasn't unadulterated rubbish.

I was heartbroken this year to lose my agent and publishing-world legend, Jane Gregory, who has unaccountably abandoned me for a sun-soaked retirement on the south coast . . . She was the first person to spot Cassie's potential and has been a wise adviser – and a good friend – over the years.

Jane's insights will be much missed, but I must also thank her for introducing me to my *new* agent, Veronique Baxter. I knew from our very first meeting that she would be a rock – straight-talking and smart, but also kind and supportive. I'm looking forward to a long and fruitful relationship with her, and everyone at David Higham Associates – especially their energetic and impressive foreign rights team.

Finally, huge thanks go to the lovely Kelly Smith, my talented, hard-working editor at Zaffre Books. She is the best possible cheerleader for the Cassie Raven series, brings great insights to my manuscripts, and is incredibly patient with my endless text-tinkering . . . Thank you, doll!